Sinners Retreat

Lauren Biel

Library of Congress Cataloging-in-Publication Data

Sinners Retreat/Lauren Biel 1st ed.

Cover Design: Qamber Designs

Editing: Sugar Free Editing

Interior Design: Sugar Free Editing

For more information on this book and the author, visit: www. LaurenBiel.com

Please visit LaurenBiel.com for a full list of content warnings.

This book is dedicated to the humble pineapple

Chapter One

Kindra

Cat peers over my shoulder as I make the final incision and wrench the warm heart from its nest in the man's chest cavity. Blood splashes into the mess of exposed organs as I tilt the heart on its side, but it isn't like the movies. This dark chunk of meat doesn't continue beating once removed. It's been reduced to a smooth, lifeless muscle.

"Sorry I was late," Cat whispers as I pour India ink through the left ventricle. "I couldn't find my gloves."

I don't respond. Not during the integral part of my mission, which is the message I plan to send. The man I killed was not a man at all. He was a monster walking among us. Now his heart is as black as his soul.

"What did this one do?" Cat asks.

"Hair," I say.

"I don't follow."

"Your fucking hair is hanging out of your skullcap.

1

Those little blonde strands of incrimination will get you caught."

She winces as her trembling fingers work to hide the offensive hair from view.

I tuck the heart into the dead man's dominant hand. Sometimes it's the left, but it's usually the right. When they're ambidextrous, I just make a judgment call.

Then I stand and answer Cat's question as I survey my handiwork. "He was a kindergarten teacher."

"Oh."

There's no need to go into more detail. The young victim has gotten the revenge the court systems can't provide, and the world is a little brighter tonight.

Wind rushes past the eaves, creating an eerie whistle as Cat squats beside the dead guy and starts examining his body. Most of the houses on this street are abandoned. Without the constant hum of electricity, every sound can be heard. Every footstep outside, every breath from my lungs.

Bllffft.

And every gaseous emission from a corpse.

"Ew, what the fuck was that? Did you just pass gas?" Cat whispers.

"No. When you moved his leg, you might have released some trapped gas. All the muscles have relaxed, so there's nothing to hold it in."

She lowers the leg with a grimace. "Why don't you cut off their dicks? That's what I would do."

I immediately regret encouraging the girl to ask more questions.

My shoulders lift in a shrug. "They aren't always men. Women can be just as vile. But they all have a dark heart in common, so that's what I remove."

She blinks up at me, and the admiration and reverence in her blue eyes make me want to vomit.

Cat is my apprentice. A serial killer in training, if you will. She created a website that chronicled my entire murderous arc—an endearing homage to my life's work. Unfortunately, that painstaking collection of commendation had to come down pronto. While I appreciated the gesture, it laid things out too plainly. The last thing the incompetent detectives need is a competent admirer to do their job for them.

I contacted her and asked her to take down the site, and she agreed . . . if I would take her under my wing and show her the ropes. This is the second kill she's joined me on, and I'm debating my life choices at this point.

"We should go get a smoothie to celebrate," she says. "This was a good one."

"Yes, I'm sure the servers down at the diner will think nothing of our black catsuits, gloves, and skullcaps. If they ask about all the red stuff on my forearms and chest, I'll just say it's a fucking fashion statement."

My god, she has so much to learn.

I kneel before the man and lower his shirt, covering the gaping hole below his sternum and the knife wound in his left side. Another signature. Well, when it all goes to plan.

Sometimes I have to stab what I can, but I prefer an initial slash to the lung. It's hard to scream for help when you're struggling for your next breath, and I want them to know what it feels like to be so incredibly helpless. Just like their victims.

Satisfied, I get to my feet and head toward the door with my blonde shadow hot on my heels. As we exit the abandoned house, I stop in my tracks. "Cat?"

"Hmm?"

"Why is your car parked in front of the scene of the fucking crime?"

She steps beside me and begins fidgeting. "Shit. I was in such a hurry that I forgot you said to park at the pump-and-dump motel. Sorry."

I sigh. What the fuck else can I do? "Just drive me back to my car."

Grass and weeds peek from the busted cracks running through the concrete walkway. I sidestep them and make my way past the rusty chain-link fence. The gate lies askew on the ground.

We get inside her beater, and I'm grateful that the busted thing blends in with the surrounding area. Which is to say, the car looks like it smokes a lot of crack.

Squatters and addicts occupy most of the houses on this street, though I use the term "houses" very loosely. These rundown buildings are mostly crumbling relics of their former selves. Long gone is their glory age—a booming mill town run to ruin when the mills had to close after the jobs were sent overseas.

I click my seatbelt into place, and the car grumbles to life. As Cat pulls the rust bucket away from the crumbling curb, her fingers flex and tap on the steering wheel. It's a nervous habit, which she partakes in—much to my displeasure—when her mind conjures a question her mouth is too nervous to ask.

The radio doesn't work, so I have two options. I can continue listening to this incessant, nerve-grating representation of her anxiety, or I can give her an opening.

"Cat, just ask the fucking question."

She needs no further invitation and promptly spits it out. "Can you tell me about your brother's murder?"

My shoulders stiffen, and my stomach clenches until

I'm certain I'll shit or vomit. Maybe both. I suppose that's a natural reaction when a mind is forced to relive a traumatic event.

Cat clears her throat. "I wouldn't ask if I didn't have a reason, but I want to be sure before I say anything."

My ears perk up. I've been searching for my brother's killer for as long as he's been in business, but even though I'm a stellar journalist with a nose like a hound, the man has been a ghost. Untraceable. Undetectable. If talking about what happened can bring me closer to finding him, she can shove a pull string up my ass and yank it to her heart's content.

"Well, I was seventeen," I begin. "The killer pulled up to the house in a black van in the middle of the night, broke in, and hung my brother from—"

"Meat hooks?" she asks.

"Yes," I say. "In the garage. I was the one who found him. The image is burned into my brain, and not just because it was the first dead body I'd seen."

"The Abattoir Adonis," she breathes.

I nod.

"So what burned it into your brain?"

"You mean, aside from the fact that my brother was levitating four feet off the ground with meat hooks through his armpits? Or maybe it was that he had no eyes to speak of, he was completely nude, and the number seven was carved into his body in several places? It certainly wasn't the copious amount of blood painting the concrete floor."

I turn to her with a deadpan stare, but she's too busy imagining my description of the scene to notice.

She nibbles her lip and takes a right turn, putting us in view of the seedy motel. I chose the place because it lacks any cameras. Its clientele doesn't like to smile for photos.

"How strange," Cat says.

"What?"

She ignores my question and poses one of her own. "What year was he murdered?"

The disconnected tone she uses when talking about my brother's demise rubs me the wrong way, though it shouldn't. It's the same way I ask questions when I'm covering a story. But then she works out the answer before I can offer it to her.

"Wait, you were seventeen, so that means . . . your brother was his sixth victim. He'd established his MO by that point. Why did he deviate?" Her eyebrows pull together as she turns in at the motel.

"That's the million-dollar question, Regis. If I knew the answer, I'd probably be closer to finding him." I scoff and look out the window.

My brother is the only Adonis victim to be stripped nude and have his eyes removed and numbers etched into the skin. He typically just hangs and drains.

She slides the car into a parking spot as a housekeeper pushes a trolley down the sidewalk in front of a row of doors outside the motel. It's a bit late for changing the sheets, so I'm fairly sure she's the on-site Hoover for hire. Instead of sucking grit from the carpet, she'll suck the soul right out of a man. Good for her.

Cat puts the car in park and turns to me. "You might be closer to an answer than you think, but before I say anything else, I want to be certain. Can you give me a couple of hours? I'll get everything together and meet you at your place."

This bitch.

"Is this another ploy to see where I live?" I ask. The girl

has been trying for weeks, and it's the one area of my life I'd prefer to keep private.

And that's a fucking lie. I'd prefer to keep *all* areas of my life private.

I have no friends or romantic connections, and I like it that way. My work relationships are just as sparse, extending far enough to keep me in business so I can pay my bills. The rest of my energy is devoted to finding and killing my next victim.

And seeking my brother's killer.

To be fair, my brother and I had drifted apart before his death. He was ten years older, and we didn't really have much in common. But he was still my brother, and he didn't deserve to die at the hands of a sadist. Killers who kill indiscriminately are not in my league.

"While I'm still dying to see your house, no, it's not a ploy," Cat says. "I lied about why I was late because I don't want to get your hopes up until I know something for sure. Even though I did a deep dive on you, there was a lot I couldn't find out regarding your brother's death. I don't exactly have a press pass."

My job certainly has its benefits, one of which is my ability to discover my next victim while getting paid to do so. I typically cover crime stories, and the dirty little perverts come across my desk on the regular.

I mull over my options. Without saying as much, Cat has essentially given me an ultimatum. If I want to learn whatever secret she's uncovered, I'll have to invite her to my house. My home. My sanctuary.

Closing my eyes, I rip off my skullcap and resign myself to defeat. "I'm at 1408 Thornwood Drive."

While I wait for Cat to arrive, I don't bother tidying up. I don't give a shit if she thinks I'm dirty because I have a few dishes in the sink or a bit of dust on the bookshelves. If she doesn't like it, she can leave.

Maybe I should shit on the carpet to encourage that outcome.

She pulls up the driveway at two a.m. by way of a ride service. This was my one condition. Considering her car could have been spotted driving away from the scene of a murder, I want it nowhere near my house.

I let her inside, and she's practically agog with wonder. I'm not sure why. It's your average home, complete with a broken dishwasher, a garbage disposal that sounds like it's choking on a long-forgotten fork, and a toilet that only flushes if you hold down the handle.

She pulls off a light jacket and folds it over her arm. Her platinum hair sticks out all over her head, which tells me she didn't even shower once she got home. Fucking rookie. Showering was second on my list when I walked in the door. After tossing my murder ensemble into the wash, of course. They can do amazing things with leather these days.

Her gaze flies from the hardwood floors to the hall tree in the entryway. "Wow," she breathes. "I never pictured you with a hall tree."

I pluck the jacket from her arm and hang it on one of the wooden dowels. "Did you ever picture yourself becoming my next victim? Because we can make that happen too."

She closes her dropped jaw and composes herself. "Right. I'll try to keep my excitement to myself."

I lead her into the living room and motion for her to take a seat on the couch.

"So, what did you find out?" I ask, impatient to learn what she's come up with. I take a seat on the leather recliner beside the couch and pull my dark hair into a low ponytail.

"Um . . . before we get to that, could I have a drink? I'm pretty thirsty." She offers a sheepish smile, but I'm onto her.

"Jesus fucking Christ. If you want to see my glassware, I'll be happy to show you later. Hell, I'll invite you for a sleepover with makeovers and a chick flick if you'll just tell me what the fuck you know that I don't!"

"I'm sorry! It's not every day that I get to see inside *the* Heartbreak Killer's house." A wide grin spreads on her face. "Once you know what I've found out, you'll probably let me look at whatever I want."

Doubtful.

"Have you ever heard of the Sinners Retreat?" she asks. A mischievous glint sparkles in her eyes.

I've covered a metric fuck ton of stories over my career—and researched far more than I've written about—but a Sinners Retreat is a new one on me. I shake my head.

"Every year, a handful of serial killers are invited to vacation on a private island. The details are pretty sparse, but from what I've gathered, they get to enjoy sun, sand . . . and murder!" She leans forward. "Could you even imagine all the fun we could have? Maybe I could even get my first kill."

I have a self-imposed rule that I must never murder the innocent, but this nitwit is about to force me to abandon that. She baited me. Knowing I would let her into my

9

private life if she had a juicy bit of info, she fucking baited me.

Before she can say anything else, I raise my hand and silence her. "First, those are old wives' tales. There've been rumors for years, but they're all unsubstantiated reports. Second, even if the rumors were true, I would rather suck off Charlie Sheen and swallow than go to that island. Third, fuck you for making me think you knew anything about my brother's killer. You can leave now."

I stand and begin marching toward the door.

"Don't be so quick to raise your hackles," she says, and I love that she assumes my hackles weren't already raised.

I turn to face her. "Even if it were real, how did you, the antithesis of a serial killer, gain access to such a secret?"

"Ouch," she says, though she knows I'm right. She's a straight-A student from Portland who flew to New York to live out her big dreams of becoming an actress.

People in the limelight do not make good serial killers. I'd say you could ask Rodney Alcala, but he died in jail.

I rest my case.

"Don't take offense," I say with a wave of my hand. "Not everyone is cut out for this life. Whether you are remains to be seen."

I'm being too kind. Like a naked man running through Times Square on a Tuesday, it's been seen. She is not cut out for this life, and I have very little hope of making anything of her.

"I'm on a message board on the dark web. I met a guy who knows a guy who—"

I roll my hand in the air, urging her to wrap this up.

"I showed a guy my tits, and he let me in."

My eyes drop to Cat's chest. Cat's very full, very perky

chest. Possibly fake, but still impressive, nonetheless. But top-secret info for a flash of nip? I don't buy it.

I raise an eyebrow.

"Okay, I let him titty-fuck me, and then I pretended to smoke some meth with him. Once he was good and gassed, he forgot I was there, and I was able to access his laptop while he talked to the men in the wallpaper. See? My acting skills come in handy sometimes."

Maybe for porn.

"Look," she says, "I've brought an offer you can't refuse. Do you want to know what I've discovered, or are you going to keep being a judgmental asshole for the rest of your natural life?"

My eyes widen, but I'd be lying if I said I wasn't at least a little curious about what has her so goddamned excited. "Go on," I say.

Her smile returns, and I feel like I've been blasted with a ray of radioactive sunshine. "For your consideration, I present the guest list for this year's Sinners Retreat."

She leans forward and pulls a piece of paper from her back pocket. I take it from her and unfold it, ready to admonish her for doing something as ignorant as printing off something so incriminating—if it's even real—but then I see the first name on the list.

The Abattoir Adonis.

Chapter Two

Ezra

I've been in America long enough to blend in—just over twelve years—but no part of me has ever stopped longing for the rainy afternoons spent in a British pub. This place is a far cry from London, but I'm not here for pleasure.

My phone vibrates in my back pocket, but I'm a bit indisposed at the moment. It's probably just my brother calling to give me the flight details for the upcoming trip. It can wait.

I lean against the bar to snag the bartender's attention. That's what it looks like I'm doing, anyway. I'm actually trying to get a better look at the guy on the last stool.

He's pressed against the wall, nursing a pint of something gold and frothy. A dark-green jacket hangs from his thin frame and drapes over the back of the stool. It's nearly eleven p.m., yet he's wearing sunglasses. Indoors. It's likely an attempt to hide his bloodshot eyes.

Has he been losing sleep?

God, I hope he has.

His receding hairline does him no favors, especially when he could charge people to advertise on his massive forehead. A few reddish-blond sprigs attempt to bridge the thinning area over his crown, but his scalp still shines through. The nose above his thin lips can best be described as a cross between a pug and a pig—round and flat to his face, with a little point at the tip. His bulging eyes top off the look.

The bartender appears in front of me, and I lean back. I've gotten a positive ID, so there's no need for false pretenses now.

"I'll take a Negroni," I say.

She smacks her gum and shakes her head. "We're out of Campari."

"Gin and tonic?"

"Soda gun is busted."

Now I can see why this bar is so empty. "Just give me a gin on the rocks. That's if you have ice?"

She spins away from the bar, but I don't miss the subtle roll of her eyes.

I start toward the man against the wall, but a woman steps in front of me and blocks my path. Her nails stretch to a length that leaves me wondering how she wipes her ass. Also, she should have stopped bleaching her hair at home about four sessions ago. There's hardly any left.

"Hey, cutie," she slurs. "Where do you think you're going?"

Probably to the nearest health department for a lot of testing if you come much closer, I think.

The woman is the human embodiment of a walking STD. A crusty cold sore obscures the left side of her bottom lip from view. Judging by the scars and sores on her face and arms, she either has a compulsive skin-picking issue or a chronic drug habit. The veins in her left arm look like they've reenacted the Great Fire of London, so I'm guessing it's the latter. They're completely destroyed.

She places a hand on my arm, and I can't wait to throw this jacket into the fireplace when I get home. "Don't you want to buy me a drink?" she slurs.

I try not to squint as her breath reaches my nose. God help anyone who lights a match within five feet of her. "I don't, but thanks for the offer."

As I try to pull away, her grip tightens. "Aw, come on. You look like a movie star, and I ain't ever shared a drink with a British movie star before."

"If you don't release my arm, you'll be sharing your next drink with a group of medical experts as they try to dislodge a chair leg from your brain. Or what's left of it." I shake off her loosened grip. "Now, if you'll excuse me."

I stride away before she can say anything else. I don't normally like to draw attention to myself, but needs must.

The man at the end of the bar brings the pint glass to his lips and takes another short pull. I'm not surprised he's drinking, but I would have expected him to hit something a little harder after the night he's had.

I slide onto the barstool beside his, hold out my hand, and muster my best attempt at a smile. "Howdy, stranger. Haven't seen you for a while."

He turns to me, perplexed. "Do I know you?"

Ah, here it is. My second-favorite part of the dance. They should have called me the Chameleon, but Rasmussen already holds that title.

"Don't act like you don't remember me, Gary. We went to school together back at Georgetown High." I clap him on the back and lean closer, holding my hand in front of me as I lay out the scene. "I certainly remember you. Fourth quarter, we were down by a touchdown against the Riverside Bengals. Thirty seconds left in the game. Then here you come, bolting down the sideline like a madman."

A smile lights his face as I pull him into the farce. "Oh, yeah! I remember that game! We had a real rager that night."

I know nothing of the party he speaks of, but that doesn't matter. My foot is firmly in the door.

"A couple of the guys are getting together for a few rounds of poker tomorrow night," I say. "You should join us."

I wish I could have said tonight, but there are too many witnesses that might recall my face. You don't fly under the radar for as long as I have by making yourself memorable.

When the bartender slides my iceless gin in front of me, I put my beliefs into practice. She receives payment, along with a tip that is of a forgettable amount.

"Aw, I can't make it tomorrow," he says. "I just started a shift job, and I'm on nights. Can I get a raincheck? I'd love to see everyone again. I've lost touch with all the guys."

I'm well aware of his new job. And his schedule. He's playing right into my plan.

Before I can respond, my phone once again rattles against my ass cheek. It's not like my brother to be so incessant, so it must be something important.

"How about this weekend?" I ask as I stand from the stool.

"Yeah, I could do Saturday." He takes another swig and smacks his lips.

I pull my phone from my back pocket and swipe to answer the call. "I'll only be a moment," I say to the man at the bar.

Heading for the front of the building, I bring the phone to my ear. "Bennett, I'm a bit busy. Is there any chance this could wait?"

"Are we talking elbows-deep-in-a-vic kind of busy? Or muff-diving kind of busy? If it's the second one, send her my way when you're done." My brother was raised in America, so he lacks my refined accent. And manners.

"First, you're disgusting. Second, neither. I've got one on the hook, so if you don't mind—"

"Two more just signed on for the trip."

I grip the phone a little tighter. With every new name that appears on the trip roster, the odds of meeting my idol increase.

HBK.

The Heartbreak Killer.

The vast majority of serial killers choose to enter this hobby as an outlet for some frustration in their lives. Strange sexual urges, a need for power—the reasons are endless. But a rare few are vigilantes like me. We kill as a way to end the suffering of so many.

And the secretive Heartbreak Killer is one of us.

"Names?" I ask.

Fingers clack on a keyboard, and then my brother says, "The Sunshine Strangler and the Cat Scratch Killer."

"The Cat Scratch Killer? What a stupid fucking name."

"To be fair, over half of the provided names appear to be made up. I haven't heard of most of these people. At this point, you may be the only one I *have* heard of."

I'm not surprised. Many of the attendees are probably first timers. Too scared to put down their real names, they prefer to make something up. By the end of the retreat, their MO will shine like a beacon in the night and tell me who they really are. I can only hope that one of them enjoys

17

cutting a heart from the chest and leaving it in the victim's dominant hand.

Discovering people's secrets is a gift, really, and I use it often. That's why I'm a private detective. The only person to elude me has been the Heartbreak Killer.

"Have you received the flight plans yet?" I ask.

"Yeah, but they canceled the private flight on Sunday because there weren't enough people to fly out. Now we need to take a commercial flight on Saturday, spend the night in Miami, then catch the private jet to the island from there."

Well, shit. Looks like I'll have to cancel that poker game.

"Don't get your hopes up too high," Bennett adds. "The odds of HBK learning about the retreat are already slim. The odds of him showing up are even lower."

"It could be a woman. You never know," I say.

"And what if HBK turns out to be a man? You gonna get on your knees and suck him off?"

I shrug. "I might consider myself an equal-opportunity sex god for the right person."

"Sex god?" Bennett huffs a single laugh into the phone. "A blind gynecologist sees more pussy than you do."

"Are you kidding? With looks like mine, I'm spoilt for choice."

"Jesus fuck. Don't start with the British lingo."

I glance back at the woman who made a move on me earlier. "I'm only stating the obvious. I could have any woman I wanted if I actually found someone worth wanting. In the interim, I have my right hand and the internet."

The man at the end of the bar tosses back the rest of his drink and eases off the barstool.

"I gotta run," I say before ending the call and stuffing the phone into my pocket.

Gary approaches me with a smile. If he knew what I'd originally planned for him this weekend, the grin would melt from his face.

Then again, maybe I can still take care of him after all.

"Hey, man," I say as I slap my arm over his shoulder. "How would you like to take a trip this weekend?"

Chapter Three

Kindra

The black cat stares into my soul as it squats in the litter box and proceeds to shit, its spindly tail flicking back and forth. Its ears lie back against its head, and its eyes stare into the distance. Whatever is coming out of its ass end seems to require more concentration than a calculus equation, because that creature is fucking focused.

"What possessed you to put the litter box in your living room?" I ask over the sound of kitty claws raking grit over a turd the size of a Snickers bar.

Cat—the person, not the animal that is now climbing out of the blue plastic box—shrugs. "I used to have two cats. The other would piss all over the furniture, so I put a box in every room, thinking it would help. It didn't, so I had to get rid of him."

I blink up at her. "You mean . . ."

"What? No! I would never hurt an animal. He lives with a nice elderly lady now. Her house already smelled like cat piss, so I figured he'd be right at home. What kind of sick fuck do you think I am?"

"There's no reason to take offense. I only ask because you want to be a serial killer, and sometimes they use animals for . . . practice."

Her eyes go wide. "I'm well aware, but I love animals. People, not so much."

I agree with her sentiments wholeheartedly, but I don't say as much. I don't want to give her the wrong idea. This current arrangement isn't a friendship, as much as she seems to think it is. Allowing her to believe we have things in common will only bolster her belief that we should be pals.

As she retreats to the kitchen, I glance around her sparsely decorated living room. Picture frames line a small coffee table, and from the center, a creepy family photo stares back at me. Cat, her mother, and her father sit on a family couch, with furry felines crawling all over them. There have to be at least five cats in the picture. It's mayhem.

My eyes land on some mail sitting in front of the pictures.

"Your real name is Caterina?"

"Did you think my parents would actually name me Cat?" she calls from the kitchen.

"I thought maybe the feline fascination was genetic," I say as I study the photo of them in horrid nineties garb. Even the cats had little headbands.

No wonder she's a bit . . . eccentric.

My foot knocks into a box. She's lived in this city for six months, but moving boxes still clutter most of the living room. When I agreed to come over this evening, I didn't expect to sit within a cardboard fort. Maybe I should just move the conversation along so I can get the hell out of here.

"You booked our flights and paid for the retreat, correct?" I ask as she fiddles with something in the kitchen. Glass clinks together, and something spills.

"Yes, everything has been taken care of. How do you take your coffee?"

I look back at the litter box and recall that she has one in every room of the house. "I'm not very thirsty right now. Besides, it's almost midnight. I'll never sleep if I have caffeine this late."

Cat enters the living room and plunks down beside me on the couch.

I motion toward a stack of U-Haul-emblazoned cardboard. "You planning to move again soon?"

"No. I thought I might have to, but I got a job today. Now I won't have to give up my apartment and head back to Portland. Isn't that great?"

To think I was so close to ridding myself of the little tick . . .

"Yes, wonderful," I say.

"Don't you want to know where I'll be working?"

Not really, but I nod.

She holds out her hand. "Hi, I'm Cat. Your new personal assistant!"

I scream in my head. "The fuck you say. I have never and will never have a PA. I don't need one."

"I booked our flights and reserved our spots at the retreat, so I've already proven myself useful. I've also spoken with your boss, who agreed to pay for the trip since it's for work."

"You *what*?" The scream makes its way to my throat, but I swallow it and force my hands to remain in my lap so that I don't gouge out her eyes with my nails. "I had vacation time saved up, which I planned to use. This isn't for work! Whatever happens on that island, I can't fucking write about it, Cat!"

The girl is unfazed. She just sips her coffee and smiles at me. "I've worked that out too. I didn't give your boss any details, but he knows you plan to reveal the identity of a serial killer. He doesn't know it's the Abattoir Adonis, but he'll probably give you a bonus when he finds out. You can get an exclusive interview, pictures . . . just think of the possibilities. And after you've outed him, he gets to spend his nights staring at a cell wall. The revenge is just the cherry on top."

"You consider jail time revenge?" I blink. It's all I can do at this point. "Do you know how many murder fantasies you've just wrenched from my grasp?"

"I mean, I just—"

"You just what? Fucked up? Ruined my life? Destroyed any hope I had of torturing this asshole?"

Tears brim at the edges of her lashes. "I'm sorry, Kindra. I didn't mean to fuck up. I thought I was helping."

Closing my eyes, I begin to count to ten. I make it to four before the urge to strangle her overwhelms me. To prevent myself from committing a second murder this week, I stand to leave.

"Please don't go," she says. She sounds almost lovesick as she pleads for me to stay. "I won't do anything else without asking for your approval first. I didn't know my idea would backfire like this."

I take a deep breath and turn around before I reach the door. "Do you realize what you've done? It's so much worse than you realize. I can't interview or bring to light any of the killers at the retreat. They will have seen my face. I'll be dead before I write the first line of the exposé. Now my boss expects a big story, so I either have to forfeit my job or my fucking life."

"Well, while you're busy murdering, maybe I can come up with a solution to this problem. We could always—"

"You will do no such thing. For the remainder of our time together—which will hopefully last only until the end of this trip—you will refrain from anything you consider *helpful*. Now, I'm going home. Email the flight information, and don't contact me otherwise."

The girl couldn't look more stricken if I'd actually struck her, but she nods and walks me to my car. I allow it because I'm not entirely heartless.

Part of me feels slightly guilty for raking her over the coals, but she stoked this fire herself. Now I'm left to make sure all the cinders are reduced to ashes.

"I'm really sorry," she says again as I slide into the driver's seat. "Maybe we can figure something out."

I grip the steering wheel and look into her eyes. "*I* will figure something out."

After slamming the door, I start the car. I need to get out of here before I become even more fucked than I already am. While I don't see how that's possible, I'm sure Cat can find a way.

As I pull onto the road, my mind is already whirling with ways to get myself out of this mess. My boss is a shrewd man. He'll likely fire me if I don't return from this trip with *something* salacious. I only hope I can come up with an angle before the return flight.

My mind clicks off a mental checklist as I drive. I'll need to do some shopping tomorrow. Never having been one for a hot-girl summer, I fear my wardrobe is a bit lacking in the swimsuit department. It's a five-day retreat, and I can't be seen in the same thing twice, so that means I'll have five swimsuits to toss in the trash when I return.

As for the activities . . . I have plenty to bring along in the way of weaponry. Throwing stars, my trusty serrated knife, my beloved garrote. The options are endless, and I don't get to use most of my arsenal because it doesn't fit with my MO.

On the island, though, I could be anyone.

I have exactly zero plans to use my usual methods. The risk of discovery is too great, and even in a crowd of people who are just as high up on the FBI's shit list, I have no desire to reveal my identity. Only one person could possibly fuck this up for me.

And now she's my personal assistant.

Chapter Four

Ezra

Bennett pulls up to my house thirty minutes early. The man is early for everything. Our flight doesn't leave for three hours, but he wants to get groped by TSA as quickly as possible.

Despite having different mothers, we look fairly similar. We both share our father's dark hair, but he has steel-blue eyes and twenty-twenty vision to rival my brown eyes and glasses. He also has numerous tattoos and a few piercings in unmentionable places. I have one tattoo that I'd love to forget.

Gary already sits in the luxury sedan's passenger seat. I told him I knew his boss and would make sure he had the time off so that he'd agree to join us. In truth, I know his boss about as well as I know American history, which is to say, not at all.

But that doesn't matter. We didn't book a return flight for him.

"Gotta hop in the back, pal," I say to Gary. "I get motion sickness if I'm not up front."

I'm not worried about hurting his feelings. The Cattle are housed away from the Sinner villas until they're needed for the activities.

Gary nods and smiles and climbs into the back seat, unaware of the strings we had to pull to have a chance to kill him some place scenic. We've given him a gift he doesn't deserve, really. Instead of dying in an abandoned warehouse, he gets to bleed out on a beach.

Bennett didn't want to bring him along, but he didn't have a choice in the matter. I refused to leave this scum on the street while I headed off on holiday. He had to make the arrangements, or I would've stayed behind. Thankfully, the event coordinator owed Bennett a favor after last year's debacle. One of the Cattle managed to get hold of a switchblade, leaving my brother with a permanent scar over his right eyebrow.

"I really appreciate you guys bringing me along," Gary says from the back. He's smiling and peering out the window like a kid on his way to Disneyland. Unfortunately for him, the animatronics at this park wield weapons. "I can't remember the last time I flew on an airplane."

"The pleasure is all ours, I assure you," I say.

Gary talks our ears off for the remainder of the drive to the airport. My brother and I aren't the talkative types, so we mostly just smile and nod. Traffic is fairly light, even close to the city, so the drive isn't half bad.

When we reach the airport, Bennett maneuvers through the winding parking garage before finding an empty spot. We grip our luggage—which is blessedly light— and make our way into the building.

The airport hums with activity. People of every color,

shape, and size tread the shining floors, none of them concerned with anything aside from their own destinations. Some are headed to far-off places while others are returning from distant shores. You can tell which are which by the looks on their faces. The arrivals look much more exhausted than the departees.

When I reach the ticket counter, I'm greeted by a smiling woman, though the grin doesn't quite reach her eyes. Ah, the good old Plasticine smile.

She takes my tickets, and the false smile doesn't drop as she says, "I'm sorry, but we've overbooked this flight. One of you will have to sit in economy."

I turn to my brother. Gary sure as shit can't be out of our sight, so that means one of us will have to give up our spot. That also means one of us will be forced to listen to him yammer on for an entire flight.

"I'll take the economy ticket," I say.

Realizing what I've done, Bennett sends the toe of his boot into my Achilles tendon. I suffer in silence because it's only fair. He'll have an awful flight, so I don't mind walking with a limp for a few days to make up for it. It's still better than sitting with Gary for three hours.

With our tickets settled and our luggage sent off with a prayer of return, we trudge toward our gate.

"I'm starving," Gary whines.

"I'm sure there will be food on the plane," I say.

"Peanuts ain't gonna cut it," Bennett chimes in, and now I'm outnumbered.

With a longing look at our gate, I follow the pair toward a fast-food booth. Bennett and I order burgers, and Gary orders the chicken sandwich.

We gather our bags and head to the gate when we realize the three measly tables in the dining area are full.

We're still very early, so we have our choice of seats. I take one by the large window, and Gary and Bennett settle in the central area. They tear into their food like beasts, but I'm not as eager to swallow the grease trap within the silver wrapper.

A pretty stewardess ambles by, probably on her way home after a flight. Bennett watches her with male amusement, eyeing her trim waist and large breasts. Gary doesn't spare her a second glance. I'm not surprised. At twenty-something, she's a bit too old for his perversions.

God, I can't wait to kill him.

It's been months since my last slaying, and my fingers itch to use the new meat hooks I purchased six weeks ago. I only target the rapists and pedophiles, so I'm forced to share some of my potential victim pool with my brother and the Heartbreak Killer. The lack of victims is a good problem to have, I suppose, but it does nothing for my bloodlust.

Time passes, and more people begin to fill out the empty seats. I study each person, wondering if they could be the illustrious HBK. Any of them could be.

Well, maybe not the little old lady clutching a sleeve of cookies to her chest. She lacks the upper body strength to crank open a chest cavity.

Speaking of cookies, a pang in my gut reminds me of the very mediocre burger waiting for me. I peel back the wrapper, inhale the sad aroma, and take the first disappointing bite.

I'm broken from my mindless chewing when two women choose to sit close enough that I can hear their whispered argument. Listening would be rude, but I never said my manners were infallible.

"I don't want to sit in the middle," the blonde says.

"Can't I have the window seat? It's my first flight, and you fly all the time."

The raven-haired woman scoffs. "You mean you drove all the way from Oregon to New York?"

"Well, yeah. You saw my boxes. I didn't trust movers with my stuff."

I snag glances as they continue arguing. While the blonde is conventionally pretty—striking blue eyes, slender waist, large breasts, mile-long legs—the dark-haired woman is what my male fantasies are made of.

She fills out her tank top and shorts, and I don't mind the bit of midsection which hangs over the waistband. I practically drool over it as I imagine what that velvet flesh would feel like as I take it into my mouth and suck. Since I wasn't paying attention when they walked over, I haven't seen her ass, but I can imagine it based on her thick thighs. And it's perfection.

She wears a pair of sunglasses to ward off the morning sun blaring through the massive window, but if her eyes are as dark as her hair, I'm in trouble. Having never minded being in trouble, I stuff the burger wrapper into the bag and turn to the women to offer a solution to their problem.

"I have a window seat, but I don't mind sitting in the middle seat if you'd like to switch," I say to the blonde.

The dark-haired dream screws up her mouth, but the blonde holds her hand toward me.

"Hi, I'm Cat, and this is—"

"Kindra." The dark-haired woman swats her friend's hand back to her lap. "And I have no interest in sitting beside a stranger for the flight."

"Well, tough shit, Kindra," Cat says, "because either you switch with me or you switch with him."

Kindra's grip tightens on the travel bag in her lap, but she says nothing.

I turn toward her. "I'm Ezra. Thirty-six. I'm a private investigator on my way to a convention. I'm traveling with my brother, Bennett, and an old chum, Gary. They plan to sightsee while I'm networking. I've lived in America for twelve years, but I'm originally from Gravesend in county Kent, right beside the Thames." I extend my hand with a genuine smile. "There, now we aren't strangers."

Begrudgingly, she takes my hand, shakes it, and pulls her clammy fingers back to her lap. She turns to her friend. "You owe me so fucking big for this," she whispers.

Afraid I'll piss her off, I stifle a chuckle. She doesn't exactly seem the jovial type who can handle any amount of good-spirited joshing. Americans can be sensitive that way.

The blonde is undeterred by her friend's sour mood, and she turns to me with a bright smile. "I really appreciate this. Maybe I can pay for a drink or two when we land in Miami?"

"I don't drink," Kindra says. "And on this trip, neither do you."

Like a scolded child, Cat closes her mouth and sits back in her seat. Her balls are only so big, it seems.

"Who said it has to be spirits?" I say. "We could all enjoy a cold glass of something non-alcoholic when we land. Like all human beings, you at least drink water, I presume?"

Before Kindra can shut me down again, a voice comes over the intercoms to announce that our plane will begin boarding soon. I paid for priority, so that means the blonde will need to get in line, leaving me all alone with the grumpy temptress. I couldn't have planned this better if I'd tried.

Cat and I swap boarding passes, and she flitters off to

claim her coveted window seat in economy. I didn't fare so terribly in the swap, as their seats are in business class, and despite Kindra's dark-cloud demeanor, she'll be nicer to look at than any view from the window.

With her friend spirited away to the plane's interior, Kindra fidgets in her seat. The poor thing can't seem to get comfortable. Her fingers repeatedly move to her temples, where she rubs and rubs until I get the impression that she has one hell of a headache.

I reach into my pocket and produce a small travel bottle of extra-strength Tylenol, purchased when I thought I would need to endure an entire flight beside Chatty Kathy. Now it seems they'll still prove useful.

"Here," I say. "You need them more than I do."

I expect her to argue or flat out refuse my help, but she surprises me when she snatches the bottle from my palm, unfastens the top, and dry-swallows three of the white pills.

"Thanks," she says as she returns the bottle to my hand.

"It's the least I could do after ruining your flight. I apologize. I thought I was being helpful."

Her shoulders loosen, and she sighs. "No, I'm sorry for coming across as a mega-bitch. I'm under a lot of stress with work right now, and nothing seems to be going my way."

I can think of one good way to relieve her tension, but she has all of her spines pointed outward, and I'm not in the mood to fuck a cactus today. She'd almost be worth it, though.

"What do you do for work?" I ask, but then it's our turn to board. I don't think she heard my question over the crackling intercom voice.

This is going to be a long flight.

Chapter Five

Kindra

Thanking the powers that be for a reprieve, I rush toward the front of the line with my boarding pass outstretched. The sooner I can get in my seat, the sooner I can pretend to be asleep. Ezra is pleasant enough to talk to and would have been an upgrade from sitting beside Cat for an entire flight, but there's just one little problem.

He's my goddamn kryptonite.

Tall, dark-haired, and handsome, with glasses perched on his perfect nose. It's very Clark Kent chic, and the only thing physically defective about him appears to be his vision.

I like my frigid persona. I enjoy being a walking block of ice. But Ezra is like a furnace aimed right at the space between my legs. His t-shirt hugs his broad shoulders and chest, and I've never wanted to be woven cotton so badly in my life. I would allow this man to use my tongue as a loofa.

The mental image of Ezra in a shower has my thighs pressing together as I walk. I can see it so clearly. Water cascading through his dark hair and catching on his long, dark lashes. His brown eyes opening as he licks a stray water droplet from his full lower lip. Me, on my knees in front of him, drowning as I deepthroat a cock the size of a Hickory Farms sausage log.

Okay, I made that last part up, but I don't see how a man as perfect as Ezra could have a gherkin down there when the rest of him looks like *that*. He is walking male perfection, and unless I'm reading the room incorrectly, he's into me.

And that's not good.

Any other day of the week, I'd be down for a one-nighter. Hell, I should be down for one now. An orgasm would disintegrate my stress and let me unwind for a few hours, at least.

But I have to focus. In less than forty-eight hours, I'll finally meet the man who slaughtered my brother.

I push onto the plane and stow my carry-on bag in the overhead compartment. I've just plopped down in my seat when Ezra appears in the aisle. My thighs clench again as he settles so close that I can feel the heat from his skin, and I silently curse myself for choosing a tank top this morning.

Raising the window covering, I stare out at the tarmac and busy myself by counting the luggage being removed from a plane in the distance. Anything to keep my attention away from the man seated beside me.

"Do you fly often?" he asks, forcing me to engage with him.

I shift in my seat. "Not as much as I used to."

"I used to be afraid of flying."

"You?" I turn and look at him. He looks like flying should be afraid of *him*. He's all muscles and mystery, and

36

that bit of scruff on his sharp jaw makes him look almost dangerous. "I can't imagine you being afraid of anything."

A laugh rumbles out of him, and even that sounds sexy. "I've never been a fan of heights. When I was young, my father took me on holiday to Dover. Standing at the edge of the cliffs and looking into the water below was all it took to start a lifelong fear."

"How'd you get over the fear?"

"How does one get over any fear? I faced it. Sometimes when you look into the face of the thing you fear, it doesn't seem so scary anymore. You tend to realize you built it up into something it's not."

Does he have to be attractive as well as intelligent? I mean, glasses make you *look* intelligent, but he actually seems to be. And that accent. He could narrate an instructional calculus video and I'd hang on every word.

Then again, he has a point. Isn't that what I've been doing since I saw him? Building him up into something that can derail me? He's just a fucking man, and maybe it won't hurt to do a little flirting until we part ways. And we will part ways, after all. When we reach Miami, Cat and I will shuffle away to a hotel, and he'll be off on some adventure with his brother and their friend.

I turn to speak, but my stomach chooses this moment to push everything I've eaten in the last twenty-four hours toward the exit. My rosebud puckers to the point of nonexistence, but I fear it won't be enough to hold back whatever waits behind that gate. Unwilling to find out if this is a fart or a shit the hard way, I simply excuse myself and try to stand.

A nearby flight attendant flitters toward me with a saccharine smile, her hands waggling at a frantic pace.

"We're about to take off, so I'll need you to stay in your seat until we're in the air."

My stomach clenches again. With Ezra's face so near the danger zone, the anxiety only adds to the urgency. Goddamn Cat for wanting to stop at that greasy diner this morning.

"I just need to use the restroom," I say. "It won't take long."

This isn't a lie. I'm fairly certain the entirety of my insides will evacuate my body in less than three seconds flat.

The flight attendant's smile doesn't drop. "I'm so sorry for the inconvenience, but we really need everyone in their seats."

"Excuse me," Ezra says as he peers around the detonation zone. "You lovely ladies haven't even given the pre-flight speeches yet. Surely she could pop off to the powder room?"

He gives the woman a smile that could melt a heart made of Antarctic ice, and she reconsiders her stance.

"Well, I'm sure your wife—"

"We're complete strangers," he says with a wink that sends a bright flare of jealousy through my chest, even though he's helping me.

The woman steps out of my way, and a breath of relief rushes out of me. Thankfully, it chooses my mouth as its exit. I clench my ass cheeks for the entire walk of shame to the toilet. God help anyone who enters the bathroom after me.

I squeeze into the tiny space and fumble with the braided leather belt pressed against my midsection. Goddamn my need to be fashionable, but also, goddamn my fingers for suddenly turning to putty. Or maybe it's my brain that refuses to work correctly, because for the first time since I was in preschool, I have forgotten how a fucking belt works.

A hot wave of regret washes over me, and I grip the sides of the metal sink until the cramp passes. Sweat collects on my brow, and I stare back at myself in the mirror. Teeth gritted in sheer terror is not a good look for me.

The intense rush of pain recedes, and I return to the belt. I unfasten the buckle, lower my pants, and flop onto the toilet. What comes out of me can only be described as that pea-soup scene from *The Exorcist*, only out the other end.

The smell, however, is indescribable.

Any hope I had of playing this off disintegrates with each inward breath I take. Now I can only cling to the prayer that the ventilation is top-notch.

Once I'm certain I have nothing left to offer, I clean up and flush the evidence of my crime away. I turn to the sink to wash my hands, all while wondering if the lessening stink is because of the sanitation liquid that rushed my waste away or if it's because I've gone nose blind to it.

Then there's a knock at the door.

"Are you okay in there?" a voice says from the other side, and based on the British accent, I'm certain it's Ezra.

"Yes, just washing my hands," I call back.

"You might want to hurry," he says. "The third passenger in our row arrived, and when they pushed their bag into the overhead compartment, your luggage started . . . buzzing."

"Fuck, fuck, fuck," I say under my breath as I swipe my hands across a few rough paper towels and toss them away. "I'm coming!"

"Judging by the sound of that thing, you probably will be later."

Is there a word in the English language that is stronger than mortified? Because there should be.

I rush out of the bathroom and head right for my stowed bag. It isn't hard to find. It's the one that's rattling the entire cabin with a low bass hum. With all eyes on me, I unzip the side pocket, reach in, and flip the switch. Only then do I look down and see who's sharing our row.

A fucking priest.

I'm not a religious woman, but something about my sex toy randomly activating a few feet above a clergyman's head fills me with an intense amount of guilt. It's not my fucking fault. Blame the TSA. They're the ones who require these things to go in carry-on only.

I slide past Mr. Judgement Journey and the British sex symbol, then flop into my seat and shrink as low as I can. The embarrassment is finally beginning to fade when Ezra leans closer and shoves something into my hand.

Looking down, I spy a packet of Imodium AD in my palm.

Just let me die.

"No need to be ashamed," Ezra whispers close to my ear. If shame didn't have a firm grip on my body, the brush of his warm breath against my ear would have sent goosebumps skating across my skin.

"For almost shitting myself? Or did you mean the sex toy going off above a fucking *priest*?" I whisper back.

Ezra stifles a chuckle. "For starters, everyone on this plane has had a case of the trots at some point. Even the priest has to exorcize the demons sometimes."

"Even you?"

"Why do you think I carry a sachet of pills in my pocket?"

His admission—coupled with a smirk that shouldn't be

that sexy, considering he's talking about explosive diarrhea —does the job and puts me a little more at ease.

"And what about the sex toy?" I ask. "How do I get over *that?*"

"When you get off this plane, you'll likely never see these people again, including the priest. You'll be a funny story at a few office parties for a bit, but then they'll forget all about it."

"And every time I use it, it will be all I think about," I say with a groan.

Ezra adjusts in his seat and turns toward me a bit more. "Maybe you just need someone to hold it against you so you can take your mind off this and focus on something a little more fun."

"If I didn't know better, I'd think you were propositioning me," I say with a laugh, though I'm only half joking. Most men are too insecure to allow toys in the bedroom, so I'm certainly intrigued by this fantasy he's conjured in my mind.

"Maybe I am." He shrugs his broad shoulders. "Would that be such a bad thing?"

Instead of answering him, I peer out the window as the plane starts down the runway.

Chapter Six

Ezra

The plane touches down in Miami, and I only want to return to the air. Once Kindra loosened up from her embarrassment, she'd been the most pleasant companion.

As it turns out, we have much in common. We both enjoy the complete works of Tolstoy and detest the vast majority of the human race. Neither of us vacation often, and we are married to our work. The list of commonalities seem to go on forever.

If I were a man who believed in kismet, I would have seen this as a sign from the heavens. Fortunately, I believe the only luck we have is that which we make for ourselves, and I plan to make my own luck with her.

As passengers shuffle around in their seats and begin gathering their things, I turn to the beauty beside me. "Kindra, we'll be staying at the Flamingo Sands Resort tonight. If you can spare the time—"

"What a coincidence! That's where my friend and I are

staying as well. Maybe we'll run into each other before she and I are forced to take off again tomorrow morning."

Again, I do not believe in kismet, but my god. What are the odds?

"Instead of leaving it up to chance," I say, "why not make a few plans? Maybe dinner and drinks in the lounge just off the lobby?"

Kindra's tongue slides across her full lips, and I've never wanted to put my dick somewhere so badly before. If I can have just one night to ravage those soft curves, I can die a happy man.

"Um . . . maybe," she says. I think she's trying to let me down gently, but then she adds, "How does seven sound?"

Visions of a night of pleasure begin forming in my mind. I can almost feel the way her body will give beneath me. I can almost taste the feral pleasure gathering on my tongue as I lap from that warm space between her legs.

"Unless that doesn't work for you," she says, and I realize I haven't responded.

"Sorry, yes. I'll meet you in the lounge at seven."

"No, Ezra," Bennett says. "Abso-fucking-lutely not. You chose to bring this shitbag along, so you can take care of your little pet yourself. I had to listen to him talk about his political stance for three hours straight, and I can't stand another minute of it."

"Can't you do this for me? Please?" I grip his shoulder to turn him toward me as we stand in one of our two hotel rooms. "I need this."

Bennett rolls his eyes and shrugs out of my hold. "You—the self-proclaimed sex god—*need* this?"

Yes, like air and water and nourishment, I need to know what it feels like to sink inside the sheer perfection that is Kindra. Something about her intrigues me, and I want to know what she sounds like when she comes. But I can't say that, so I just give him a deadpan stare and hope for the best.

His shoulders stiffen, and he turns to me. "Actually, fine. You can have the single room, but I get to kill Gary on the island."

"What? No! I did all the legwork on this one, so it's my kill."

Bennett shrugs and reaches across the bed to close my suitcase. "Then I suggest you grab your things and get out of my room. It's the kill or the room. You can't have it both ways."

A knock silences our debate for the time being, and I let Gary into the room. He's dressed in a loud-as-fuck Hawaiian shirt in a shade of yellow that threatens to give me a migraine. At least one pound of gel forces his hair to stand in short spikes, but the style does the man no favors. His pink scalp peeks out in too many places.

"What's the plan for the night, fellas?" Gary rubs his hands together, and with his bulging eyes, he's the caricature of a human fly.

Bennett turns toward me with a knowing smile. "Yeah, what are our plans tonight?"

None of this would even be an issue if we weren't forced to babysit Gary. Getting a third room and leaving him to his own devices isn't an option, and judging by the swim trunks swallowing his pasty legs, he plans to venture down to one of the resort's three pools.

Where there are pools, there are children.

I glance at my wristwatch and groan internally. It's already half-past six. If I want to shower and ready the room for potential female company, I need to shake a leg.

My options stand before me. On one side is a child predator who offends all the senses and begs to be slain. On the other stands an attractive, intelligent woman who tantalizes me in every way and begs to be fucked. Thoroughly.

I close my eyes and take a deep breath before I say, "I'm probably going to have an early night, so you boys are on your own."

"Such a shame," Bennett says. "You could have had so much fun. But I guess the fun is all mine now, huh, Gary?"

He claps a hand on the wheedling man's back and nearly sends him onto the bed. Gary just grins. He doesn't even realize he won't have teeth to grin with by the time Bennett finishes with him.

"Yes, well, I need to shower and ready myself for bed. If you boys don't mind shuffling out of here, that would be great." I motion them toward the door.

As they exit the room, I catch Gary mentioning a karaoke machine in the attached bar. Bennett turns to me with a final pleading look, but I just smile and usher him out. Hopefully it's not the same lounge where I plan to meet Kindra.

I close the door behind them, return to the bed, and sift through my suitcase. Everything is folded and bagged for ease. My hand fishes around until I pull a clump of dark denim from inside one of the bags. Despite trying to avoid them, wrinkles glare back at me. Maybe they'll loosen while I shower.

I hang the jeans and a dark-grey button-up on a rack in the bathroom. An iron offers a reproachful look from the small closet across the way, but I'm not exactly domestically inclined. The steam will have to do.

I turn on the hot water and step into the large walk-in shower. As I lather my body with the provided hotel soaps, I curse myself for not bringing along a travel set of my own making. Instead of smelling like a man, I get to sit beside a goddess while I give off the aroma of a funeral parlor. Who chooses the fucking scent for these things?

Once I've rinsed off as much of the stink as I can, I step out of the shower and glare at the empty towel rack. I probably should have noticed that when I hung my still-wrinkled clothes there, but I was too consumed by thoughts of Kindra.

Like her ample breasts. And the way her bottom lip forms the perfect landing zone for my cock. She's a bit tightly wound, which leads me to think she'll be the type to let loose in the bedroom. A man can dream.

I slosh water over the carpet as I head toward the phone in the room. After calling room service and requesting some fresh towels, I hurry back to the bathroom and use a rag to dry my body. Only then do I realize I've forgotten to grab a pair of boxers from my bag. I exit the bathroom once more and nearly run into a frail housekeeper.

The gray-haired woman in front of me isn't the least bit fazed. She holds a towel toward me and stands there as if seeing a naked man isn't at all concerning to her.

"Please speak of this to no one," I say before rushing to the bathroom.

After securing the towel around my waist, I open the door to apologize to her properly, but the woman must be part apparition because she's disappeared. I step into the hall, but she's not there either.

Then the door clicks shut behind me.

I turn and rattle the handle, though I know it won't open. My room key lies on the other side of the door, along with my clothing, cell phone, and dignity.

Well, fuck.

With no other option, I head down the hall toward my brother's room. I can only hope he and Gary haven't yet gone out for the evening.

I rap my fist against the door and am flooded with relief when it opens. My brother steps back to allow me to enter, but I don't miss the questions firing in his eyes. I have a few questions of my own when I glance at one of the two beds and see Gary in a deep sleep.

"Bennett, you didn't," I whisper.

"Oh, I did. I have zero interest in karaoke or any activity which involves public attention. I also didn't relish the idea of spending an entire evening listening to his voice, so I did myself a favor and slipped a little something into his pre-game cocktail."

While I prefer for my prey to be fully awake and aware of whatever I have in store for them, Bennett enjoys knocking them unconscious and putting them in precarious situations before they wake up. When it comes to our shared pastime, I am a creature of habit, but my brother is a creator of chaos.

"You can't do anything until we reach the island," I remind him.

"Yes, and how unfortunate," he says as he stares at the sleeping man on the bed. He turns back to me. "Why are you in my room dressed in little more than a thin strip of scratchy cotton?"

"It's a long story, but suffice to say, I have locked myself out of my room. Did they give you a spare key at the front desk?"

Bennett shakes his head and covers his mouth to hide his smile, but his eyes give away his sheer enjoyment of my folly.

Fuck him.

I move toward the phone on the nightstand between the beds, but my brother stops me before I can reach for the receiver.

"No use trying to make a call. The phone doesn't work. It makes this god-awful sound whenever you mash a button. I'm afraid you'll have to waddle down to the front desk and ask for a key." He makes no effort to hide the way his chest shakes with laughter when he's doomed me to roam the halls in the nude.

I turn to look at him. We're roughly the same size, and while I don't enjoy wearing a t-shirt on a first date, it beats the hell out of what I'm wearing now.

"Give me your suitcase," I say.

"What? Absolutely not," he says, and all humor has left him now. "You've already taken my room. I won't have you stretching out my shirts too."

When I say my brother and I are roughly the same size, I mean that in the most hopeful sense. In reality, he could stand to spend some time in the gym. He isn't skinny by any stretch of the imagination, but I don't blame him for worrying that I'll ruin his clothing.

"I just need to wear something long enough to pop down to the lobby," I say. "I'll pay for it if I ruin it."

Bennett sighs, then points to his suitcase atop a large red chair. "Damn right you will."

I rush to unzip the luggage. I've frittered away far too much time already, and I'm cutting it too close for comfort. Kindra strikes me as the kind of woman who won't wait around for a man who's running late, even if his excuse is as good as mine would be.

Near the top of the monsoon wreckage of clothing thrown into his bag, I find a maroon t-shirt and a pair of black sport shorts. I can only assume these are my brother's pajamas for the evening. He dresses much too casually for my taste.

I rush to the bathroom to dress. The shirt is at least one size too small, and the shorts display my dick outline like a neon sign. It's still better than the alternative, but I can't help dreading the walk of shame I'm about to embark upon.

"Hurry back," Bennett says as I leave the hotel room.

The cheeky asshole can kiss the tip of my dick.

Angling my offensive front away from a pair of children returning from the pool, I head toward the elevators. They pay me no mind, but their exhausted mother finds the strength to look twice. I swallow and continue on.

Lady Fortune smiles upon me, because the lobby is blessedly empty. Aside from an elderly man sitting by the empty fountain, it's just me and the employees behind the desk. I approach the dark oak counter and display my best smile.

"I'm afraid I've locked myself out of my room. Could I have a spare key, please?"

The spunky blonde behind the computer monitor smiles and nods. "Of course. I'll just need your room number and identification."

"Unfortunately, my identification is in my room," I say.

"No problem!" Her enthusiasm makes me want to throttle her. "Just return to your room, grab your ID, and I'll have the key made by the time you return."

"How can I return to my room when I don't have a key? You see the problem with your plan, don't you?"

"Oh, goodness. Silly me," she says as she smacks her fingers against her forehead. "I can get a housekeeper to allow you into the room long enough to grab your ID."

Gathering all of my remaining composure, I take a deep breath, glance at her shiny silver name tag, and lean closer to the counter. "Listen, Stephanie, I only checked in an hour or so ago. I'm sure at least one of your fellow employees remembers me."

The ancient housekeeper from earlier appears around the corner. While I'm loath to bring her into this and risk exposing myself further, I see no other option.

"That woman there just brought towels to my room," I say as I point toward the housekeeper. "She can clear this up."

Stephanie motions the woman over. "This gentleman says you brought some towels to his room just now. Is that true?"

The woman looks me up and down, then says, "I've never seen him before."

I grip the counter to stop myself from screaming as she gives me a sly wink. The woman has made good on my request that she keep what happened private, but screw her secrecy in this moment.

Just when I think things can't get much worse, footsteps approach behind me, and a familiar voice reaches my ears.

"Fancy meeting you here."

Chapter Seven

Kindra

He turns to me with a sheepish smile. I'm a bit shocked to find him at the lobby desk instead of the lounge where we agreed to meet. His choice of attire also surprises me.

The maroon shirt threatens to cut off the circulation to the entirety of his upper body, and the black sport shorts have officially usurped gray sweats in the Cock-Showcase Olympics. The man is packing a grenade launcher in those things, and I'm prepared to offer myself as sacrifice.

"Kindra, I'm terribly sorry," he says. "I've locked myself out of my room, and this nice lady at the desk refuses to make a copy of my key."

I flash the girl a cotton-candy grin. "Oh, that's okay. I'll just give the resort owners a call."

As I pull my cell phone from my pocket, the girl at the desk begins typing something into her keyboard.

"No need," she says. "Since you've confirmed that he's Ezra Carter, I'll get the key made right away."

I slip the phone back into my pocket. "Thanks, sweetie. I'll let Cheryl know what an excellent employee you are at our next mimosa brunch."

The desk girl shuffles away to a back room, leaving me alone with Ezra.

"Thanks for that," he says as he runs his hand through his damp hair. "I'm so glad you know the owner. What a stroke of luck."

"Oh, I don't know any such person, but the resort owner waxes on about herself for about an hour in the intro video on the television. I just snagged some of the info I overheard while I was getting ready."

"Stunning and sly. What else will I learn about you this evening, Miss Amato?"

He eyes me with a smirk that turns my pussy into a Slip 'n Slide, and his gaze assesses me as if he knows what I look like without any clothes on. If any other man looked at me this way, I'd eat him alive, but something tells me I'm the one on the menu tonight.

There is something to be said about a man who drips with natural masculine energy. Most men put on a front. They posture and parade around like gorillas when they're nothing more than kittens in costume. Ezra has no need for any of that. The beast within him lingers just below the surface, hiding behind his dark eyes and waiting to pounce.

The blonde scurries back to her post and holds a key card toward Ezra. He takes it with a nod, then turns to me.

"Would it be too much of a bother if I pop up to my room for a quick change? These are my brother's clothes, and I fear my bits will make an appearance the first time I dare to sit down."

His "bits" are already making an appearance, and I'm thoroughly enjoying the view.

"No bother at all," I say. "In fact, I'll come with, if that's okay?"

Like the devilish beast I pegged him as, he catches my meaning and offers another of those sinfully delicious smirks. There's no need for false pretenses. We didn't plan this evening so we could hang out and share a meal. The only things we want to share are our bodily fluids and a couple of orgasms.

Part of my brain still screams that this is a bad idea. I should spend this time preparing Cat for the island. She'll be as obvious as a pubic hair on a bar of soap if I'm not careful, and this is one short-and-curly I can't risk exposing. She could ruin everything.

But then I look back at Ezra, and all rationality evaporates. When will I have the chance to enjoy a one-night stand with someone as attractive as the man walking beside me? There's no risk of feelings or attachments. Just raw, primal need. It's pretty perfect.

We head toward the elevators, and I can practically feel the sexually charged energy bouncing between us. With one look as he presses the call button, he's turned my nipples into tiny pink pebbles held back by thin lace. The anticipation of what's to come is almost too much to bear.

The elevator doors glide open with a *ding*. We step inside, and as soon as he's pressed the button for his floor, he's on me.

His mouth meets mine with a hunger that sets my skin on fire. I'm caged between his arms as his body presses me against the mirrored wall. My fingers glide up his chest and wind around the back of his neck as his hands drop to the backs of my thighs. With little effort, he lifts me and wraps my legs around his waist.

I'm not exactly a svelte supermodel, so I'm surprised he's chosen to manhandle me like this. Surprised, but not at all disappointed.

"God, you smell incredible," he says as he lowers his mouth to my throat and nips the sensitive skin.

I tilt my head to give him more access, and he rewards me by massaging my pulse point with the tip of his well-muscled tongue. The power and precision behind that thing makes me want to rip off my clothes right now and shove his face between my legs.

If it weren't for the cameras I'm sure are hidden some-where in here, I'd do exactly that.

The car begins to slow, and my stomach does a flip as the elevator settles on his floor. He lowers me to my feet, places his hand on the small of my back, and guides me toward his room.

Using his new room key, he unlocks the door, and we step inside. I expect a moment of awkward fumbling before we get back to what we were doing in the elevator, but this man is all calculated precision. His lips are on mine as soon as the door clicks shut behind him.

His hands find my hips. He grips my love handles as he guides me backward until my legs meet the edge of the bed. I sit, and only then does he pull his mouth from mine so that he can kneel in front of me. He lifts the hem of my shirt, nipping and licking the sensitive strip of skin just above the waistband of my shorts.

"Let me grab a condom," he whispers over my skin.

"I'm allergic to latex," I say. "If you're worried about kids, I have an implant. If you're worried about STDs, I suggest not seducing random women you meet at airports."

A low laugh rumbles out of him. "Fair point."

His fingers work to unfasten my shorts, and I'm glad I chose to venture out sans belt tonight. Every second without his mouth on my skin is torture.

He slides my shorts down my legs and gazes at my black lace panties with a look that turns my insides to molten lava.

"You're fucking perfect," he whispers against my thigh.

Men often say these things in the heat of the moment, but it's usually a desperate attempt to keep the woman engaged so that they can get off and get out. But Ezra's voice drips with sincerity and awe.

"Are you leaving your glasses on?" I ask.

"Take them off and miss seeing any of this? Absolutely not." He adjusts the tilted frames until they're situated back in their rightful place.

Yeah, it's a very good thing I'll never see him again after tonight, because I could see him becoming a big problem for me.

"Take off your shirt," he commands. "I want to see more of you."

Happy to oblige, I grip the hem of my top and pull it over my head. A low groan of approval rumbles from his chest as he eyes my nearly naked body.

"I want to taste every inch of you," he says as he leans forward and bites my inner thigh. He uses just enough pressure to send a jolt of pleasurable pain through my body. Then he stills and gazes up at me. "Can I tie you up?"

I've always been curious about bondage, but it's not something I've ever tried. Considering my line of work, warning sirens should be howling in my head, but my pussy has turned off the alarm system.

I nod.

He stands, putting me at eye level with his erection. I

didn't feel any fear when he asked to tie me up, but seeing that thing up close has me a little nervous. I worry I'll be forced to tap out the moment he puts more than half of that monster inside me.

I don't have time to think about that, though, because he's brought a bag to the bed, and now he's binding my wrists above my head. Why does this man have a bag of ropes, and why do I hardly give a fuck as to why? He could be a fellow serial killer for all I know, and I'm his most willing victim.

"I can't wait to play with you," he says as he attaches the red rope to the post on the headboard. "You're going to be my little toy tonight. Are you okay with that?"

"What does that entail?" I ask.

He grips my hips and pushes me up the bed so that he can crawl between my legs. "It means I'll do whatever I want with your body. I'll give you pain, but I'll also give you pleasure. Can you trust me with that?"

I don't imagine I have much of a choice, now that I'm bound to the bed, but honestly, the hint of danger is turning me on more than I could have imagined.

"I trust you," I say as he drags his tongue across my thin panties.

"Good girl."

Without warning, he grabs me and flips me onto my stomach. His arm slides under my hips, and he raises me until my ass is in the air. He pulls my panties to the side and bites my ass cheek, alternating between painful nips and gentle licks. I squirm against the restraints.

"Be still or I'll have to punish you," he growls.

His palm cracks against my ass, and I cry out. I feel the sting of his strike long after his hand moves away, but he soothes the pain by rubbing the warm skin. Fabric rips as he tears my panties away, and I'm almost upset that he's just destroyed an expensive undergarment.

Then his head is beneath me. His glasses land on the bed, and all is forgiven when he says, "Sit on my face."

He doesn't have to tell me twice. I lower my hips, trying to give him some breathing room so that he doesn't suffocate, but it's not enough for him. His arms band around my thighs, pulling me down until my pussy creates a vacuum seal with his mouth.

My mind goes blank as he laves my clit with warmth and pressure. An occasional groan leaves his lips as he devours me, sending heavenly vibrations through my core. I fight the urge to grind on his face, because I fear he'll stop as punishment. The spanking I could handle, but I'll die if he pulls his mouth from me.

His nails dig into the small of my back, and my thighs begin to quiver. I can only hope I'm allowed to move while I'm coming, because I have a feeling I'll lose all control over my muscles.

"Fuck, I'm close," I whimper.

I don't know why women tell men when they're close, especially when being eaten out. It usually results in the man completely changing what he's been doing, which ruins the orgasm. But Ezra is a pro, and I never should have doubted him. He keeps that same pressure between my legs until I'm a shaking, shivering mess.

Unable to keep still any longer, my hips move of their own accord and grind my pussy against his mouth. He tightens his grip around my waist, pulling me down and keeping me in place as I come on his face.

Stars dance behind my eyes, and I'm pretty sure I lose consciousness for a few seconds. I bury my face in a pillow and moan through the waves of pleasure. My pussy spasms around nothing, and now I want him to fill me.

"Please fuck me," I beg. "I need you inside me."

He moves off the bed and turns me onto my back again. If my wrists hurt from the pressure, I can't tell. I'm numb from the explosive orgasm, and I can only feel my pulse throbbing between my legs. I can only feel the intense need to have him pound into me until I can't see, massive cock be damned.

He reaches over, picks up his discarded glasses, and puts them on his face as if he *needs* to see me clearly. Why is such a simple motion so fucking sexy? I've seen people put on glasses a million times, but never with such villainous finesse.

He moves to my wrists and releases the rope. "Sit up and put your hands behind your back."

I do as he commands, and he removes my bra before securing my hands, then wrapping the rope around my chest. My breasts begin to swell from the pressure, but it's surprisingly pleasurable, especially when he closes his mouth around my nipple. The skin is so much more sensitive now.

"You're being such a good little toy," he says, then bites my breast.

My body jerks as a jolt of pain stabs through my chest, but I don't pull away. I want this. I want all of this. There's something so freeing about being bound and having all control taken away.

His hand cracks against the outside of my thigh. "Open your legs or I'll have to tie them up too. For tonight, I own you, and I want to see what belongs to me."

I keep my thighs pressed together, but not because I don't want him to fuck me. I just want him to tie my legs to the posts. It sounds hot as fuck, and I want him to thoroughly use me.

"Very well," he says with a smirk.

He stands and removes his shirt before digging through his bag of tricks. A light sweat slicks his chest. When he returns to the bed, he fastens a rope around each ankle, then places me exactly how he wants me before hoisting my legs as high and wide as they can go.

I didn't think this through. While I'm very secure about my body, I don't relish the idea of my asshole getting this much light. He doesn't seem to mind, though. He just pulls off his shorts, kneels before me on the bed, then leans over me, pressing the head of his cock against my dripping entrance.

"I'm going to use you now," he whispers into my ear. "Just remember to trust me."

He sits up and closes his hand around my throat, and I worry I've reached my limit. This is getting a little too David Carradine for me as he applies pressure to the side of my neck. Before I can open my mouth to voice my concerns, he grinds his hips forward and pushes inside me.

I'm not ashamed to admit I've shoved some questionable objects inside my pussy over the years. Don't we all experiment a little before we gain the courage to purchase a dildo? But nothing has ever filled me as completely as Ezra's cock.

With each slow pump of his hips, his grip tightens on my neck. He isn't cutting off my air, but I still feel a dizzying darkness creeping around the edge of my vision. If I have to die today, I suppose there are worse ways to go.

Just before I black out, he releases his hold and moves his hand to my pussy. He rubs my clit, massaging at a steady pace until another orgasm lingers on the brink of detonation.

"I can feel you getting close," he says. "Don't hold back. I want you to come on my cock. Give me what I demand, or I'll stop pleasing you."

Oh, fuck. Each gravelly word rushes straight between my legs and pushes me closer to the edge of oblivion, but the pressure of being made to come on command is too much.

"I can't," I moan. "Just keep fucking me. Please."

His free hand shoots toward my neck, and the blood choke resumes. "I won't let go until you come, so I suggest you figure it out."

A bolt of panic seizes my chest because he sounds really fucking serious. This doesn't feel like something kinky anymore. But for some strange reason, his threat is just the nudge I need. Right before I black out, I'm overcome with a full-body sensation like I've never felt.

Stars blaze across the ceiling, and the darkness gives way to a rush of blinding light. I want to scream that I'm coming, but my voice refuses to cooperate. Cries of pleasure fill the air on my next breath, but my mouth can't form words.

With the way I'm tied up and quivering, I probably look like a trussed pig having a seizure, but I don't care. I've never experienced such an intense orgasm, and if I have to get tied up and choked to the point of hilarity to feel something so amazing, so be it.

Ezra also doesn't seem to mind. As my eyes focus once more, he releases my neck and I see him above me. Sweat glistens on his chest and forehead. Breath saws out of him as he continues pummeling my pussy, and a dark glint shines in his eyes.

He leans forward, bracing himself on powerful forearms

as his thrusts stutter to a stop. His cock fills me so completely that I can feel each pulse as he comes inside me.

When he's fully spent, he sits up and begins untying my legs. I'm just as breathless as he is, and all I did was lie there and take it. He helps me into a sitting position and unties my wrists. My shoulders are going to ache for the next few days, but it's so worth it.

With my arms and legs finally free, I flop back on the bed and smile. "That was incredible," I say on an out breath. "I'm almost sad it's over. Could you hand me my clothes? I don't think I can walk."

Instead of gathering my things, he drops beside me on the bed. "Over? The night is still young, pet, and we have miles to go before we sleep."

Chapter Eight

Kindra

Six. That's the number of times I came before I hobbled back to mine and Cat's room at three a.m. She'd been fast asleep as I crawled beneath the covers and slid into a dreamless sleep, and I was glad for it. After such an amazing night, I didn't want it spoiled by mindless conversation.

Not that I had much mind left to contribute by the time Ezra finished with me.

Now it's seven in the morning, and I'm exhausted as I trudge to the bathroom to shower before heading off for our flight to the island. My shoulders feel like they've been beaten with a hammer, but the ropes left no marks on my wrists. With the way I was squirming, I'm surprised I didn't saw them clean off.

As for my hips, legs, and pussy, I don't think I'll ever walk normally again.

"Morning, sunshine," Cat says as I step out of the bathroom. "I brought up some breakfast from the lobby. For a resort, they didn't have much to choose from."

Her bright demeanor so early in the day would normally grate my nerves raw, but the multiple orgasms from the previous night have left my tolerance much improved.

"Thanks," I say as I towel off my hair. I dress in something comfortable for the plane ride—another tank-top-and-shorts ensemble, no belt—and sit on the edge of the bed.

Cat grabs her laptop and sits beside me. "I received a link to a video from the Sinners Retreat last night, but you were still out, so I haven't watched it yet. I figured we could watch it together."

"What kind of video?"

She shrugs and opens the laptop. "I dunno. Probably some kind of orientation."

After clicking a link, a pink-and-orange logo fills the screen and a male voice comes through the speakers.

"In a few short hours, you'll be on Devil's Horn Island, home of the Sinners Retreat."

The image fades to black, then fades back in on a wide shot of a large island set in the middle of the ocean. The images look like they were shot with a camera from the seventies. Even the music sounds like something from a bygone era.

"While on our island, please observe a few simple rules. First, keep your kills confined to activity events. We have several to choose from."

Short clips flash across the screen. In one, a couple rides a pair of horses down the beach at sunset. As they break into a canter and move away from the camera, we can see the ropes attached to each horse. Two bodies bounce along behind them, leaving a trail of blood to be washed away by the incoming waves.

In another shot, a group of people laugh as they mill about a kitchen. The camera zooms in on a blender, which holds a severed hand and what appears to be a few organs. Maybe a liver and some kidneys, based on the coloring. The blender whirs to life, and the body parts turn to mush.

"I am not partaking in the cooking class," Cat says.

"Now there's something we can agree on."

I lean forward and watch as the video continues.

"For the safety and privacy of our guests, we do not allow any photography or videography on the island. All guests must consent to have their devices wiped clean of all images before departing our little slice of heaven."

After an image of a camera with a large red X over it, the shot showcases a large mansion set within a jungle.

"We look forward to seeing you at the welcome dinner. And remember, we're all sinners here."

The camera backs away and rises, revealing a group of people on the beach, who all smile and wave as the shot fades to black.

"Well, that's three minutes of my life I'll never get back." I stand and move to the sink to begin packing away my toiletries.

Cat does the same, and we're ready to leave when our car arrives out front a few minutes later. I grab the small bag of breakfast Cat chose for me and peek inside. A dry muffin stares back at me. It's a good thing I'm not very hungry. After last night, I don't think I'll crave anything other than Ezra for a while.

We make our way to the lobby, then out the front doors. I look back at the resort and bid a silent farewell to an evening of fantasy fulfillment. At least something good came out of this.

Now it's time to focus.

Once we're settled in the back of a long black limo, I turn to Cat and keep my voice low so the driver can't eavesdrop. "Listen, while we're on the island, I need you to keep a low profile. You have to help me keep a low profile as well. That means you can't bring up my real identity. Got it?"

She nods. "My lips are sealed."

I wish she spoke in facts instead of cliches. We wouldn't be in this mess if she had some strong epoxy to hold her mouth shut.

"Also, no matter how excited you are to witness or participate in these activities, you have got to keep your cool. If you look like a first timer, you'll blow our cover."

I can see it now. Someone slits a throat, and Cat's eyes go wide with wonder. If they get a single whiff of her naïveté, we'll be the ones to have our throats opened.

Cat groans and looks out the window. "I wish you had a little more faith in me. I'm not completely useless."

While I'm sure she's good at many things, she has yet to divulge any of them to me, either by words or actions. But I keep this to myself. I'll have to watch her like a mother hen for the next five days, and I don't want to upset her too much.

We arrive at a small airport after a short drive through Miami. Our driver takes us straight onto the tarmac, where a sleek silver jet awaits our arrival. A man dressed in black takes our luggage, then leads us to the stairs, where we enter the most luxurious travel accommodations I've ever experienced.

The space looks more like a futuristic living room than the inside of an aircraft. White leather seats dot the interior, with what looks like a couch on one side. The ceiling is one big screen, which showcases a night sky. It's so realistic that I feel like I'm standing in the open instead of crammed inside a tin can.

I turn to Cat, expecting her to be as awestruck as I am, but she's playing it cool. She glances around like she flies in one of these on the daily, then takes a seat in one of the white leather chairs.

I choose a seat near the back of the cabin, preferring to sit by myself. If anyone else joins us, I can only hope they'll sit with her. I pull out my phone and begin scrolling so that I look as unapproachable as possible.

A few minutes later, footsteps trudge up the stairs, and an elderly man shuffles into the cabin. Cat notices him and turns to me. We share a look of raised eyebrows, then return to watching him.

There's no way he's on the right plane.

For starters, he's a wiry little antique. I can't imagine him killing anyone. He looks more like someone's grandfather than their worst nightmare. Then again, maybe that's why he's good at what he does.

He takes a seat near Cat and pulls a large bowie knife from beneath his suit before wiping it with the handkerchief from his breast pocket.

Appearances can be deceiving, I suppose.

Cat engages him in conversation, but they speak too quietly for me to hear what they're saying. Now I wish I'd sat closer. If she makes a misstep, I won't be there to save her.

"Do you know how long until we depart?" I say to the man, hoping to interrupt their conversation before anything can go wrong.

The man shakes his wrist, freeing his watch from his

suit sleeve so that he can look at it. "Maybe ten minutes or so."

He has a hint of an accent, possibly German.

I nod in acknowledgment and return to my phone when I see Cat pull a magazine from the small table in front of her. Good. She's much better suited for celebrity gossip.

Exhaustion creeps up on me. I tip the back of my head against the leather headrest and close my eyes. With no idea how long this flight will last, I toy with the notion of a cat nap. Even thirty minutes would do me some good.

But then footsteps clang on the staircase once more, and Ezra steps into the cabin.

Chapter Nine

Ezra

The woman I fucked into oblivion is a fellow serial killer? What are the fucking odds?

I smile and stride toward her, even though she doesn't look nearly as happy to see me. When the shock wears off, I hope she'll be more enthused. Or at least slightly amenable. The only thing I love more than killing is fucking, and if I can do both on the island, this will be the best Sinners Retreat yet.

"This is quite the turn of events," I say as I take a seat beside her.

She blinks up at me and struggles to speak. "You . . . your brother. I mean, you're one of us?"

"Gooble-gobble, one of us," I chant.

She raises an eyebrow.

"You'd have to see the movie, I guess." I clear my throat. "Yes, my brother and I are serial killers, just like you and, I'm guessing, your blonde friend."

"What are the fucking odds?" she breathes.

"That's exactly what I thought when I saw you."

My brother and Gary choose to sit near Kindra's friend, which is all right by me. A little more alone time to admire this woman isn't exactly a bad thing.

"Have you been to this thing before?" she asks.

"Yeah, my brother and I have been attending since its inception ten years ago."

"And your friend?" She points toward Gary.

I lick my lips and lean closer. "Can you keep a secret, my pet?"

Goosebumps rise on her skin. Even if she's trying to play it cool, she can't disguise her body's reaction to my breath rushing over her. "Yes, I'd like to think I can. You don't get very far in this hobby if you can't."

"He's not our friend, nor is he of our ilk. He's slotted to become Cattle for the island, though his killer will be my brother. The event coordinator owed us a favor, and we couldn't leave the pervert on the streets."

"He's a—?"

"Sick man, yes. Very sick. Just a few days ago, he kidnapped a small girl who was walking home from school. The details are enough to turn my stomach, so I won't reveal them. Just know that my brother will ensure he gets the end he deserves."

The engines whir to life outside the cabin, and everyone begins fastening seatbelts and settling in for the flight. Moments later, we're taxiing down the runway and rising into a blue sky.

I look toward my brother, who's lost in conversation with the blonde. Or an argument, rather. She keeps shaking her head, her arms folded over her chest as she gets increasingly heated. That's Bennett for you. He's much better at making enemies than friends.

I recognize the small German fellow near them. He's known as *der Sensenmann* in his homeland, but we just call him Grim. While he looks like a college professor, he's a wild man with a knife. Or a hatchet. Anything with a sharp blade will do where he's concerned.

Kindra shifts beside me and rests her head against the seat. Her lips part in a wide yawn, which she covers with her hand.

"Tired?" I ask.

She smiles for the first time since I arrived on the plane. "Someone kept me up late last night."

"I hope it was worth it, at least."

"Very much so."

I lower my voice. "Any chance of a repeat performance? I'd love to experience another night with you."

The smile drops from her face and takes my heart down with it. "As much as I'd love to, I'm kind of on a mission here. I'm looking for someone."

"Maybe I can help. Who is it?"

She lifts her shoulders in a shrug. "That's the problem. I'm not sure. He killed my brother several years ago, and I want to make him pay for it."

"That's going to be hard to do. They have pretty strict rules about killing fellow guests."

"I'm not that stupid." She shakes her head. "I just want to know who he is so I can find him when we get back. I'll need more than five days to torture him, anyway."

"Stop it. You're turning me on."

She smacks my shoulder like she thinks I'm kidding, so I grip her hand and place it on my lap.

Her eyes widen.

Then an idea strikes me. "I get that you'll need to focus

once we're on the island, but we aren't there yet. Maybe we could slip off to the loo?"

She unfastens her seatbelt and stands. "And maybe after that, we could have tea and crumpets."

"Why do you Americans always go straight to the tea and crumpets?" I release my lap belt and follow her.

We trot off to the small bathroom with everyone's eyes on us, but she doesn't seem to care, so neither do I. If Bennett has something snarky to say later, I'll know it comes from a place of jealousy.

Once we're inside with the door closed behind us, Kindra drops to her knees and begins lowering my shorts. "It's my turn to show you what my mouth can do," she says.

Not one to turn down a blow job, I don't argue.

She wraps her hand around my dick and goes straight for the undercarriage. Her mouth bathes my balls in wet heat as she runs circles with her tongue, all while staring up at me.

"You're a naughty thing, aren't you?" I growl.

Her tongue slides up my balls and travels the length of my shaft, but she doesn't go right for the head. She stops just below it and slowly trails back to the base. Pleasure grips my spine.

"I want you to fuck my face," she whispers against my cock.

Gripping her dark hair, I press the head of my dick against her lips. She opens her mouth and lets me inside. I've only been this close to heaven once before, and that was last night.

"Fuck," I groan as I push to the back of her throat. "I love the way you let me use you."

She stares up at me, a smile in her brown eyes. The girl likes praise, and I'm happy to provide it.

Her full lips expertly guard her teeth, so I pick up the pace and fuck her mouth a little faster. A low moan climbs up her throat and tickles my dick. I look down and realize she's slipped her hand down her shorts to play with herself as I use her, and it's all I can do to stop myself from blowing my load right now.

I push hard against her face and hold myself in place. Tears fill her eyes, but she doesn't gag or struggle away. She takes me. All of me. The poor thing can barely get her mouth around me, but she gobbles my cock like it's her job. Well, she's about to get a raise.

"When I come, don't swallow. Hold it in your mouth. Do you understand?"

She nods her head gently.

"Good girl."

Another moan flies up her throat. She must be as close to coming as I am.

I begin fucking her throat again. "Don't come yet," I say through gritted teeth. "The only orgasm you have will be the one I give you."

Her hand moves faster in her shorts, and her thighs begin to shake. I grip her hair tighter and angle her head back as I pound into her mouth even harder.

"Don't be a naughty pet," I say.

Her eyes close as she pants around my cock, sending me over the edge, and I fill her mouth with my come. I hold her in place until I've finished. With puffed cheeks and tear-filled eyes, she leans back and waits for my next command.

"Stand."

She does as she's told, and I pull her against me and kiss her. As our tongues tangle together, my pleasure transfers from her mouth to mine. I'm sure she's more than happy for the load to change hands. Come doesn't exactly taste pleasant, but I didn't do this so that I could taste it.

I kneel before her and snatch down her shorts. I'm pleasantly surprised when I realize she's wearing no panties. She steps out of the denim, then leans back against the wall, spreading her legs to give me access to her perfect mound.

Gripping her full hips, I bury my face in her sweet scent and force my come inside her with my tongue. I push two fingers into her to drive it deeper as I suck her clit.

A moan rolls off her lips as she grips my shoulders. Her thighs quiver against the sides of my face, and this is probably the fastest I've ever gotten a woman off. To be fair, that blow job was probably the fastest I've gotten off as well.

As her orgasm recedes, I help her into her shorts. She steadies herself by holding on to me, but she looks completely done in.

"You should be able to get in a nice nap now," I say with a smirk.

She laughs, then moves toward the sink to clean herself up. I grip her arm and stay her hand.

"I want you to finish the flight with my come between your legs," I say. "Call it weird if you'd like, but just knowing you're sitting there with my mark on you . . ."

She licks her lips and considers my request. "Okay, and what if I get a fucking yeast infection? Will you be the one to request some Monistat be flown to the island?"

"Way to ruin the moment, pet." I place a kiss on her forehead and look into her eyes. "Just do this for me."

She lets out a laugh and shrugs. "Okay, but only if you let me leave a mark on you as well."

"Anything you'd like," I say.

Without hesitation, she pulls me closer, raises my shirt,

and begins to suck the skin above my left nipple. I can only stand there and watch as she leaves a hickey the size of Denmark on my chest.

Leaning back, she studies her handiwork and finds it satisfactory. She lowers my shirt and pats my chest, then turns to exit the bathroom.

As we return to our seats, the gallery erupts in a series of applause and raucous cheers. Kindra blushes a shade of red I've never seen before, but I just stare at the others and shake my head.

"Did you fuck her?" Gary calls across the cabin.

Cat leans forward and smacks the top of his balding head. "What the fuck is wrong with you?"

Kindra flops into her seat and covers her face with her hands. "Are you positive your brother has dibs on that guy? Because I'd really love to be the one to kill him."

I need some way to take her mind off this embarrassment. The poor thing might never fly again after this trip.

"Tell me a little more about your brother's killer," I say. "Maybe I can help you find him."

She lowers her hands and stares at her lap. Embarrassment has given way to depression, and I kick myself for picking such a sore topic.

"I don't know anything about him," she says. "He's a ghost. Only one person has ever seen his face and lived to talk about it. That's how he got his name. The Abattoir Adonis."

Ice crystalizes in my veins, and my heart ceases to beat. The man she's searching for, the man she wants to kill . . . is me.

Chapter Ten

Ezra

They've made several upgrades to the retreat since last year. A new floating dock for swimming. New furniture inside the villas, which gives them a homier feel.

Home would be nice right now, actually.

A pain rips through my stomach, and I lean against the brand new chairs in the kitchenette's dining space. I gave Kindra my last precious sachet of pills, and now I feel as if my bowels may evacuate from the sheer irony that has become this trip.

When I got on the plane and saw her, I thought the good fortune of her being there too was cute. Sweet, even. But now I think it's a load of tosh. How did it turn from one of the greatest nights of my life to absolute horse shit?

I killed her brother, which is shitty enough, but then you factor in the knowledge that I only kill predators, and it only gets worse. It means her brother was one of them.

There is no solution that will allow her to hate me less when she finds out.

I remove my glasses and strip off my shirt. The heat from the island makes the waves of stomach pain even more unbearable. Sweat drips down my temples.

"Ezra?" Bennett's voice drifts through the windows.

I open the front door and get him inside before he alerts Kindra to our whereabouts. We really need to fucking chat. We didn't have a chance once we left the jet. The host ushered us to our private villas and scurried away.

"Get in here," I say.

He enters and closes the door behind him. "Whoa, you look like shit."

"Then I'm sure I look exactly how I feel. Where's Gary?" Even in my panic, I can't take my mind off that bellend.

"He's Cattle now. Don't worry about him. I wish I could have taken a picture of his face when I handed him over, but no photo ops, unfortunately. So what's got you looking like you've seen a ghost?"

It's an interesting choice of words because I feel like her brother's ghost has come back to haunt me after so many years.

"Remember the woman I met on the plane?" I say.

"And back at the hotel?"

I squeeze the bridge of my nose. "Yes. We had the most incredible night."

"Then what's the problem?"

"She's here to find her brother's killer."

"And?"

"I'm her brother's killer."

Bennett blinks an innumerable amount of times before uttering two words. "What? How?"

"Her brother was clearly unsavory. I wouldn't have killed him otherwise."

I brush a hand through my hair. If she'd found this out before we had sex, this would have been so much simpler. Instead, I had to listen to her spew her hatred for me while my come was still inside her. That's fucked, even by my standards.

Bennett shifts his weight between his feet. "Just tell her the—"

"I'll do no such thing. She can't know. She mustn't find out."

Bennett laughs, and I envision punching a hole in his throat. "The regulars know you as the Abattoir Adonis."

"Well, we need to make them not know."

"How?"

"We'll tell the organizer I want to remain anonymous this year. Then we just need to find the regulars and encourage them to keep schtum."

"I mean . . . I guess. But this sounds like a waste of time."

"Bennett, she can't find out." I've never been one to beg, but I'll get on my knees and lick boots if it means I can get a handle on this situation.

His eyes roll as he raises his hands skyward in a show of defeat. "Fine, I'll help."

How is it so difficult to find these people? It's an island, and only a small portion has been cleared out for guests.

Knocking on the villa doors proved unfruitful, though I did find Grim cleaning a knife while wearing only his

Speedo. When the older man answered the door, one testicle hung from the scanty hammock of navy-blue fabric. I couldn't get him to close the door on my face fast enough after I'd told him to keep my identity a secret.

With Bennett off to tell the organizer, I head to the beach. A huge pavilion stands on a strip of sand. New benches and chairs sit inside, and the outside shines with a new coat of sky-blue paint.

Ice Pick sits on the beach nearby, a beer balancing on his reddening belly as he sleeps. I step closer, and when my shadow eclipses him, he jerks awake. Before I know what's happening, there's an ice pick aimed at my gut. Where did that even come from?

Ice Pick lifts his dark sunglasses and laughs. "Hey, Adonis."

The Ice Pick Killer is a Texas phenomenon. He's brutal, willing to stab first and ask questions later, and I came a fraction of an inch from feeling that sort of evisceration.

"Can you do me a favor?" I ask.

We don't usually ask each other for favors. This is a very selfish profession, and we are very selfish people. But I don't see what other options I have.

"Depends what it is," he says as he tucks his ice pick beneath his hairy thigh.

"I need you to pretend you don't know me on this trip. Forget who I am. I'm nobody."

He takes a hearty swig of sun-warmed beer. "Can I call you the Crumpet Killer?"

Why do Americans *always* come at the crumpets?

"That's not your name, is it?" asks a sing-song voice behind me. It's not the lusty, mildly bitchy tone of Kindra, which means it's her blonde friend. The only other female killer on the island is Maudlin Rose, and she doesn't speak at all.

I turn and hope she only heard the tail end of this conversation.

"Yes, I am the Crumpet Killer," I say, because what the fuck else can I do? I'm now tied to this stupid name. Though I'm enraged, I'm equally amused and hysterical, and I struggle to keep a straight face. My happiness is on the line if I don't. "Where's Kindra?"

"She's over there with . . . um . . . the guy with the mullet."

I follow her finger to the pavilion and spot Kindra just within the comfort of the shade. Her dark hair whips around her face as she tries to hold it back with her hand. She looks angelic and so out of place compared to the man beside her on the picnic bench.

His wild blond mullet blows behind him as he points toward me, laughing with lips that are covered by one of the worst porno mustaches I've ever seen.

"Eighties Man." Fuck, I haven't gotten to him yet.

"Yeah, that's him," Cat says.

I'm typically a very calm person. You don't survive this career by allowing emotions to control you. But I am at their utter control as I watch Eighties' squirrelly finger pointing at me.

What has he told her? All I imagine is him saying, "*Oh, there's the Abattoir Adonis!*"

And my god, I'm panicking inside as I make my way over to them to see if Kindra will try to kill me. No amount of orgasms will stay her hand once she learns who I am. Judging by the scowl on her face, I may already be too late.

Chapter Eleven

Kindra

Ezra and Cat head toward me, and Ezra can hardly look me in the eye. Why does he look like someone just pushed his puppy into a puddle?

"Did you know he's the Crumpet Killer?" Cat says with a laugh. Right in front of him. She's shameless.

The man beside me—Eighties, as he's asked me to call him—shifts in his seat and opens his mouth, but Ezra interrupts him.

"You two never told me your killer names," he says in that smooth British accent.

Cat raises her chin, more than happy to have a chance to use the backstory we've created. "I'm the Cat Scratch Killer and she's the Sunlig—"

"Sun*shine* Strangler," I blurt before she blows our fucking cover.

I throw daggers at her with my eyes, and she mouths, *I'm sorry*. She made up the damn names. She should be able to remember them.

The man beside me scratches his head. "I'm confused."

"Why don't we grab some drinks, Eighties?" Ezra says.

The mulleted wonder stares at Ezra before getting up and walking with him toward the pavilion's tiki bar. As I watch the two men walk away, my chest tightens as memories of my time with Ezra flash through my head.

Even though I planned to cut him off once we reached the island so that I could focus on finding my brother's killer, it still hurts that he beat me to the punch. He's been distant since we joined the mile high club. What changed?

"I'd love a vodka tonic!" Cat yells toward them.

I turn to Cat. "Are you even old enough to drink?"

"I'm twenty-two."

Ezra brushes sweat from his forehead, still avoiding my gaze as he turns around. "They only offer beer and wine coolers until after the welcome party."

"Fine, but nothing berry!" Cat calls. "I'm allergic to berries."

"Not liking them isn't an allergy," I remind her. She's so melodramatic. The first time I met her, she acted like her throat was closing up from the sight of some blueberries in a bowl. I can't abide the theatrics.

Cat flops beside me on the bench. She wasted no time throwing on her tiny bikini and sheer pink wrap. She's treating this like an actual vacation when it's anything but.

"You really need to be more careful," I say to Cat. "I can't be with you all the time, especially since we don't share a villa. If you don't want me to put you on a leash, I suggest you learn to stop barking."

"When do we get to kill someone?" she asks as she gazes out at the water. "I thought this was a murder retreat."

"I don't know. I haven't read the event brochure yet because I've been a little busy."

"Making eyes at Ezra?" She waggles her eyebrows.

"No. That was a fling, and it's over now."

She licks her lips and fights off a grin. "I dunno. I saw the way he was watching you."

I smack her arm as the men approach. Mullet guy hands a drink to Cat, but Ezra is empty-handed. Which is fine by me. I want to keep my head for the remainder of the week, and alcohol won't help me do that.

"Kindra, do you fancy a walk on the beach?" Ezra asks.

I turn to face him. "Only if you aren't planning to avoid my eyes the entire time."

"Eyes are overrated, pet. I have other things I want to look at."

His words are meant as a joke, but I don't find them funny. I'm still mad at him. He went from an endearing British man who gave me endless orgasms to . . . well, this.

If he has an issue with banging a psychopath, then I don't know what to tell him. And I don't know that a walk will help. It's not my fault that his radar is off. I knew what he was the moment he pulled out his bag of tricks. I guess he could have been going to a BDSM conference or something, but I just knew this man and I had more in common than our intense desire to explore each other intimately.

But closure is always nice, and the only way I'll get any answers will be by talking to him.

"Fine," I say. "I'll go for a walk with the man who's shrugged me off like a used jacket."

What else am I going to do? Spend time with Cat? I'd rather die.

Ezra winces and holds his hand toward me, but I ignore it and stand under my own power and start toward the water.

The sand darkens where the waves have lapped against

the shore. It feels better on my feet than the loose granules. Sandpipers rush in and out with the water, skittering around on toothpick legs as they search for food.

Ezra catches up to me, and we walk alongside each other in silence as the ocean gathers around our feet. The water is surprisingly warm. I don't know what I was expecting, but I've never been to the beach before. I've always been landlocked or surrounded by lakes and rivers, never a vast ocean like this.

Despite the serenity, one question nags at me.

"Why?" I ask.

Well, that was shorter than I expected.

"Why what, pet?"

"Don't say that sweet word with your endearing British accent. You fucked me and then acted like you wanted nothing to do with me."

"It's complicated, Kindra."

"Then uncomplicate it, *Ezra*. Don't want anyone to know you're fucking the fat chick? Is that it?"

He takes a deep breath, his dark eyes scanning the water before jumping to me. "Fucking you was a privilege and not something I would ever be ashamed of."

"Then what happened?"

He stops, shakes his head, and strips off his shirt. He tucks it into the back of his jeans, and I've never seen anything so sexy. The sun gleams off his body.

I'm about to press the issue and ask the question again, but a scream breaks through the ocean's roar. As a serial killer, I home in on that sound.

"Why do I hear screams?" I ask.

Ezra looks around. "Probably the Cattle."

"The what?"

"For fireworks tonight, after the welcome party."

"That explains absolutely nothing." I drag my toe through the sand and watch as water fills the depression with the next wave.

"Each year, they bury a few of the Cattle—the prisoners—in the sand. Well, they bury their heads in the sand so they can shoot fireworks from their bums."

"So why can I hear them screaming?"

"I'm guessing some haven't been buried yet."

I follow the sounds like a fucked-up moth to a macabre flame and find an area cordoned off by low rope fencing. Several nude people lie side by side, most with their heads buried beneath the sand. Leg irons keep their ankles the perfect width apart, and their hands have been secured behind their backs. Their asses poke into the air, just like Ezra said, and light-pink fabric lies crumpled beside each one.

A man in a clown mask grips a screaming woman by her hair and shoves her face into a hole in the sand. A sand mound beneath her abdomen keeps her in an angled position as he dumps buckets of wet sand over her head, filling the hole and essentially drowning her. Her screams become muffled gurgles. Then she goes silent and still.

Is it terrible that I feel a little bad for her?

Ezra must notice the odd expression on my face, because he steps in front of me so that I don't have to see it any longer.

"They're wearing pink jumpsuits. Don't worry about it, pet."

"She's wearing nothing, but okay." I shake my head and turn to walk in the other direction, away from the line of exposed assholes. "I'm going to need you to explain this whole thing to me. I'd have asked sooner, but I was being ignored."

Ezra offers a sinful smile. "The retreat allows us to explore our murderous tendencies in a beautiful beach setting."

"You sound like the infomercial we got last night."

He shakes his head and chuckles. "I can't believe they're still sending that out to new guests. Did you see the dapper man on the big black horse? He was holding hands with the beautiful woman."

"Wait, that was you?"

"It can be, pet, if you play your cards right."

I roll my eyes. "Back to the jumpsuits. What do the colors mean?"

"The jumpsuits tell us their crimes. Yellow are your normal, everyday crimes, like robbery and battery. Red jumpsuits are sex crimes. Pink are child predators. The jumpsuits help discerning Sinners choose which Cattle they'd like to slaughter."

"Do you care about color?"

"Always pink, but I'll slaughter a red. And you?"

Telling the truth could out me as the Heartbreak Killer. It's widely known that I only target accused and convicted sex offenders. But then my mind returns to the naked people in the sand. If I say I kill indiscriminately, I'm locking myself into a box I don't want to be in. I'll have to take a risk.

"I exclusively kill those who attack the weak, so red and pink," I say.

"Here I was, thinking my brother and I would be the only killers with morals."

"I never said I have morals. I just choose to save my energy for those who deserve it." I stop walking and turn to him. "Whether you deserve more of my energy remains to be seen. You can start mending fences by telling me how you obtained such a shitty pseudonym. Which, by the way, I've never heard of."

"I've never heard of the Sunshine Strangler, either. What are you implying?"

Well, shit. I should have thought of a believable back-story before I started poking holes in his. Don't throw stones from glass houses. That's what my mother always said, and I never listened. Now my glass house is about to come down around me.

"I don't like to shit where I sleep," I say. "I do most of my work on the West Coast, then fly back to New York for my day job. I told you, I used to fly a lot."

I release a silent sigh of relief when he seems to buy my half-baked lie.

"Someone witnessed one of my crimes." He shrugs and starts walking again. "When the cops got wind of my accent, they dubbed me the Crumpet Killer. I can only assume they meant to embarrass me, but I don't care what they call me."

How odd. I have several contacts in police stations across the country, but I've never heard of this guy. Then again, I haven't heard of most of these people, and some of them are using their genuine pseudonyms. That's what sets us apart, I suppose. We fly so far beneath the radar that we can't get caught, but some fly low enough to avoid any sort of notoriety as well.

"And your brother?" I ask. "Who is he?"

"Ah, he's the Chaos Killer, though you need to keep that between us." Ezra taps the side of his nose twice. "He's never revealed his identity in all the years we've made the trip. Everyone just knows him as Bennett."

I stuff that little tidbit away for later. If Ezra chooses to get out of line and piss me off, I have no problem pulling it out and exposing his family.

We find ourselves back at the pavilion again. Cat is still talking to the man with the mullet, and they've been joined by the old German guy. I cover my mouth to stifle a laugh, which is more than he's stifling in that tiny Speedo. His balls are three times the size of his gherkin, so I imagine his motive for killing is related to sexual frustration. I doubt women (or men) are beating down his door to experience that.

"So nice of you to join us," the German says as we approach the three of them. "Your little friend was just telling us about your proficiency with a blade. I'm interested to hear more."

Ezra steps forward and holds out his hands. "There'll be plenty of time for that later, Grim. For now, she probably wants to get back to her villa so she can shower off the trip."

Mullet guy laughs and tips more beer into his mouth. "Looks to me like she just wants to get back to the villa so she can make a sandwich. Since when do—"

A fist to the mouth interrupts whatever he planned to say next. Ezra grips the back of the man's mullet and raises him into the air.

"Didn't your mother ever tell you to say nothing at all if you can't say anything nice?" Ezra asks. He sets the man on his feet and pats his swelling cheek. "If she didn't, I'm telling you now. As far as the women on this island are concerned, keep your comments to yourself."

I'm too stunned to speak, so I just stand there until Ezra takes my arm and begins leading me toward the villas. Cat jumps to her feet and hurries to catch up, but I don't miss the hate-filled glare she tosses toward the asshole behind us.

"I really don't care what people think of my body, so

that was unnecessary," I say as I shuffle along beside Ezra. "I like the way I look, and you aren't responsible for defending my honor."

Ezra stops and turns to face me, his teeth gritted and his eyes filled with malice. "No one will talk down to you in my presence. I've made my stance clear, and I don't foresee it being a problem going forward, but this will be the outcome every time if it does." He turns to Cat. "Take her to her villa, and both of you stay inside until the evening meal at the mansion. My brother and I will escort you there."

He rushes back toward the pavilion before I can argue. This is shaping up to be the longest five days of my life.

Chapter Twelve

Ezra

As I prepare for dinner, I've swapped my beachy attire for something a little classier. I roll down the purple collar, folding it at the crisp seam. As I dress, I feel dapper as hell, which is why I prefer suits to t-shirts and jeans. Also, despite my earlier setback, I've renewed my devotion to wooing Kindra. The whole murdering-her-brother conundrum will sort itself.

Eventually.

A knock on my bedroom door tells me that Bennett has let himself in.

"What's taking so long?" he yells through the flimsy wood separating us.

"I'll be out in a jiffy, Bennett."

"Yeah, yeah. You better not be dressed like a—"

I cut him off when I whip open the door dressed precisely the way he hoped I wasn't. He's in Hawaiian bathing shorts and a sleeveless black shirt. We are not the same.

"You look like an advertisement for a midlife crisis," I say.

"Yeah? You look like a James Bond villain."

"That good, eh?"

Bennett scoffs.

"Can we get going so we can escort the ladies to the party?" I ask.

"I've been waiting on you! But now I'm feeling insecure about my clothes."

"Most people don't dress up. You're fine."

"I'm trying to be as unattractive as I can to your girl-friend's little friend."

"I don't think that's an issue, as the dislike appears mutual. What was that kerfuffle on the plane about, anyway?"

Bennett begins to pace because that's what he does when he's mad. Whatever those two fought about must have been big.

"She thinks Kemper is the superior serial killer. And I think he's not even playing the same game as Bundy. What is Kemper known for? Banging his mom's skull? Bundy escaped from prison. *Twice.* He also killed three people while on the lam."

I stare at him with my mouth gaped like an imbecile. Really? That's what has his hackles up?

"Who the hell cares?" I say. "And who's the superior killer between us?"

"Obviously me."

I laugh. "And why's that?"

"Because I change up my MO. I'm chaotic. I'm untrace-able. You? Calculated. MO is well known. Have you seen your wiki page?"

"You do know anyone can put anything they want on

Wikipedia, right? In fact, I've made my own personal contribution to your page. I added that you were a weapons-grade cockwomble just last week."

"Mature."

"Says the man arguing with a pretty lady over who's a better serial killer instead of trying to wine and dine her. She's not my cup of tea, but she's very much yours."

Bennett scoffs. "She looks like she'd be a great ex-girlfriend, I'll give you that, but she's insufferable. And she has a cat! You know how I feel about those fleabags. I've never met a nice one, and they stomp all over you with their gritty, shit-covered paws too. Useless creatures. Cat women are an insta-no for me."

"Seems like Cat gave the insta-no this time."

"She'd have fucked me, Ezra."

"Sure looked like that on the plane."

"Whatever. Your girlfriend doesn't look like she wants anything to do with you either."

I take steps toward the door before turning around. "That's not the same thing, and you know it. I *have* to push her away."

At least, I thought I did. Now I'm not so sure. If I can pull off the con of the century, I could at least keep fucking her for the duration of the retreat. If I decide I want more . . .

I step out of the villa. The sun has nearly set, casting a pink glow along the horizon. The gulls and pipers have retreated inland for the night, and only a few stragglers linger at the water's edge. I start down the beach as thoughts of Kindra wind through my mind.

Bennett catches up with me as I approach her villa. I knock on the door, then adjust my sleeves as I wait for her to step into the glorious twilight.

When she opens the door, she's wearing a long black dress that accentuates each dip and curve of her delicious figure. I want to get my hands on that extra bit of stomach and squeeze.

And I would, if she didn't have a bit of a distaste for me at the moment.

Her dark eyes scan me up and down, and the corners of her lips twitch as she loses grip on her million-dollar smile.

"You look striking, pet," I say, low enough that only her ears can hear.

Cat slips out behind her, dressed casually like my brother. As much as he hates her, they sure are Tweedle-deepthroat and Tweedle-dumbass.

Kindra's hand rises to my face before grazing my ear. When she pulls her fingers away, I catch the glimpse of red on the tips. Realizing it's blood, I swipe it away.

"Must have cut myself shaving," I say. I can't tell her the truth. I reach for her fingers and wipe the tips of them on my sleeve. "Nothing to worry your pretty head about."

"I guess," she says, but she hesitates before looping her hand through the crook of my arm.

She seems like she'd rather I pull her teeth out one by one than take her to this party. I sure hope she can loosen up and enjoy herself. We're at a retreat after all.

The retreat owner—Jim Madigan—lives on the island year-round. He calls himself the Siesta Hunter, and he's a present-day Butcher Baker. He started by bringing prisoners to the island so that he could hunt them, but he ended up going a little stir crazy from being so alone.

I get it. It's a lonely profession.

Several years later, he started hosting these retreats to bring like-minded people together. This fancy mansion, which is located in the island's interior, is his home. It's a centerpiece, and a beautiful one at that, with massive columns standing like sentries in front of the entrance.

Kindra, Cat, Bennett, and I pass the large fountain in front of the mansion. In its center stands a woman gripping a severed head. Beside her, water shoots from a decapitated marble man's neck stump. In October, Jim likes to drop red food coloring into the pump. It's quite the sight, but his groundskeepers pay the price when they have to scrub the pink tinge from the marble each November.

The four of us pass through the columns and enter the house. Having been here enough times, Bennett and I take the lead and guide the women into the dining hall.

Soft classical music plays from overhead speakers near the fireplace. Jim didn't light the logs this year, and I'm grateful. We nearly sweated to death last year. This tropical heat and humidity are no joke.

I pull out a chair for Kindra, and she throws me a half-assed *thanks* as she plops down. She swipes a hand across her forehead to snag an errant bead of sweat, and I fight the temptation to bend down and lick the salt from her fingertips.

I ease into my seat and begin unfolding my napkin to place it into my lap. Kindra plants her elbows on the table and drops her forehead to her arms. She lacks refinement, but I find this more endearing than off-putting.

Bennett and Cat argued the entire walk over here. About the history of the domesticated feline, of all things. No one should have that much to say about cats, let alone two people, but I'm grateful for the silence that falls over them as Kindra and I sit between them. If they want to argue over our heads, however, this seating arrangement may need to change.

When I look around the table, every seat is full.

Except for the chair directly across from us. That place setting remains untouched.

The retreat owner enters the dining room, and all eyes turn to him as he struts to the table. He isn't in his finest attire, as he saves that for the last night of the retreat, but he's still resplendent in a tailored suit.

Kindra glances around the dining hall, then leans close to me and whispers, "Where's the guy with the mullet?"

"He's probably lost track of time. I'm sure he'll join us at some point. He was pretty drunk earlier."

Kindra stares at me for an unnecessary amount of time before she finally looks ahead again. I swallow as soon as her eyes leave mine.

"Welcome, Sinners," Jim says, raising his hands toward the ceiling. "I'm so glad you all have chosen to join me this evening." He looks toward the empty chair. "Where's Eighties?"

I clear my throat. "He was drinking down by the beach. He was pretty lairy when we left him."

"Right." As Jim sits at the head of the table in what can only be described as a throne, I don't miss the annoyed glance he tosses at the empty seat across from me. "Chef Maurice has been in the kitchen all day preparing a feast for us, and I would expect everyone to be excited and on time, but here we are."

Our attention turns to the front of the room as the two double doors swing open and Maurice rolls a cart from the kitchen. The first course is salad, and when he sets it down in front of Kindra, she frowns down at the leaves drizzled in Italian dressing.

"I'm not a big fan of salad," she whispers as she pushes the plate forward a bit.

"Just put some on my plate so it looks like you ate from it."

"Does the chef care that much?"

"Cooking is his sole reason for breathing, so yes."

While the chef is busy placing plates in front of everyone else, Kindra transfers half her salad to my plate. I stab into the green lettuce and bits of mozzarella and baby tomatoes, then bring them to my mouth. I've hardly made a dent before Maurice retreats to the kitchen and appears once again.

He tootles around the table and sets a serving dish in front of each of us. When Kindra goes to grab the cloche, I place my hand over hers and guide it back to her lap. Her eyes go wide as she registers just how serious Maurice is about table manners.

Once Chef Maurice has placed the last dish, he turns to us with a smile and a nod. Everyone reaches forward in unison, and like actors in a play, we perform our parts and reveal delicate slices of roasted meat lying on a bed of mashed potatoes.

Before I can warn Kindra, she picks up her fork and knife and heads straight for the meat.

"Kindra," I whisper, but she's already bringing the food to her lips. And, well, down the hatch it goes.

She's going to regret that.

She can't be saved, but I still have a chance. "Thank you so much for your service, Maurice, but have you forgotten that I'm a vegetarian?" I ask.

Maurice flicks a pointed finger toward me and scurries back through the doors, disappearing into the kitchen.

With her mouth full of meat, Kindra turns to me. "Since when are you a vegetarian? I'm pretty sure I saw you double-fisting a cheeseburger before the flight here."

I'm interrupted as Chef Maurice places some kind of bean soup in front of me.

"You need to use the loo?" I say to Kindra.

"No," she answers.

"Yes you do," I whisper.

"I guess I do." She takes another bite before setting her utensils on the thick fabric napkin beside her plate.

"I'll show you where they are."

I help Kindra out of the chair and smile at everyone as we walk by. We follow a long, dark hallway lined with candlelit lamps.

"This is creepy," Kindra says, her gaze roving around the hall. "I think I'd have pissed myself if I actually had to go. What is this, a mile long?"

I pull her toward the bathroom and put my hand on the handle. "You'll need this."

"I told you, I don't have to go."

"You just ate someone's arse."

Kindra chuckles. "I think I'd remember doing that."

"The roast."

"Yeah?"

"Do I have to spell it out for you, Kindra?"

"I have no clue what you're talking about."

I guess I do. "C-A-N-N-I-"

I don't get to finish the word before she turns and bolts into the bathroom. Without closing the door behind her, she flings the toilet seat open and falls to her knees.

"I cannot believe you let me eat a person!" she says between heaves.

"I tried to get your attention."

"Cannibalism deserves a bit more effort than a whisper, don't you think? Grab my fork and throw it across the room. Yell fire. Do *something*!" she screams, then retches again.

"I couldn't make a scene, pet."

She raises her head and looks at me with steel eyes. "Make a scene? Make a fucking scene? I'm about to make a bigger scene than anything you could have done." She wipes sick from her lip. "And don't call me that while I'm vomiting up the contents of a person's ass. A human person."

"I'm sorry."

"And wait until Cat finds out!"

"Something tells me that girl would eat arse willingly."

She stands without taking her eyes off me as she steps into me and pushes my chest. "This was non-consensual cannibalism. You know that, right? I didn't choose to eat this."

"You dove right in."

"Because I didn't know Jeffrey Dahmer was cooking tonight!" Her eyes narrow. "No wonder you didn't eat it. You and Bennett both had burger bags at the airport. Vegetarian my ass."

"Many apologies," I say as I guide her back to the dining hall. "But I'm pretty sure the dessert will be safe."

"Pretty sure?" she whispers, her eyes widening as we enter the dining room once more.

We take our seats again, and I stifle a laugh as Kindra tries to hide the shreds of meat beneath the mashed potatoes. The bean soup is immaculate, though, and I make a mental note to request it again.

Halfway through the main course, Jim excuses himself from the head of the table. He's likely concerned about our missing guest. If he plans to find Eighties in his room or on the beach, he'll be looking for a while.

Because I lied.

Well, I partially lied. He was definitely drunk when I last saw him, but he wasn't lounging by the seaside.

Someone will discover the body soon enough. I don't know what I was thinking. When I walked by the Blood Grotto and saw his smug face looming above the water in the hot tub, his cruel words to Kindra had repeated in my mind until a figurative red curtain fell over my eyes.

I normally prefer for my kills to be regimented, with each chess piece placed strategically for maximum odds of victory. Securing an alibi typically occurs before I've even lured my target to his or her demise, but I killed Eighties in the heat of the moment. I have no cover.

Turning to Kindra, I clear my throat. "Listen, I need to ask a favor."

"After allowing me to eat braised butt cheek, you have the audacity to ask me for help?" She shakes her head with a laugh. "Ain't happening."

Seeing no way out but through, I push on. "I killed Eighties, and I need an alibi. Can you say I was with you before dinner?"

Kindra lowers her hands to her lap, and I can't read the expression on her face. Then she turns toward me, and her words leave no room for misinterpretation. "Absolutely not."

My skin goes clammy, and a light sweat slicks my forehead. For the second time in my illustrious career, I'm faced with the risk of exposure. I once allowed a witness to escape after seeing me, and I worried for years that her description of my face would give me away. But my face was one of thousands, and the police never put the meager pieces together.

This time? This time, I'm well and truly fucked.

There are only so many people on the island who are capable of killing, and we're all seated around this fucking table. Jim is a smart man. He'll have me sussed out before the sun comes up in the morning.

The rules for the retreat are clear. No killing fellow guests. If Jim knows I killed Eighties, not only will he remove me from the island posthaste. He'll also make sure Kindra knows my identity.

I pull my glasses from my face and wipe the lenses. "I wouldn't ask if it wasn't important," I whisper. "Jim won't allow me to stay if he knows the truth."

"You should have thought about that before you let me eat someone's roasted ass meat. I'm on a mission here, and lying to the head of the event won't get me any closer to finding the Abattoir Adonis."

She doesn't realize how right she is.

Jim returns to the dining hall before I can say anything else. He takes a seat at the head of the table, then raises his glass and gives it a few clinks with his butter knife. An immediate hush overpowers the quiet conversations.

"My dear friends," he says, "I regret to announce that someone has broken my most cherished rule and has killed a fellow guest. Eighties was just discovered in the Blood Grotto, and while I'm thrilled the sacrificial slab has received an offering, I'm displeased that it is one of our own. Does anyone care to own up to this travesty?"

All heads begin turning toward me, and I can't blame them. By now, everyone will have heard about my beef with Eighties in the pavilion.

"Ezra, it seems the fingers are pointing in your direction," Jim says. "Would you care to say anything?"

I look at Kindra, pleading with my eyes, but she looks away.

"Eighties and I had a bit of a dust up earlier, but I didn't kill him," I say, hoping I sound convincing. "As I previously stated, I last saw him on the beach when I was on my way to Miss Amato's room."

Jim places his glass on the table, then steeples his fingers in front of his mouth as he turns to look at Kindra. "If you were with Miss Amato, perhaps she can vouch for you?"

Kindra shakes her head and stands.

Chapter Thirteen

Kindra

I place my hands on the table and shake my head again. A mental war wages on inside my brain.

Yes, this incredibly attractive man has given me some of the most mind-blowing orgasms I've ever experienced, and he makes this horrible retreat almost bearable, but he's also a distraction I don't need. If he's thrown off the island, I'll regain my focus and get that much closer to discovering the identity of my brother's murderer. And after allowing me to eat human meat, he deserves to be cast out.

I raise my head and look at Jim. "Ezra was with me. I don't enjoy airing my personal business, so that's as much as I'm willing to say."

My ass drops back to my chair. I curse myself for providing his alibi and securing his place on the island, but I couldn't rat him out. My pussy overpowered my brain. That's my only excuse.

Just as forks begin clinking against plates and I think we

can put this whole thing behind us, a chair scoots across the floor, and Cat gets to her feet.

"I can vouch for him too. I was there," she says.

Fucking fabulous. Now it sounds like we were engaged in some hedonistic threesome on Murder Island. I close my eyes and mentally will her to have a brain aneurysm.

"Well, I can't argue with two people providing an alibi, can I?" Jim says with a smile. "I suppose we'll just have to keep our eyes peeled, hmm?"

Cat nods and sits down, but not before looking at me and shoving a conspicuous wink in my direction. I'd have kicked her shin beneath the table if she'd been in front of instead of beside me.

The remainder of the dinner passes without much fanfare. Dessert is served—a fabulous tiramisu, which I demolish—and many of the guests retreat to the sitting room with Jim for after-dinner cocktails. A cocktail sounds amazing right about now, but so does a good night's sleep.

I walk toward the front of the mansion and step into the night. Instead of the hum of New York traffic, I hear only the sound of waves rushing over sand as I pause at the foot of the steps. Above me, the sky is a tapestry of starlight like I've never seen. The lack of artificial light allows the universe to glow more brightly.

A breeze blows off the water and races over my skin as footsteps approach behind me. I turn and see Ezra drawing closer. Before I can scurry off, he spots me.

"Wait up," he says as he jogs until he's at my side. "I need to thank you for that. I was sure you were about to reveal my secret."

"If you want to return the favor, you can start by helping me figure out which of these killers is AA." I sigh and begin walking down the jungle path toward the villas.

"If I agree to help you discover his identity by the end of the trip, will you go back to the fun Kindra from the hotel?" He keeps pace beside me, and I wish he wouldn't stand so close. His body heat is like waving a packet of cocaine in front of 1980s Bobby Brown. I'll slip and do a line of Ezra's dick if I can't get some space.

"I don't think that's a good idea," I say.

"And why is that?"

I stop walking and turn to face him. "Because I find you incredibly attractive and instead of looking for my brother's killer, I'm afraid I'll spend the entire retreat in bed with you."

"And miss all the fun activities? I won't let that happen." He smirks, and I can't decide if I want to kiss him or slap him.

"I don't plan to participate in any of the activities, so that's off the table."

"Not even the basket weaving with intestines demonstration?"

I grimace. "Especially not that one."

We start walking again. As someone who prefers quiet to meaningless conversation, I've never experienced an uncomfortable silence until this moment. It's as if the universe is waiting on two actors who've forgotten their lines. We amble along the overgrown path, our faces occasionally lit by the glow of a tiki torch, but we don't speak again until we reach my villa door.

Standing on the steps, I feel as if I'm preparing to say a final goodbye to a longtime lover. I've known this man for mere days, but I feel as if we've been brought together from another lifetime. His sighs, his smirks, his every expression —I know them all.

Ezra grabs my arm when I turn to go inside, and his firm

grip prevents me from moving away from him. "I don't want to go without seeing you again," he says, his voice low. "I'm used to getting what I want, and what I want is you. Multiple times and in every position. The ropes I used on you were just a sampling of the new world I can show you. Just think about that before you make a decision."

My back presses against the door to my villa as I try to keep my legs from collapsing and sending me to the roughly hewn boards under my feet. I want to scream yes, that he can take me right now and help my mind go numb for a few hours, but that's just my vagina talking again.

Sensing my weakening resolve, he steps closer and brushes my hair behind my ear. I'm caged between his powerful arms, and I don't want to escape. He could take me without my consent if that's what he really wanted to do. He's strong enough to break me in half. Yet it's his restraint that drives me wild with need.

Like the slacks cloaking the rock-hard erection pressed against my stomach, he's holding himself back. He's practically shaking from the sheer desire pumping through his body, and that virus is catching.

He leans down, bringing his lips close to mine, but I don't turn my head away. I close my eyes and tilt my head toward his.

"Okay, you two. Time to tell me what the fuck is going on." Cat's voice cuts through the silence—and my sanity.

"What the fuck! You scared me!" I duck beneath Ezra's arm. "How are you so silent now? Any other time, you'd be clomping around like a goddamn Clydesdale, but *now* you want to live up to your namesake?"

Cat bites her lip and looks between Ezra and me. "I'm interrupting something. I am so sorry."

And yet, she doesn't leave.

"No, nothing to interrupt," Ezra says as he starts down the porch steps. "I was just leaving. I need to get to bed early if I want to do the sunrise horseback riding in the morning."

Cat grabs his arm before he can slink away. "Not so fast. What was all that shit at dinner? If I provided your alibi, the least you can do is tell me why."

I hold up my finger. "Technically, I provided his alibi. You just stuck your nose where it didn't belong."

She ignores me and continues staring at Ezra, who runs his hand through his hair and looks toward the ocean.

"Then again," I add, "I'd also like to know what happened."

With no way out, Ezra turns to us and steps closer so we can hear him as he whispers his misdeeds. "This is the last we'll speak of this, understood?"

We nod, eager to hear about his murderous rampage.

"And if I tell you," he says to me, "you agree to at least consider what I was saying before we were interrupted?"

Fuck, fuck, fuck. "Fine."

Cat and I listen as Ezra spares no details. He spotted Eighties in the hot tub at the Blood Grotto, where he pushed him beneath the frothy water until he stopped moving. Once he was dead, he hoisted him onto the sacrificial slab and painted the stone with Eighties' entrails.

"Doesn't that go against your whole motto to kill only those who deserve it?" I ask.

Ezra turns to me, and the sincerity in his dark eyes sends my stomach into a loop. "If someone hurts you, they deserve to be hurt in return."

"Wow, that's hot," Cat says as she fans her face with her hands.

The moment thoroughly ruined, I groan and turn for the villa. "I'm going to bed. You two have a nice evening."

"Good night, my pet, and remember that you agreed to consider things." Ezra heads off down the beach, and I shake my head as I open the front door.

"Wait, I needed to talk to you about something." Cat follows me inside before I can stop her.

I'm all talked out, and I just want to go to fucking sleep. She's been just as busy as I have, so how is she so bright-eyed and bushy-tailed this late in the evening?

"Make it quick," I say. "I'm starting to get another headache."

She sits at the breakfast nook and begins rapping her nails on the table.

"Cat, just fucking spit it out!"

"Okay, okay." Her fingers still and she looks down at her lap, the picture of an admonished child. "Could I spend the night on your couch?"

My mouth falls open.

"It's just . . . There was a murder today, and now I'm a little scared."

"We literally know the person who murdered him. He just told us. Not to mention the fact that we're all on this island so that we can kill people."

"I know, but it's just so quiet in my villa, and it's so dark outside and—"

"Just sleep on the couch," I finally say, if for no other reason than to stop her incessant rambling.

Before she can say anything else, I go to my bedroom and close the door, cutting off any more communication. Everything is a mess. I can't keep my panties dry or my brain functional when I'm around Ezra, I've just lied to the event organizer, which almost guarantees he won't be of any help in my search for AA, and now I've been forced into a sleepover with the bane of my existence.

As soon as I've changed into a thin tank top and a comfortable pair of granny panties, I crawl beneath the covers and close my eyes. My brain continues to whirl with thoughts of how I can find the Adonis. A few people can be ruled out, such as the old German guy who likes to air his undercarriage in a Speedo.

I can also ax the guy they call Ice Pick. Unless the woman had nineteen shots of Patron before witnessing the man leaving the scene, there's no way she found him attractive. Per the single witness, the Adonis could melt panties with a single smoldering gaze.

Ezra and Bennett are also off the suspect list. They aren't indiscriminate killers. Like me, they have more discerning palates. If I pay attention to who kills the yellow jumpsuits, that will narrow the options even more.

Satisfied that I've gained some ground in the planning phase of my mission, I try to let my mind drift to sleep.

It's no good. I'm too wired.

Maybe if I get myself off, I can clear my head and stop thinking. I always sleep well after a good orgasm.

I ease out of bed and retrieve my toy from the bag. My thumb fiddles with the buttons until the little device buzzes to life. It's a lot louder than I remember it being, and I shut it off before Cat can hear. I'll have to work myself up to the climax, then use the toy for the big finish.

After climbing into bed, I lie on my back and allow my mind to linger on visions of Ezra. How he looked with his shirt off as he stood on the beach. The way his arms glistened when he reared back and pushed a fist into Eighties' face. The wild way he must have looked while disemboweling the guy for speaking ill of me.

God, he's so perfect.

My right hand dips into my panties, and my left hand cups my breast. I begin working myself up to thoughts of Ezra over me, his sweat dripping onto my skin and his hand around my throat. He unlocked a new kink for me, and I want to experience it again, even if only by myself.

I raise my hand to my throat and try to choke myself the way he choked me, but it's just not the same. I even consider looping a belt around the bedpost and choking myself that way, but that isn't how I want my life to end.

Frustrated, I grip the toy and push it below the comforter. If I throw a pillow over my lap, maybe it will muffle the sound. I try it, and it seems to work.

In my overexuberance as I lose myself to good vibrations and more thoughts of Ezra's sweaty body, the pillow eventually slides off my lap. I'm too close to stop now, so I keep going. I'm about to fly off the edge when a light knock comes from my door.

I scramble to shut off the toy and lower my legs before the door opens. Cat enters just as I'm shoving myself to an inconspicuous sitting position.

"Did you hear that?" she whispers.

I look around. "Hear what? The peaceful silence? The lullaby of the ocean? Why aren't you sleeping?"

She comes and sits on the edge of my bed. "I was almost asleep, but then I heard what sounded like someone running a buzz saw. What if they're dismembering people out there?"

Instead of covering my face with a pillow and screaming, I try to remain calm. To be fair, she looks genuinely frightened. "Cat, they probably *are* out there dismembering people. Because this is a murder retreat. Where they kill people. Remember?"

"I know, but it's still scary. You're used to this stuff. I'm not. Maybe I've gotten myself in over my head. Maybe I'm not cut out for this."

Truer words have never been spoken, but now is not the time.

"Would it help if you sleep in the bed and I sleep on the couch?" I ask.

She nods. "Yeah, because you'll be closer to the door. Not that I want you to get murdered first, but you have a better chance of fending off a killer than I do."

The girl has an odd way of handing out compliments, but I'll take it. And she's not wrong. I bet she doesn't even sleep with a weapon by the bed.

I grab my things, sneak my toy into my bag, and shuffle off to the couch as Cat situates herself in my comfortable king-size bed. The couch isn't what I would call a luxury accommodation, but at least it's quiet out here.

A little too quiet, I realize as I settle in.

Maybe that's why Cat was so unnerved. When you've grown used to living in a busy city, the lack of manmade noise can leave you feeling a little uneasy. That must be why I feel eyes on me right now.

"There is no one outside the window," I whisper to myself. "Don't let Cat's insanity rub off on you."

But even as I close my eyes and drift off to sleep, I can't shake the feeling that someone is standing just outside. Watching.

Chapter Fourteen

Ezra

I feel so dressed down this morning, but riding a horse in khakis and a stiff dress shirt isn't exactly comfortable. Then again, wearing jeans in eighty-degree weather won't be fabulous either, but here we are.

I rap my knuckle against Kindra's door, but she doesn't answer. She's going to kill me. The sun is hardly peeking over the horizon and I'm trying to drag her out of bed.

After a few minutes, I turn to leave, but the door whips open and Kindra stands in the doorway. Her palm grinds into her left eye as she tries to adjust to the sunshine. Black hair pokes in all directions from her head, and her cheeks are puffy from a terrible night's sleep.

"Why the fuck are you here at . . . ?" She leans back and looks at a clock on the wall, but I don't think she can read it. "The exact time doesn't matter. It's early as shit."

"Horseback riding on the beach awaits, pet."

"I'd rather die, thanks."

"I promise it will be better than eating butt cheek by

117

candlelight. Just give it a shot." I hold my hand out to her, but she shakes her head. "Come on, Kindra. Let's go have a bit of fun. We're killers, and we came here to kill."

"You already got a kill in," she says through a yawn. "And if you don't leave right now, I'm going to get a kill in. Which I should do anyway, after what happened last night."

"I didn't bring the fork to your pretty lips. Can't you let it go?"

"Absolutely not. You didn't feed it to me, but you didn't stop me from eating it, either. And I don't think anyone can truly 'let go' of becoming a cannibal against their will."

"You aren't a cannibal because you ate a person one time."

"How many times makes you a cannibal, Ezra? Two? Four?"

"It has nothing to do with frequency and everything to do with desire. You didn't enjoy it; therefore, you are not a cannibal." I spare a glance at my watch. If she doesn't dress soon, we'll miss the ride altogether.

I push my way inside her villa. A blanket and pillow lie on her couch, and the cushions appear rumpled.

"Do you have a visitor?" I ask. An odd pang of jealousy hits me in the face.

"Shh, you'll wake it."

"It?"

Kindra points toward her bedroom. "Cat."

"Why is Cat in your bed?"

"Because she's too scared to stay in her own villa. She's one step up from a child."

"Can't someone else babysit her?"

"Unfortunately, she's my responsibility."

Bennett should be the one shacking up with her, not

Kindra, but those two can't seem to get past their menial differences. Having Cat in Kindra's villa poses problems for me, though. She's a cockblock. That's if Kindra wasn't already blocking my cock herself.

Kindra plops down on the couch with a yawn, and I walk over to the coffee pot and begin brewing a cup. Maybe it will give her the strength to face the day.

"Thanks," she says as I slide a warm mug into her hands. "How'd you know what I like in it?"

"You seem like a cream and sugar kind of girl."

"What's that?" she asks, pointing to the manilla folder rolled up in my back pocket.

"The Cattle menu."

I pull it out and place it on the table in front of her. She flattens it with her palms and opens it. The Cattle are listed based on jumpsuit color, and it even lists their crimes.

"What is this for?"

"We need to pick who we want to drag behind our horses."

Her eyes land on a circled mugshot in the pink category. Paul J., a fifty-three-year-old pedo from North Carolina. He murders his small victims, and I can't wait to murder him.

Kindra flips the pages and drags her finger along the paper until she finds a red she likes. She taps her finger on George S., a thirty-two-year-old with multiple rape charges against adult victims. One of which was an incapacitated adult.

Good choice, Kindra.

"I'll call up to the mansion and let Jim know," I say. "He'll send down our chosen targets."

"I still can't believe I'm doing this."

Once she's had a few sips of coffee, she rises from the couch and goes to the bathroom to dress, carefully tiptoeing past the bed in her room. I stay in the living room.

I'm surprised when she emerges only fifteen minutes later. Like a butterfly, she's managed one hell of a metamorphosis.

She tamed her hair into a high ponytail and traded her baggy t-shirt and sleep shorts for a snug green blouse and a pair of jeans. Her ass looks good enough to eat, though I withhold the compliment. The fewer reminders about last night's meal, the better.

We exit the villa, and Kindra yawns beside me as we walk toward the beach.

"Were you up late?" I ask.

"Cat showed up, and then I *tried* to get some me time in so I could fall asleep, but she heard me and interrupted that. So no, I didn't sleep well."

"Brave move to use that toy with her there. Did you hear how it rattled an entire 747?"

She swipes her hand across her face. "I *almost* forgot about that. Thanks."

"I'm sure the priest is kept up at night thinking about it."

She socks my bicep. And I deserve it.

We step onto the beach and follow hoofprints to the ocean. A chill nip hides within the breeze, and it seems to have kept other retreat participants from going on today's ride. They've probably opted for one of the many indoor activities.

The stable master holds a rein in each hand. One attaches to a stunning black Percheron gelding I rode a couple of times last year. I walk over and stroke the horse's big head, and he nickers softly in shared recognition. Kindra's horse is a stout white mare. She must be new this year.

"What's her name?" I ask.

"Sophia."

"Is she a safe ride? The lady here isn't familiar with—"

Kindra stomps her way over to me. "Bold of you to assume I've never ridden."

"She isn't Fynn, but she's a good mare," the man says.

I turn toward Kindra. "Please take Fynn."

"I'm fine with Sophia."

"Fynn is a safer ride."

"No."

Before she can hop on, I grab the saddle horn, put my foot in the stirrup, and hoist myself onto Sophia. The horse's muscles tighten beneath me, and she takes off, ripping the reins from the man's hands. I'm stuck atop a bucking bronco, and I'm too English for this very American sport.

I'm flung forward and backward as I grip with my thighs and try to stay atop the bloody psychopath. I'm in the air as all four feet rise with every pissed-off buck.

Just when I think all my years of riding have made my rear sticky enough for a rank little mare, I fly over her shoulder and land on my back. The mare stops bucking the moment I come off, and I lie in the sand as I struggle to catch a breath. All the wind has vacated my lungs.

Kindra comes over and stands above me, and now my dignity hurts more than my body.

"You can have her," she says with a smirk. She reaches toward me and helps me to my feet.

"That could have been her!" I say, pointing to Kindra. If looks could kill, the stable master would be dead.

The stable master slips Fynn's reins into my hands, grabs Sophia's, and leads her back to the stable. He returns with Aspen, a dead-broke gelding I'm actually familiar with.

Regardless, I hand the reins of my beloved Fynn to Kindra. He'll take care of her like he takes care of me, and I can trust the big gray quarter horse to behave when I'm on his back.

A masked man leads our selected Cattle toward our horses. My selection wears his pink jumpsuit, and Kindra's wears red. They squirm and try to scream, but the sound is a muffled plea barely heard over the crash of water against sand.

Plus, their mouths have been sewn shut.

The masked man takes out their knees and wraps a chain around each of their legs. The chain connects to the saddles via a special hook system so that the restraints don't impede or injure our horses. The Cattle, however . . .

We mount up, and it's much less eventful this time. Kindra looks like a natural seated atop Flynn. With her dark hair and dark eyes, she looks like she was made for that horse.

I look behind us and smile. Our Cattle strain and writhe against the restraints as the whites of their eyes show within widened pink lids. I hope they suffer worse than their victims.

"Ready?" I ask Kindra.

She nods, and I squeeze Aspen's sides. The horses take slow, even steps while the Cattle bounce behind us. Kindra and I laugh at their muffled screams.

They'll fall silent soon enough.

"Can we trot?" Kindra asks.

"We can do whatever you want, my pet."

Kindra squeezes Fynn, and he steps into a trot. Aspen, afraid to be left behind, begins that pace on his own. Kindra posts the trot, lifting herself out of the saddle with each rise of Fynn's massive shoulders. She looks incredible, and I've never wanted to be a four-legged creature more in my life.

Our baggage bounces and spins, their bodies banging against every ridge of sand or rock we fly over. My Cattle rips the stitches from his lips by straining his jaw as wide as it will go, and his screams ring out among the clop of hooves on sand.

It's delicious.

A sign with an arrow guides us down a path. Logs lie along the trail. I turn to ask Kindra if she's ever jumped, but she flies out ahead of me. Fynn effortlessly leaps over the logs, and Kindra's Cattle flails through the air before crashing down on the forest floor. I follow her, my own Cattle becoming a projectile with every jump.

"Oh god, please, stop!" he yells behind me.

"I'm sure your victims said the same thing!" I shout. "And you didn't stop, did you?"

The path takes a sharp turn, and the Cattle bash into trees and rock ledges as we round the bend. Mine hits a rock pretty hard. His body audibly scrapes the craggy surface, which creates a lovely background accompaniment to his screams. Moments later, he goes quiet.

Damn. I was really getting into the music.

We reach a clearing that opens onto a private corner of the beach. A large red-and-white blanket lies on the crystal sand, with a basket sitting in its center.

"Is that a picnic?" Kindra asks as she brings Fynn to a stop.

"It appears so."

I dismount and offer my hand to Kindra, but she hops down without accepting my assistance. I need to remember she neither likes help nor wants it, but it's hard to stop myself from offering. I've never wanted a woman to find me useful, aside from my ability to give toe-curling orgasms, but Kindra is slowly changing my mindset.

123

Before we check out the picnic, I stroll to the back of the horse to observe what's left of my Cattle. It's not a pretty sight, which is marvelous.

At first glance, he looks dead, but his bloody lips move, forming circles as he tries to speak. Blood weeps from innumerable gashes and scrapes on his body, made visible beneath what's left of his jumpsuit. Twigs and leaves poke from his skin, and his right eyeball has vacated his head. He must have caught it on a branch. I hope it hurts terribly.

"Mine's dead," Kindra says, nudging the body with the toe of her shoe. "I was hoping I'd have a chance to take a stab at him." She draws her knife from her hip, and I nearly come in my pants at the sight of it.

My urge to kill is strong. Stronger when a man such as this is at my feet. But my need to let her kill is even stronger.

"Mine isn't gone yet. He's all yours."

I step back and watch the excitement creep over her face. Her smile is worth giving up the kill.

She hurries over, as if she fears he'll expire before she can get to him. With a gleeful laugh, she plunges the knife into his abdomen and rotates the blade inside him until I'm sure she's nicked every organ at least once. Her hands hover over him like she's fighting an urge, but instead of doing more, she just tugs her knife from his gut and heads toward the water to rinse off her blade.

I don't get in her way. There's a certain high you get just before, during, and right after a good kill, and I let her have that dopamine hit while I tie up the horses and head for the blanket.

She bends at the waist and rinses her blade, then stares at the ocean for a long moment before she joins me on the blanket and peeks inside the basket.

"Please tell me Chef Dahmer didn't prepare any of this?" she says with a grimace.

"He doesn't make turkey sandwiches, so we're good. But don't take his cooking classes while you're here."

Kindra pulls a sandwich from the basket as if it's unexploded ordnance. She lifts the bread, smells the meat, and takes a bite.

"Does he actually teach people how to cook . . . other people?" she asks through a mouthful of turkey.

"That he does. He also has a YouTube channel called 'Crazy Cooking with Chef Maurice.'"

We eat in stifled silence as we listen to the nearby gulls squabbling over a discarded bit of bread. By the time we've finished eating, we've hardly said more than a few sentences. I search my brain for something to talk about, but this is new for me. It isn't often that my love interests and I do much talking.

As we unhook the literal deadweight and mount our horses, a topic finally comes to me.

"Did you know I'm obsessed with a killer too?" I say. "Albeit for different reasons."

Kindra pulls a bottle of water from the saddlebag, then pauses before taking a sip. "Who?"

"Don't laugh at me, but I'm on a mission to find the Heartbreak Killer. I really admire them."

Kindra chokes on her water, her hand wrapped tightly around the flimsy plastic bottle. "I've heard of them," she finally spits out.

"Do you think it's a man or a woman? My brother insists it's a man."

"I think HBK is a woman. She's too good at what she does to be a man."

"Thanks a lot."

"You're welcome." She nudges the horse forward, ending the conversation.

We ride back to the pavilion, and I'm surprised to see Bennett in the same vicinity as his arch nemesis. He and Cat stand under the shade as they seem to discuss something rather amicably. Maybe they're turning a corner and becoming friends.

We hand off the horses to one of the workers and approach the pair. As I draw closer, their conversation reaches my ears, and hopeful thoughts of friendship evaporate.

"Having different MOs makes you not even seem like a serial killer," Cat says. "What's the point without notoriety?"

"Because it makes me impossible to catch. What's the point of being a notorious serial killer if I'm in prison? I don't think you've ever killed a damn thing in your life. You shouldn't even be here." Bennett folds his arms over his chest.

"You don't even know me," Cat snarls.

Bennett turns toward Kindra. "Is Cat a killer?"

"In training," Kindra answers.

"See! She should be taken off the—"

"Piss off, Bennett," I say. "We all get our start somewhere."

Cat sits back in her chair and crosses her arms, mirroring Bennett's posture. I bet those two would have amazing hate sex.

"Why don't we all go for a round of mini golf?" I regret making the invite as soon as it leaves my mouth. Spending an hour with them would do my head in.

"Pass," Cat says. "I planned to take Chef Maurice's cooking class."

Kindra's back stiffens as if she's just been thrust into a war scene in her mind. The Battle of the Buttocks, perhaps?

"Chef Maurice cooks people!" Kindra blurts.

Much to her dismay, Cat doesn't react. "I know."

"You knew?"

"I've eaten human flesh before, Kindra. I once went on a few dates with a self-proclaimed cannibal."

"Weren't you worried he'd eat you?" Kindra asks.

"Oh, he ate me, all right." Cat flicks her blonde hair over her shoulder and smirks. "No one eats human flesh like a cannibal, that's all I'm saying."

Bennett's cheeks flame a shade of red I've never seen. "Instead of listening to the gross sex life of a wannabe killer, let's go play some golf."

Kindra stares at me for a moment before dropping her gaze. "I'm actually pretty tired. Mind if I head back for a nap?"

"Of course not." I'm sure she wants alone time away from her friend. And by alone time, I mean time to bang one out with her toy.

God, I want to be that toy.

There has to be some way I can win her over before the end of this trip. Even though I murdered her brother, whoever he was, I can't deny the driving urge to hear her speak or see her face in moonlight. I'd also like to have her beneath me just once more.

Who am I kidding? Once more would never be enough.

As the ladies wander toward their villas, my brother and I head toward the mini golf course behind the mansion. We grab our balls and putters and head to the first hole.

I set up my ball and smack it down a thin alleyway. It loops around a windmill and comes to a stop about six feet from one of the heads buried in the sand. The setup is pretty perfect. I'll probably knock out at least three of the Cattle's teeth when I make my next putt.

That's the goal of the game, after all. Sure, there are holes to putt toward, but battering the Cattle heads poking from the hot sand is the real reward.

"I'm glad the girls didn't come. I'm kind of sick of them." Bennett lines up his shot.

"I think Kindra would've had fun." Though I know she's probably having fun by herself. With that buzzing between her legs. Those vibrations. Her moans . . .

"Did you hear me?" Bennett says.

"What?"

"I asked why you're so hung up on Kindra. She doesn't want you, dude."

"Oh, she does. But she's got too much on her mind."

Bennett hits the ball. It goes through the windmill and thwacks flesh on the other side. Based on the yelp, it was a nice hit.

"You mean finding her brother's killer, right? Need I remind you that you're him? How do you think this is going to go, Ezra? Do you think dicking her down will be enough to make her forgive you?"

I wish that was enough.

Without answering him, I head around the windmill to find my ball. Bennett's blue ball rests just beside the bruised head. Five of the Cattle's teeth sit beneath his mouth on the "green." He begs and pleads, blood dripping from his lips, but I ignore him as I line up behind my ball, swing my arms back, and blast the purple ball forward. It collides with a satisfying *thunk,* right between his eyes.

"Ignore it all you want, but you're wasting your time with her." Bennett lines up his shot. "There's no future there. You murdered that option when you murdered her brother. And the longer you go without telling her, the worse her reaction will be."

"I'm going to tell her, Bennett."

"When?"

"The last day of the retreat. I'll tell her on our last day together."

I speak before I even know what I'm saying, but now that I've said it, now that I've put it into the universe, it just makes sense. On the last day of the retreat, regardless of how things go with Kindra from this point forward, I have to tell her the truth.

Chapter Fifteen

Kindra

I finally have some time to myself in the late afternoon. Ezra and Bennett haven't bothered me since they went to play golf, and Cat is probably still at her cooking class for cannibals, leaving me with some much-needed peace and quiet so I can think.

The Abattoir Adonis is on this island, yet no one seems to know who he is. Whenever I ask, I'm met with sideways glances and shrugs. This leads me to believe he's not here . . . or he's using a different name.

When Cat presented the list of attendees back in New York, I'd promptly destroyed it once she'd left. It made no sense to keep something so incriminating. Now I wish I'd at least taken the time to memorize the names so that I could compare them to those on the island.

As I sit on the uncomfortable couch and sip a warm mug of tea, I recall what I can. Which isn't much. Aside from Ice Pick, Grim, and Maudlin Rose, it seems everyone else has gone by a different name.

So lost in thought, I barely register the knock at the villa door. I place my tea on the coffee table and hurry to the window to learn who's come to interrupt my solace this time.

Cat stands in front of the door, a large suitcase dragging behind her. She raises a small fist to knock again, but I open the door before she can.

"You can't move into my villa," I say. "If you're that frightened—"

"No, that's not why I'm here," Cat says as she hoists her bag through the door. "I can't decide what to wear."

"Wear? To what?"

"Dinner. At the mansion."

"You're really going all in on this cannibal thing."

"Maybe, but when in Rome . . ."

"I don't think that counts when we're discussing eating human flesh."

Cat shrugs and opens her suitcase. "What happens on the island stays on the island, so I might as well go big."

"Regardless, I fail to see why you needed to bring your closet to my villa. I'm not exactly fashion forward." I motion to the baggy t-shirt and loose shorts I slipped into as soon as I returned from the horseback ride.

Undeterred, Cat pulls a few options from her suitcase and drapes them over the back of the couch. "I respect your opinion. Plus, I know you won't let me walk around looking like a clown."

The girl places far too much blind faith in me.

She nibbles her finger and considers what she's pulled from the sea of fabric. Her decisions made, she plucks three from the lineup, returns the rest to the luggage, then retreats to my room.

Moments later, Cat emerges in a shimmering red dress.

The neckline plunges between her breasts, and I'm fairly certain I see a flash of pink nipple every time she moves. It's pretty, and it looks amazing on her, but it's also an attention grabber. We're trying to find my brother's killer, and that means we can't draw too much attention while we're here.

"It's a bit much," I say. "Stunning, but better suited for the red carpet. Plus, remember that we need to lie low."

She holds up a finger. "Right. Got it."

The door clicks shut behind her, and like a butterfly, she emerges changed. This time she's chosen a sky-blue spring dress. It flatters her figure just as much as the first, but it's less ostentatious. The color also brings out her eyes.

"That's the one," I say. "Subtle, yet still very alluring."

Cat's eyes light up and she spins in a half circle. Her excitement is almost contagious. "Now that I have the fit, I just need to situate the rest of my look. Will you help me with my hair? I was thinking about a cute French braid, but I can't braid my hair myself."

I start to tell her no—I don't do anything with my own hair, let alone someone else's—but her wide, hope-filled eyes tug at the few heartstrings I have.

"Fine."

Cat grabs a comb from her suitcase, then sits on the couch. I stand behind her and begin sectioning her hair. I haven't done anything like this since I was in grade school, but my fingers pick up the rhythm as if I never stopped.

Though I did stop.

When my brother died, things like hair and makeup and cute clothes lost their luster. Friends didn't seem so useful anymore either. I boxed myself off from the world because everything in life had become so pointless. What was the point of wasting hours on relationships and appearances when it could all be snatched away by a psychopath with a few meat hooks?

"What's killing feel like?" Cat asks, pulling me from my self-dug hole of despair.

I clear my throat and blink away the mist in my eyes. "It feels good, I guess. If it didn't, we wouldn't do it so often, especially considering the risks. It's like the best sex you've ever had."

And I'd know because I experienced the best sex of my life just a few days ago with the man I now have to shrug off while I'm at this retreat. What I felt while lying beside him before I went back to my room was the closest I've come to the killing high.

Cat offers a slight nod. "I think I'll get my first kill tomorrow."

"Why tomorrow?"

"Did you even read the brochure, Kindra?"

"No."

"It's the Island Olympics! We slaughter Cattle in a relay obstacle course. I think the competition aspect will prevent me from overthinking the actual murder part."

Thinking about the murder is part of the high, though. The anticipation just before ending an evil life is what makes that end so sweet.

I pull a few strands of hair taut and motion for Cat to hand an elastic band to me. "Did you ever think maybe you aren't a killer? You're fascinated by what we do, but that doesn't mean you have to join this very exclusive and fucked-up club. There's a word for people like you."

"Hybristophilia. The sexual attraction to killers. While that's accurate, I don't think that's all there is to it."

"So if you're attracted to killers, how are you not attracted to Ezra's brother?"

Cat rips her hair from my hands as she whips her head around to stare at me. "I would *never* date a man who hates cats. Bennett is a menace, and it will be a cold day in hell before I ever let him near my vagina. We can't even be around each other for two minutes without me wanting to claw his eyes out, but judging by the scar through his eyebrow, someone else got to him before I could."

"But could you imagine the hate sex?"

She rolls her eyes and faces forward again. "What about you and Ezra? You're perfect for each other, yet you keep pushing him away. Now *that's* insanity."

I get back to work on the second braid. "It was supposed to be a fling. You know, the sort of thing where you never see the person again unless you're hiding behind a menu when they happen to come into the same café. It never would've happened if I'd known he'd be at the retreat. And besides, Ezra is clearly obsessed with someone else."

Cat rips the braid from my hand as she turns to face me. "Who?"

"The Heartbreak Killer."

Cat's eyes narrow on me, and the wheels turn in her head. "But . . . that's you."

"No, I'm the fucking Sunl—"

"Sunshine," she corrects. "Why don't you just tell him who you are?"

"I don't want *anyone* knowing who I really am, especially Ezra."

I don't even think Ezra would be mad if he learned my identity. Based on how enamored he looked when he spoke the name, he'd probably just come in his pants. If anything, he'd become even more obsessed with me.

And I can't have that.

135

I need to stay focused. I *need* to find my brother's killer. And I won't find him in Ezra's bed.

"So, the murder relay race . . ." I say, desperate to change the subject.

"The races are in groups of four. If you'll partner with me, we just need to find two more. I don't care if you recruit Ezra, but I veto Bennett."

"Pass. I'm not interested in anything that involves running on sand in the heat."

"Please?" she begs, and there goes her silky hair, ripping from my hands again as she turns to look at me.

"I'm about to let you go to dinner with half your hair done, Cat."

"I'm sorry. I just need you there."

"If you need an emotional-support serial killer, then you aren't ready for your first murder."

"I don't need an emotional-support person. I need a friend."

A friend?

I've fought that word since the moment I met her. Friends don't write extensive blogs about their friends. They don't document every morsel of crime their friends commit. They don't make it easier for the police to catch their friends.

But she speaks with such genuine human emotion, making it difficult to deny her assumption that we *are* friends. I suppose it wouldn't kill me to be a little kinder to her.

"Fine, I'll do the damn relay race."

I finish the second braid, and Cat gets up to admire it in the mirror.

"It's perfect!" She turns back to me. "Are you sure you don't want to come to dinner?"

"I am absolutely certain."

"Then I guess I'll see you tomorrow morning, bright and early." She crinkles her nose, grabs her suitcase, and totters out the door in a pair of sparkling heels.

The door closes behind her, and just as I sit down on the couch, there's a knock. Cat must have forgotten something.

"What did you—?" I say as I whip open the door.

But it's not Cat. It's Bennett.

"Uh, hi," he says. He peers into the room, his head on a swivel. Almost as if he's ensuring there's no one around to witness him murdering me.

I glance at the couch and make a mental note of the blade tucked beneath the middle cushion. Just in case.

"Bennett . . . come in, I guess."

I haven't actually said more than a handful of words to Ezra's brother. He's been too busy arguing with Cat since we met. Despite our limited engagements, he's entirely candid with what he says next.

"You need to stay away from Ezra."

I wouldn't mind staying away from Ezra, though he's drawn to me like a handsome fly to a pessimistic piece of shit. But I don't like being told what to do.

"And why would I do that?" I ask.

Bennett brushes a hand through his hair as he enters the villa and begins pacing in front of the door. "Because he's a playboy. You're being used. Don't you see that?"

Considering I'm the one shrugging off every single one of his advances, I'm pretty sure I'm not being used. And who cares if Ezra sleeps around? I'd be more surprised if a man who fucked a stranger he met in an airport *wasn't* that type of person.

"I'm an adult, Bennett. I think I can handle myself. I

don't know if you noticed, but I've skirted every one of your brother's attempts at this retreat. But even if I hadn't, what we do is none of your goddamn business. Are you worried we'll get married and have fucked-up little children with poor coping mechanisms? No. This is just a fling, and it's not even that anymore. I have one thing on my mind at this retreat, and it's finding my brother's killer."

Bennett grips the door and swings it open, letting the heat and humidity seep into my villa. "This won't end well for you two. And don't say I didn't warn you," he says before disappearing like a ghost of flings past.

I suck in a breath as the door closes, but I can't stop thinking about what Bennett said. Even as I sit on the couch and remind myself of my reason for being here, thoughts of Ezra creep into my mind.

Bennett's words were a ploy. That much was clear. Ezra may be a playboy, but that's not enough of a reason to stop allowing him to get me off. So why is Ezra's brother trying to warn me away from him?

I get up, lock my villa on the way out, and head to Ezra's. He could be at the dinner for all I know, but maybe he decided to skip out on tonight's human delicacies.

Sand crunches under my feet as I march down the boardwalk. The sun has started to set, but the tiny grains grip the last strands of warmth and use them to burn my arches. It'll be worth it to see the look on Ezra's face when I knock on his door.

And I'm in for a treat, because his wide eyes and dropped jaw don't disappoint as he sees me standing on his little porch.

Surprise, motherfucker.

I bully him into the villa with my body language alone

and close the door behind me. It's all an act. I just want to see him squirm.

"So you're a playboy type, Ezra?"

"I beg your pardon?"

"You sleep around? Love your one-night stands?" I step into him as I talk.

He scratches the back of his neck. "What are you talking about, pet?"

The panic in his eyes nearly makes me laugh. I don't actually care. He's not mine, and this is just a fling gone weird. An extended-stay one-night stand.

"Wait, who told you I was a playboy?"

I flop onto his couch and pick a grain of sand from beneath a fingernail. "Your brother."

"Bennett told you that? Oh, pet, you can't listen to a word he says. He's out to protect one person and one person only, and that's himself. He's just worried I'm getting attached."

I flick the grain of sand onto the floor and look at him. "Are you?"

"Of course not." He wears a poker face as he speaks, but I don't miss the way his voice has risen an octave. "Are you?"

"Not a chance in hell." I'm a much better liar, but if he called my bluff and told me to get undressed right now, I absolutely would.

He steps closer and leans down, placing an arm to either side of my head. "Then I see no issue with resuming our little arrangement."

His warm breath rushes over my neck and chips away at my resolve.

"I'm not a playboy, but I'm not out to make you fall in love with me, either. I like this push and pull between us."

"Mostly push these days."

"Yes, regretfully. What do I have to do to get a little more . . . pull?" His hand grips my hair and yanks back my head, giving him access to my neck.

I don't push him away as he lowers his lips to my skin. I don't protest as his hand falls to my breast. Like the little slut I am, I moan and encourage him to keep going as all thought evaporates from my mind.

But just as I reach to undo the pesky button separating me from pleasure, the villa door flies open.

"She's the bane of my existence, Ezra! If I have to hear her—" Bennett freezes beside the couch and looks away as Ezra and I scramble to put space between us.

"Have you ever heard of knocking?" Ezra shouts, and I don't think I've ever seen a human turn that shade of red.

"I didn't expect you to have company," Bennett says.

I sit forward and smirk at him. "And why is that? Because you told me to stay away from him? You should have known that would only push me toward him, Bennett."

Remembering why I'm there in the first place, Ezra turns toward his brother. "Speaking of that—"

"Nope, we can discuss this later." Bennett shakes his head and turns for the door.

"At least tell me why you're back so early," Ezra says before he can leave. "The dinners usually last well into the evening."

Bennett balls his fists at his sides, more than happy to vent about the blonde stranger who ended his evening. "Her little *friend* ruined everything. When Chef Maurice brought out brain puffs as a nice little hors d'oeuvre, she refused to try it."

Ezra winces.

"When Maurice came at her and tried to assault her, I had to step between them. Do you know how difficult it was to defend the thing I hate?" Bennett shivers and looks at the ceiling. "I should have let him beat her to death, but I enjoy the food."

So I have both Cat *and* Bennett to thank for interrupting what was sure to be an evening of moaning, writhing, and a lot of pleasure? Well, I know just how to thank both of them.

I turn to the men and smile. "How would you boys like to team up with me for the Island Olympics tomorrow?"

Chapter Sixteen

Ezra

Bennett and I pass the pavilion on our way to a wide stretch of sand that will be home to this year's Island Olympics. The site where we usually host the games was made into a nude beach this year. No one liked the idea of watching Maudlin Rose and Grim—the two oldest participants—stripped down to their birthday best, so we opted to move the festivities.

Unfortunately, we still have to pass the old site on the way, and Bennett and I are treated to a rare display as both Rose and Grim aim their buttholes toward the rising sun. They claim it's spiritually cleansing.

"Why did I agree to do this?" Bennett asks as we try to avert our poor eyes.

"Because you want to win? That's all you cared about last night." I pull off my t-shirt and let the sun's warmth sink to my bones. Maybe the two nutters on the beach are onto something.

"Some of these other killers need to be humbled." Bennett turns toward me. "Kind of like you."

"I beg your pardon?"

"You need to realize how stupid you're being. Both of you." He brushes a hand through his dark hair. "You keep saying it's just sex, but it's not, and you know that."

It's literally just sex. We made sure of that last night. She was very clear. She doesn't have feelings for me, and that's fine. It's a mutually beneficial arrangement. Rather, it could have been, if Bennett hadn't decided to cockblock me for the entire retreat. If he'd arrived a half-hour later, I'd have already tied her up and we'd have been well on our way to bliss.

Sigh.

She had a moment of weakness last night, but I don't know if I'll catch her in the right mood again.

"Thanks for last night, by the way," I say. "Kindra and I had a wonderful discussion after you tried to tarnish my name. A playboy, Bennett? Is that the best you could come up with?"

"Would you rather I told her the truth? That you're the Abattoir Adonis?"

I look around to be sure no one heard what he said. That's when I spot Kindra and Cat only a few paces behind us. We were so lost in conversation, I didn't hear their feet rustling through the sand. I can only hope the waves muffled what my brother just said.

"Ladies," I say, testing the tense air for any turbulence. My heart resumes beating when Kindra graces me with a bright smile.

"Gentleman," she says.

A black one-piece bathing suit and blue shorts cover her body from view, leaving what lies beneath to my imagination. And I'm imagining her beneath me now. And on top of me. And on her knees in front of me.

I could keep going all day. I have a good imagination.

Cat has chosen a tiny pink bikini top and short jean shorts, leaving nothing to the imagination. She's the definition of Bennett's type, and I don't know how he doesn't see it.

Probably because he thinks ignoring her might make her disappear.

"Are you ready to get this show on the road?" Kindra says, clearly not enthused about getting any show on any road.

"My brother and I were just talking about the Olympics, weren't we, Bennett?" I say, putting my arm around his shoulder.

He couldn't look more miserable if he tried as he shrugs out of my grasp.

Kindra doesn't even send a peep of breath his way. I guess she didn't appreciate being told how to live her life. He needs to mind his own business. He's gathering enemies as if they're collectible cards.

Bennett walks a little faster and pulls ahead of us.

Does anyone want to be here? Because it doesn't seem like it. Cat, maybe. As the obstacle course comes into view, she's a veritable powder keg of excitement.

"Wow," she breathes. "Look at the Cattle in the pen behind the course. That's a lot of dead men walking." She gives a little giggle, and I can almost see Bennett's cock retract into his body with disgust.

"Is the baby making her first kill on the course?" Bennett asks, finally looking at Cat.

"If I don't make it here first," she says through a smile.

Bennett rolls his eyes and turns to offer a rebuttal, but

Cat is quicker. And more lethal. Before anyone knows what's happening, she's stepped toward my brother and driven her knee into his groin.

Kindra lets out a soft gasp as Bennett keels over from the pain. I feel it in my nuts too, though I don't blame Cat. He was being a sod. We all started somewhere as killers. What better place to start than on an island?

"You're dead," he says through gritted teeth.

"Hopefully, so is your ability to reproduce." Cat steps around him and continues toward the course, closely followed by Kindra.

I place my hand on my brother's shoulder. "You know, if you stopped sticking your nose where it doesn't belong, it wouldn't get bitten off so regularly. Couldn't you just play nice for one day? Hell, one event?"

He straightens and glares at the ocean. "If you stopped sticking your dick where it doesn't belong, you might find the solutions to your own problems. Fuck off."

He's made his intentions clear enough, so off I fuck.

We're the first to arrive, which means we'll be the first to pick our team colors. And by we, I mean Kindra. She's already begun gathering the purple accouterments. She sets to work on the baggy t-shirts, cutting them up with the provided scissors so that we can all make a smashing fashion statement.

As the other teams arrive, I take stock of our competition.

Maudlin Rose and Grim have abandoned the butthole sunning in favor of partnering with Ice Pick and Jeff, who is one of Jim's sons (the family has a penchant for generic male names). They choose yellow as their team color.

Three men I don't recognize—nor can I remember their nicknames—team up with the Stocking Strangler. He is not to be confused with the notorious serial killer of the same name, for Bob is neither notorious nor dead. He's not even called the Stocking Strangler away from the island. Only Jim, the event coordinator, knows his true identity, though I don't know why he chose to idolize Carlton Gary as his cover. Disgusting. Regardless, he chooses blue for his team.

I lose interest in studying the fourth and final team because Kindra approaches me with a shirt that has been sliced to resemble something akin to a tank top. Wearing swim shorts daily is enough of a struggle for someone as fashionable as I consider myself, but the monstrosity she dangles in front of me is almost more than I can stand to look at, let alone wear.

But then I see the glint of excitement in her eyes, and I can't put it on fast enough. If it pulls a smile out of her, even better.

"Wow, that looks a lot worse than I thought it would," she says through a laugh as I model it for her.

"What the fuck is this?" Bennett says from a few feet away, and I turn to look at him.

Cat has handled his shirt design, and she's done an excellent job. I can't wait to see my brother racing down the sand in what can only be described as a crop-top-*cum*-sports-bra. Despite my initial reservations, I definitely came out with the better deal.

"We're matchy matchy," Cat says when she's stopped laughing long enough to take a breath, and she's not wrong, though the cut is much more flattering on her.

Bennett grumbles something under his breath, but he decides to be a good sport and puts it on.

We move toward the starting line and choose our order of play. Bennett will go first, followed by myself, then Kindra, and lastly, Cat. I would have preferred to finish a bit stronger and position myself as the closer, but the obstacles in the final leg are much easier than the others, and she doesn't exactly boast a lot of muscle.

The rules of the game are simple enough. Each participant must complete a small section of obstacles, then murder their target at the end. One team is eliminated at the end of the second round, then again at the end of each consecutive round.

But there's a catch. There's always a catch.

The way in which the Cattle must die is partially randomized. There are four stalls at the end, and as each player crosses their "finish" line, they then choose which stall to use. And that's the beauty of the game, especially if you know your opponent.

For example, Maudlin Rose gravitates toward poisoning her victims. She lacks the upper body strength to grapple or stab or strangle. Knowing this, whoever goes against her should aim to take the easiest kill, thus forcing her to take a more complicated option and add time to her team's clock.

As the teams begin lining up in their chosen order, I hurry to formulate a plan. The four initial stalls have been set up, complete with Cattle. The first stall houses a pit of sea water, which means drowning.

It's not a quick death, especially considering the target in that stall looks like he's taken his prison workout routine very seriously. I worry Bennett will choose that stall, if for no other reason than to be a showoff.

"Which are you keen on?" I ask him. "And don't you dare say the first one."

He lets out a sigh. "I guess I'll go for the machete. But what if it's dull like last year?"

"Don't even test it. Open the jumpsuit," Kindra says. "Go right for the gut, and you won't have any issue. Even a dull blade can cut through the abdomen if pushed hard enough, and you look like you can handle it."

Bennett nods. "And what if Ice Pick beats me to the end? Despite the fact that he's already drunk at seven a.m., he's alarmingly fast. He's liable to go for that stall, leaving me with a difficult decision."

I study the stalls again and realize what he means. If he can't get to the machete in time, that leaves him with drowning because the other two stalls hold Cattle of the wrong color. We want to win, but we won't sacrifice our meager scruples for a tin medal and a clap on the back.

"I suggest you lace your shoes tight and haul ass, then," Kindra says. "Make it to that machete."

Jim blows a whistle, signaling for Bennett to take his position. Ice Pick, Bob, and a no name join him. When Jim blows the whistle again, they're off.

The race to the stalls isn't a fair one. Bennett and Ice Pick leap over logs and crawl under razor wire like their lives depend on it. Bob opts for the thirty-second penalty when he reaches the razor wire, choosing to go around it rather than under it. His entire team groans. The no name is still struggling to get over the logs by the time Bennett and Ice Pick emerge from the far end of the wire jungle.

There are no rules about cheating, so I'm not surprised when Bennett trips Ice Pick and sends him to the sand. All's fair in murder and mayhem, and my brother makes it to the machete stall with a shit-eating grin.

The Cattle have been chained to an iron rod which runs behind the stalls. A shackle around one ankle keeps the targets in place. Their hands have been tied behind their backs, and their mouths have been superglued shut, but they still have the use of their bodies.

The Cattle in the machete stall tries to make the most of

his weight, throwing himself around as Bennett reaches for the line of snaps at the front of his red jumpsuit. The wooden walls rattle and threaten to collapse.

It wouldn't be the first time. I don't know why Jim sets them up at all.

Bennett finally rips the jumpsuit open and drives the machete into the exposed skin. Our fears were unfounded. It's definitely sharp.

Blood spills on the sand, and the target drops to his knees. Set free, his internal organs dangle from the wound like long pink slugs. The target looks down and screams, but the sound is a hollow whimper from his nose.

"It's sharp!" Cat screams. "Cut off his head! It's faster!"

"Shut up!" he screams back, but he takes her advice and drives the target onto a blanket of guts and gore before raising the machete over his head and bringing it down on the man's thick neck. The head doesn't detach fully on the first swing, so he does it again, coating the wooden side walls in a spray of jugular joy.

The timer stops for our team. One minute, seventeen seconds.

Ice Pick finishes his kill soon after, having chosen the stall with the garrote. Suffocation isn't quick, but when you use the wire as a saw, it's a bit quicker.

The no name goes for the stall on the end, and he kills his target after several shots with a gun. It takes several shots because it's a BB gun. He must've thought it was a weapon of much better caliber. What a bellend.

Having fallen so far behind, Bob gives up entirely, granting his team a whopping ten-minute penalty and all but ensuring they'll lose as he stomps back to the starting line with his bottom lip leading the way. The man is a total twat, and I laugh to myself as the rest of his team exits the beach, refusing to waste any more time.

The remaining team of nobodies isn't a threat, but I'm concerned about my opponent as I line up at the start of the next race a little ways down the beach. I'll be facing Grim.

He may be a wiry old man, but he has more strength in his stringy muscles than one would expect. He also has a bit of an advantage over me in this leg of the competition.

For the first stretch, we must run through a mud pit. It sounds simple enough, but I'm not exactly light. I'll sink down, making it harder to push through the thick sludge.

Just beyond the mud pit, four logs have been driven into the sand, though we'll only utilize three, since Bob's team abandoned ship. At the top of each log sits a weapon, and only one will result in an expedient kill. The chainsaw. The other options include a hammer, a nail gun, and a drill.

I have to make it to that chainsaw.

I'm formulating a plan when I feel a light tap on my shoulder. I turn and find Kindra gazing up at me.

"Good luck," she says with a coy smirk. "If you can put us even further ahead, I might make it worth your while."

"Hmmm, does my pet have a competitive spirit?"

"Maybe a little." She licks her lips, and now I must win. If I have to kill a man with nothing more than a grain of sand, I'll make it happen so that I can receive her as my prize.

I lean down and kiss her. "For good luck," I say against her lips.

"Oh, for fuck's sake," Bennett moans from the other end of the course.

Ignoring him, I go for another kiss . . . and the whistle blows.

I turn and race for the mud pit, but Grim is already two

steps ahead of me. Using his spindly legs and the power of his shining silver Speedo, he races across the mud like a goddamn Jesus lizard. Meanwhile, I'm neck and neck with one of the no names. How embarrassing.

My mind fills with images of a naked Kindra, tied up and squirming as I bury my face between her thick thighs, and it's all the motivation I need. With a raging erection, I barrel through the mud pit and emerge on the other side as Grim reaches the midpoint of his chosen log.

And he's picked the chainsaw.

"Go for the drill!" Kindra shouts. "Aim the bit at the base of the skull and press as hard as you can!"

God, her bloodlust is like foreplay for my brain. I don't know how I'll climb this log with a cock like a steel rod in my board shorts, but we're all about to find out.

I grip the log and begin to climb, every thrust of my legs bringing me that much closer to the drill at the top. Grim has already secured the chainsaw, but I'm happy to see him struggling to get it down from the top of the log. He decides to toss it into the sand, then leap after it.

When I reach the drill, I don't waste time thinking. I hold it in my hand and pray my ankles can withstand the eight-foot drop. They survive, but my shins will hurt for the next week after this.

As I race toward a pink jumpsuit in one of the stalls, I'm overjoyed to see that Grim's prized chainsaw doesn't want to start. He yanks the pull cord like it owes him money, but he's rewarded with a pathetic burble each time. I depress the drill's trigger to be sure I haven't fallen prey to one of Jim's sneaky traps, and the bit whirs to life.

My target is a woman, and I'd hoped she'd be here today. She molested her niece for years, and a drill bit to the brain is much kinder than she deserves. Had I more time, I would make her suffer.

I kick the backs of her knees and send her to the sand. She doesn't fight. She just looks out at the ocean and cries. If she'd had as much pity for her victim as she has for herself, she wouldn't be in this situation.

I certainly have no pity for her.

I press the drill bit to the back of her skull and let the fun begin.

Her stoicism fades as the metal sinks into her flesh, and she begins to squirm away. Grim has nearly gotten his chainsaw started, so I don't have time for this.

I straddle her back and press my weight against the tool. After a satisfying *pop*, the bit breaks through bone, and the Cattle begins to twitch. I've severed the spinal column from the brain, and that counts as a death. Our clock stops.

As does my target's.

Grim's chainsaw finally lets out a low growl, and the no name is busy bludgeoning his Cattle with a hammer, but I don't pay attention to that. I jog back toward the start of the race, my eyes set on Kindra.

From the corner of my eye, I catch a glint of color. I turn my head and blink several times, but my brain can't rationalize what I'm seeing.

A man in a yellow jumpsuit has broken away from one of the handlers. In his hand, he wields a large blade that looks awfully similar to the machete Bennett used on his Cattle. Judging by the dark stains on the handle, it must be the same one. But that isn't what steals the breath from my lungs.

His glazed eyes are trained on Kindra, and he's heading straight for her.

Chapter Seventeen

Kindra

A blur of yellow flashes in the corner of my eye, and I turn to see one of the Cattle dashing toward me. Not one to cow to danger, I square up, raise my chin, and try not to think about the machete in his hand. Feigning confidence is a natural gift of mine, and it's not like I can outrun him. He's nearly on me.

I close my eyes and brace for impact, but then I hear a grunt. I open my eyes as the man is speared to the sand. Ezra grabs the machete to stop the attack, but blood drips down his wrist. He's been cut.

I should go and help, but I'm frozen in place. I can't seem to make my feet do their only fucking job. Instead, I'm destined to watch the rolling mass of muscle as Ezra fights off a man who wanted to kill me.

Where's the fucking event coordinator? Don't they have a response team for this kind of thing?

Grunts and groans overtake the sounds of the ocean as

Ezra fights the Cattle. His muscles tense and flex, but he holds his own against a man that's twice his size—weight wise, that is.

The machete skitters across the sand, and Ezra's hands wrap around the man's throat. He lays his weight into him as he strangles the ever-loving shit out of his body.

Sometimes watching him in his element feels like a fucked-up episode of *Black Mirror*. It's like watching a golden retriever maul someone.

Ezra switches tactics and releases the man's throat so that he can begin beating him until his features become a mixed-up sliding puzzle. I'm certain I couldn't put him back together. I don't even think doctors could help at this point.

His muscles flex and weaponize, all because of me. That's fucking sweet, but what do I say after someone just saved my life? Thanks? Can I buy you dinner? Good game? I don't fucking know.

Ezra goes back to choking the life from him. The man's legs kick in near-death spasms, but Ezra doesn't climb off his round body until he's certain he's dead. Once the threat to my life has been eliminated, he seems to heave a sigh of relief as he stands.

Jim picks up a bullhorn, and the feedback rings out and buffets my ears. "Due to unforeseen circumstances, the rest of the Olympics are canceled for today."

Not very unforeseen. I could have seen this happening if I was blind. Pitting criminals against criminals is a recipe for a shit sandwich.

"No!" Cat says behind me. She stomps her foot in the sand, the picture of a child who reached the front of the line only to be told the ride is closed.

I turn toward her. "I'm sorry that me almost dying is ruining your opportunity for a kill."

"It's just not fair."

"Neither is Ezra taking a machete for your friend."

Her eyes sparkle, and the loss of the kill is all but forgotten. "You admitted we're friends."

Jesus Christ. I wasn't thinking. It just came out. Near-death experiences will make you say some crazy things. I'm probably more shaken up than I thought. She's just an annoying stranger who follows me around, and that doesn't qualify as a friend.

I turn back to Ezra. He's standing there looking like a bloody Greek god who's just risen from the ashes after an earth-shattering fight.

No one should look that good after committing a homicide.

No one.

He walks over to me, taking my face in his hands as if he's completely forgotten he's coated in red. Warm crimson smears across my cheeks as his lips press against mine.

Bennett scoffs behind me.

Ezra pulls away. "Sorry, pet," he whispers. He clears his throat. "I'll show you where to clean up."

I follow him to a shower station tucked behind some fencing. Rust clings to the drain in the concrete floor, but it's otherwise clean.

"Are you okay?" he asks as he puts soap on his hands and begins to clean himself off.

"I'm fine," I say. "I'm not a damsel in distress, though. If it was my time to go, it was my time to go."

"If you have a death wish, it won't be fulfilled in my presence." He leans closer and gently scrubs the blood from my cheek, but it only gets bloodier because his wrist is still bleeding.

"Can you be a love and hold this together for me?" he says, gesturing toward the gaping wound.

I press the wound together. "If you pull a needle and thread from your pocket, I can't promise I won't laugh."

"It's super glue. We use it when we aren't quite done killing one of the Cattle. It buys us a little more time."

"Yeah, use it for them, not *you*. That gash needs stitches, Ezra."

"Are you saying you care about what happens to me, pet?"

I scoff, but I can't respond. My arctic heart would like to remain frozen when it comes to feeling anything for him. There is no room for feelings in my world. Feelings distract you and make you soft. His dick is distracting enough, and I refuse to let emotions sully the waters any further.

He glues the wound together, then keeps his hand outstretched, letting it dry, but I don't miss the way he's struggling to keep from laughing. I fail to see the joke.

Just before we exit the shower area, the sand begins to rumble and the smell of diesel smoke chokes the ocean's salty perfume. I round the shower wall just in time to see the mangled body of that yellow-clad Cattle rolling in front of the bucket of a Bobcat tractor.

Someone blind, drunk, or high—maybe all three—uses the machine to push the body through the sand before trying to scoop up the massive man. All the forceful rolling around has detached his arm, and it lies in the sand as the tractor backs away with its prize.

"Will you grab that arm for me?" he says. "I think I want to take a trophy for once. This arm was from the man whose death made Kindra say she cares. Do you think I could make it through TSA with it?"

"You're an asshole." I leave him behind as I stomp toward my villa.

None of this is funny to me. I don't care that I nearly died, and I meant what I said. I'm not a damsel in distress, and I don't need anyone to save me, even from myself.

Pounding footsteps come up behind me, and I flinch and wheel around.

Ezra stops in front of me, his hands behind his back as he rocks on his heels. "Sorry for sneaking up like that. Listen, I know you're completely fine, but I'm a little shaken up. Do you mind if I come with you to your villa?"

He's lying. He's about as shaken up as an empty soda can. Also, letting him into my villa almost guarantees we'll end up in bed, and I'm running out of time here. The orgasms are great, but they aren't bringing me any closer to my goal.

Ezra steps toward me, then holds his hand against my cheek, weakening my resolve. I close my eyes and lean into his touch.

His oddly cold touch.

I open my eyes and discover why. I shout and slap away the hand in Ezra's grasp, and it drops to the sand. I back away from it as if it will Thing its way across the granules and worm around all over me.

"Gross!" I say, wiping at my skin. "I thought you were kidding about that hand."

"I thought you needed a laugh."

"And you think my sense of humor extends to being lovingly caressed by the dismembered limb of a man who tried to kill me?"

A small laugh escapes my mouth, then grows louder as my eyes ping-pong from the sinfully gorgeous man to the

159

pale hand. Ezra's momentary doubt recedes as we both discover that yes, my sense of humor extends just this far.

Ezra steps closer and takes me into his arms. Despite everything, I let him. The laughter has loosened something inside me, and I'm back to being putty in his hands.

"That laugh does something to me, pet," he says. "I want to hear more of it."

He leans closer, until his breath brushes against my mouth. I was almost gutted and yet, here I am, wanting those lips on mine. I'm so fucked.

His hands travel over my body. One grips my hip and pulls me closer, but the other goes to my throat. His hold tightens, and a wave of pleasure thrums through the arteries in my neck.

Does he strangle his victims? Staring into his pretty eyes as he chokes the life out of me wouldn't be the worst way to go.

"We can't keep kissing in public," I say.

"I don't care who sees."

"I do, Ezra. Remember why I'm here. People won't open up around me if they think we're more than just friends."

"Did you just call me your friend, pet?" he asks, mimicking Cat.

I hate both of them.

But the truth is more complicated than that, and the truth is that I don't hate either of them. That's a fucking problem.

No matter how much my brain tells me not to fuck with this man, my vagina usurps any rational thought. I'm a serial killer who is fucking a serial killer at a murderous retreat.

There's nothing rational about any of this.

Maybe one more distraction won't be such a bad thing. I'll buckle down and focus after that.

I lick my lips and say something I hope I won't come to regret. "Listen, I don't want to do this in public, but behind closed doors . . ."

Before I know what's happening, he's scooped me into his arms. Like a crazed juicer prepping for an intense competition, he begins jogging down the beach toward the villas.

Chapter Eighteen

Kindra

He demands I undress as soon as the villa door closes behind us, and I'm happy to obey. I yank off my shirt, and my shorts and panties come off next. My clothes are pretty much melting off me at this point.

His clothes don't hold up much better, and we're both butt-ass naked in less than thirty seconds.

His hands slide down my body, hanging up on every roll before passing lower. He grips my ass and digs into my flesh as he pulls me into him and picks me up again. I've never felt small in someone's arms, and as a big girl, I never thought I would, but he holds me up without a breath of difficulty as he beats back my insecurities.

He steps forward until my back meets the wall, then pins my hands above my head, keeping me in place as he kisses me. Honestly, if he dropped me right now, I wouldn't even be mad.

His mouth eases away from mine. "Relax, love. You won't fall. I'm not going to drop you. Just get ready to hang on to whatever you can grab."

I can't even react before he lowers me onto his cock. A feral sound leaves both our lips, as if our bodies were equally desperate for each other.

Ezra drops my hands, and I drape them over his shoulders. My fingers interlace behind his neck. He lifts and lowers me until my eyes are crossed, and I no longer care if he drops me. If I die, I die.

"We can't keep doing this," I say through a moan.

"Doing what, love?"

"Fuck me like it's the last time," I whisper.

"It won't be. But I'll still fuck you like I'll never see you again," he growls.

How can his words hammer my clit like this? I'm already close to coming, but then I get an idea.

"If I'll never see you again, can we play out a little kink of mine?" I ask.

Ezra stops bouncing me on his dick. "Does it involve the Priest-Exorciser Five Thousand?"

Heat flushes my cheeks as humiliating core memories are unlocked. The vibration. The priest. While I'm lost in the throes of my own embarrassment, I figure it can't hurt to pile on more.

I've never shared this kink with anyone else. It's strange, to say the least, so I've only indulged solo while fantasizing about a second party. While I'm sure Ezra will make jokes about it at some point, it's a small price to pay to bring my fantasy to life.

"I want you to take a bath with me," I blurt before I can change my mind.

He lowers my feet to the floor. "That's tame compared

to what we've already done."

"I'm not finished." I take a deep breath. "I want you to wash me up."

"Oh, I'm loving where this is—"

"And then I want you to drown me."

He blinks and looks down at me. "Pardon me, I think I misheard you. I thought you said you want me to drown you." He chuckles awkwardly because we both know that's what I said.

"Don't kink shame me, Ezra. I didn't say shit when you wanted to truss me up like a goddamn Christmas goose."

"Okay, fair, but how does one figure out they want to be drowned? Is it by accident, or . . . ?"

"If you must know, I masturbated a lot as a teenager. We didn't have one of those fancy shower heads you could pull down and press between your legs until you collapse, so I had to settle for the tub's faucet."

"And how did this translate to drowning?"

"The house was older, and the drains were shit. As the water slowly rose, it was a race against getting off or accidentally unaliving myself. Thus, a kink was born."

"And what am I supposed to do while I'm . . . um, while I'm drowning you?"

He's really struggling with this, but at least he isn't laughing me off or telling me no.

"You just have to fuck me," I say. "Fuck me and hold me under."

He thinks for a moment, then shakes his head. "I always said I'd try anything once, but maybe not this."

"Don't you trust yourself to let me up for air? I trust you." The moment it comes out, I know it's true. I trust him. And I might die because of it.

He pulls me into him and kisses the top of my head. "Let's run a bath."

Ezra's cock goes flaccid as he walks me toward the bathroom. The wall-to-wall tubs in these villas are massive, leaving plenty of room for both of us. We draw a hot bath, and I climb inside.

Ezra gets in behind me and pulls me against him as he kneels to grab the shampoo. He washes my hair, his fingers lacing through the wet strands. He's hard again, and I'm glad to feel that stiffness against my spine.

Next, he washes my body, cleaning every curve with dedication and admiration. Little compliments slip from his lips.

"God, you're so perfect."

"Your skin is so soft."

I mentally preen under his attention as I anticipate what's to come.

I sit up on my knees and let his hands drop between my legs. With his cock rubbing against my ass, I bend over for him, and he pushes inside me. I grab both sides of the tub as my nipples sink beneath the waterline. I'm so close to the surface that each exhale ripples the water. Excitement creeps up my spine.

"Drown me," I say.

His hand moves up my back and stops at the back of my head. A killer never hesitates, yet he can't bring himself to do it. But I *need* this.

"Don't think about it like drowning me," I say. "Instead of drowning, think of it as holding me underwater."

"So . . . drowning you."

Frustrated, I try to sit up, but he thrusts into me and holds me in place.

"I didn't say I wouldn't do it, and I'm not done fucking you yet." He wraps my hair around his hand. "We can't use a safe word, but we at least need a safe gesture. Something you can do to let me know you need air if I hold you down for too long."

"We don't need—"

"That's my rule. You want to be held underwater while I rail your pretty pussy, and I want a safe gesture. If you need me to pull you up, hold up a fist. Do you understand?"

I nod.

"Tell me you understand."

"I understand. I'll raise a fist if I need you to back off."

"Good girl."

"Are you going to keep your glasses on?"

"Do you want a blind man to watch for your life-saving hand gesture, or . . . ?"

He stops thrusting, leans forward, and pushes my face beneath the water. A dark emptiness surrounds me, and the world goes silent. The oxygen in my lungs begins to dissipate. Depleting. Depleting. But he's not fucking me. He's literally just drowning me without doing the other steps.

I hold up a fist, and he pulls me out of the water.

"Are you okay?" he asks.

I suck in a deep breath and swipe water from my eyes. "Is this like when you rub your belly and pat your head? You can't drown me and fuck me at the same time?"

He thrusts into me, knocking me forward and dipping my chin below the water. He pushes my head down again, and this time, I get both parts of the action I need.

My hand goes between my legs, and I rub my clit while my lungs start to scream for air. But I won't give up. I want this orgasm more than I want to breathe.

Unfortunately, my body doesn't get the memo. My faithful right hand drives steady circles over my clit, but my deceitful left hand joins my legs in an underwater struggle. Fighting against impending death is part of the thrill, but Ezra doesn't realize this and pulls me up.

"I didn't . . . make a fist," I say through coughs and gasps.

"You were actually drowning!" he says, though I have to give him a few bonus points because he keeps pile-driving his cock into me.

"That's . . . part of it. Don't let me up unless I give the—"

I'm driven under the water again without time to gasp for a final breath. The clock starts ticking, but I have less time now. I furiously work my clit as he fucks me senseless.

Without warning, he pulls me up again. "Do you like me inside you as you drown, pet?" he asks.

"Yes," I whimper before I'm pushed under the water again.

This is more like it. He's losing his grip on his reservations and really going for it, and as the risk of death intensifies, so does the pleasure between my legs.

I grind against every thrust of his powerful hips, chasing my pleasure. I moan in my mind, unable to release the sounds trying so hard to free themselves from my throat. My lungs won't part with an ounce of scarce air.

Darkness encroaches on the edges of my vision as my chest begins to burn. I'm losing consciousness, and if that happens, I can't hold up a fist to stop him. It's the one thing neither of us considered when setting up the safe gesture, and I'm fucking glad. It's just the push I need.

My lips spread against my will, filling my mouth with water as I come. I hope and pray to the gods that he doesn't pull me up. It'll ruin my orgasm.

I swallow water, gulping liquid into my stomach instead of air into my lungs. It's just enough to trick my body into relaxing, so I allow myself another millisecond before I raise a weak fist above the water.

I'm a coughing, satisfied mess as he snatches me back by my hair and finishes inside me while I'm still spasming around him.

He sits down, and I turn to face him. He pulls me onto his lap and we both stretch our legs.

"We have got to stop this," I finally say into his neck.

"We don't have to do any such thing."

Now that I'm not just thinking with my vagina, I need to remind both of us why I'm here. "I have a mission, Ezra. I have to find my brother's killer. I need to focus. And I can't focus with you in the picture."

He places a kiss on my head. After a few moments, he says, "I promise I'll help you find his killer. Two sets of eyes are better than one."

It's a nice gesture, but he fails to see the problem with his plan. "Unless the Abattoir Adonis lives in my vagina, I don't think we'll find much of anything if we try to do this together."

He begins to chuckle. "You're looking at it the wrong way. The sex is just a nice bonus we can enjoy after a hard day of hunting for clues."

A sigh escapes my chest. "That would be nice, but I don't know how it's possible."

"Just give it a try," he says.

I want to, but the risk of developing feelings for this man is the one risk I'm not willing to take. It's bad enough that I'm beginning to care about Cat. Caring about two people will occupy too much of my time.

But with his naked body glued to mine, I come to the

most horrifying revelation. How did I not realize? How did I miss it before this moment when it's been in front of me all along?

I can't stop myself from developing feelings for Ezra because it's already happened.

I'm falling for him.

Chapter Nineteen

Ezra

Dark storm clouds dapple the sky just above the far horizon on the third morning of the retreat, but I'm hopeful we'll still get to enjoy the fishing excursion. Grim is already behind the captain's wheel, prepping for launch, and Bennett is busy helping load the Cattle into their restraints below deck.

I stayed at Kindra's villa until well after midnight, so I can only hope she got enough sleep to make it out this morning. She wasn't exactly keen to wake up at the crack of dawn to sit on a boat all day, but I convinced her by saying we could discuss a strategy for sussing out the Abattoir Adonis.

Who is, of course, me, but she doesn't know that. Yet.

I still plan to tell her the truth on the last day. It's selfish of me to steal this time with her before coming clean, but I can't help myself. She'll get what she wants in the end, and I'll probably get what I deserve.

Until that moment, I'll make the best of my time with her.

Staring down the shoreline, I spot two figures making their way toward the dock. Judging by the bright neon-green swimsuit, one of them must be Cat, which means the other figure is Kindra.

Excitement and dread take up equal space in my chest. I look forward to spending time with her, but the topic of her brother's killer will come up at some point, and the lying is what I don't look forward to.

She raises her hand in a wave as she reaches the dock, and I wave back. She's stunning in a black one-piece swimsuit and short denim shorts. I feel a bit overdressed in khaki shorts and a polo, but I have no plans to go in the water. That's what the Cattle are for.

"I plied her with coffee, so she's a little less angry than she was twenty minutes ago," Cat says as she boards the boat.

Kindra rolls her eyes. "I wasn't angry. I was groggy. There's a difference."

The girls each carry a large beach bag with snacks, drinks, and supplies. They haul these to the front of the boat and take a seat on one of the benches. Bennett joins us, and we give Grim the thumbs-up. Instead of starting the engine, he comes toward us.

"Are you sure you want to go out this morning?" he says. "The waves in the distance don't look very friendly, and the skies are getting darker."

We all turn our heads toward the horizon, and he's right. The sporadic spots of darkness have pulled together to form an ominous inkblot over the water.

"Couldn't we go out for a bit, then turn back when it

gets closer?" Cat asks. "I've never been deep-sea fishing before."

Bennett scoffs. "You've never done a lot of things before. Like killing someone."

"Play nice, children," Kindra says. She turns to Grim. "How serious is it, really?"

Grim pulls off his glasses and begins cleaning them with his shirt. "I am not afraid to go toward the storm, but I have lived a long life. Take from that what you will."

"I'm still in," Bennett says.

"Me too," Cat says, though I hear the tremor in her voice. She's only doing this to show my brother that her balls are as big as his are.

I look at Kindra, but she's still considering her options. I can't leave Bennett and Cat alone and trust that Grim will stop them from killing each other, so I can only hope she'll still tag along.

Finally, she nods. "Okay, I'll stay too."

Grim retreats back to the wheel while we settle in.

No one talks on the way to the fishing spot. Cat is too busy puking over the side of the boat, and the rest of us wouldn't be able to hear each other anyway. The waves are choppy as hell, and Grim plows into them like he has a death wish. Maybe we should have heeded his warning.

When the boat finally stops and Grim drops anchor, Kindra and I head below deck to get some bait. We brought along three Cattle, all of which are currently nude, but they belong to the pink- or red-jumpsuit corral. Metal collars circle each of their necks, with a chain running from the collar to a steel bar attached to the wall.

Kindra moves toward one of the men. I chose him because he murdered his wife and two sons, then kept his ten-year-old daughter around for his nefarious purposes.

He's a real piece of work, and I'm glad I'll witness his suffering.

"Do we just chop off whatever we want to use for bait?" she asks.

I step toward a cabinet and pull an electric cauterizing iron from inside. "Yes, and then you use this to stop the bleeding so that we can keep going."

"Perfect," Kindra says as she plucks the tool from my hand and plugs it into a nearby outlet. "I know just what I'll take off first."

The man's hands are cuffed behind his back, and his feet are shackled to a stiff rod, so there's no chance he can injure her. That means I can just relax and watch the show.

She steps toward him and grips his flaccid cock in her hand. Even though she's about to chop it off, a flare of jealousy rockets through me. Seeing her handle another man's bits shouldn't bother me. Someone needs to remind my heart that she isn't mine forever. She'll hate me in a few days.

Kindra pulls a blade from her pocket and saws off his penis. When I say she saws it off, I mean it in the most literal sense. The knife must be incredibly dull by design, because she hacks away for several minutes until it's off. The Cattle screams through his nose for the entire ordeal— their lips have been superglued shut—then falls unconscious once he's been separated from his tiny ego.

"Shit, the iron still isn't hot enough," she says as blood spurts onto the metal floor. "Can you put pressure on this thing while I wait?"

If holding that raw stump means she'll stop touching him, yes, I absolutely will apply pressure.

I step forward and encircle the remnants of his cock stump with my hand. The man looks at me as he regains consciousness, pleading with his eyes as he screams through his nose again.

"I have no sympathy for you," I say. "You're a dirty nonce, and you deserve all of this and so much more."

"Nonce?" Kindra asks.

"Sorry, pet. I use my native slang on occasion. It means he's a filthy child predator."

Her eyes light with understanding. "Speaking of your British heritage, why do you and your brother have different accents?"

"Our father was a bit of a philanderer. We probably have siblings on every continent, including Antarctica. When my mother died, she told me she knew I had a younger brother in America, so I hopped across the pond to find him."

"How long did that take?"

I shake my head and smile when I recall the hoops I jumped through to learn his identity and location. "Too long. I only knew his first name and that he was three years younger than me. But the journey showed me that I'm very good at discovering things most people wouldn't want discovered. That's how I started my private detective business."

She holds the penis toward me as she steps closer to the man. "Hold this. I'll need both hands."

With a grimace, I take the offered appendage. I don't imagine a penis is the most attractive part of a man, but when it's reduced to a limp slug of flesh, it's even less appealing.

Kindra doesn't hesitate as she presses the tip of the iron to his exposed meat. Smoke billows toward the ceiling and fills the small room with the nauseating scent of burning flesh. The man bucks and twists in his chains, but Kindra keeps chasing his wound with the iron.

"If you don't hold still, it's going in your ass next," she says.

Could she be any sexier?

When she finally has the bleeding under control, we start up the stairs.

"So why did you decide to stay in America?" she asks.

"England just didn't feel like home anymore. I'm not close with my father, and I didn't have any fast friendships. I'm kind of like you. I stick to myself."

"At least you have your brother," she says.

It's a stab to the heart. I still don't recall killing her sibling, but it had to be me. He was strung up on meat hooks, and no one else uses my MO. If I knew more about his death, maybe I could recall why he had to die by my hand, but I don't want to drag up such a painful topic just yet.

Cat and Bennett have gone to the back of the boat to set up the rods. We should have known better than to leave them to do anything, because fuck-all has been accomplished. Instead of readying our equipment, they've engaged themselves in a heated battle of cruel words.

Kindra steps between them. "Can you two just fuck already?"

"Kindra, ew!" Cat squeals. "I would rather fuck myself with that ghost peen in your hand than come within an inch of Bennett's herpes magnet."

"Herpes magnet?" Bennett's eyes go wide. "I'll have you know I use protection, and I've never had an STD!"

"Never?" I say.

Bennett's shoulders drop, and he shoots daggers at me with his eyes. "I've never had an *incurable* STD."

Kindra and Cat both take a step away from him.

"Fuck all three of you," Bennett says as he pushes past me. "I'll be in the wheelhouse with Grim if anyone needs me."

Unable to stop herself, Cat delivers a parting blow. "If we need to know the best antibiotic for gonorrhea, we'll be sure to come find you."

It was actually chlamydia, but I've done enough damage, so I keep my mouth shut. Everyone makes a mistake when visiting Thailand.

With Bennett gone, we begin setting up the rods. It isn't long before the rocking waves send Cat rushing for the edge of the boat again. Kindra suggests she go below deck to lie down. The cabins lie in the ship's center, so the rocking will be less evident. She nods and heads down.

And then there were two.

With no one around to see us, I step into Kindra and place a kiss on her forehead. "I'd bend you over the railing if the others weren't around," I whisper into her ear.

"You'd do it even if they were," she says with a smirk, and she's not wrong. "Let's get a line in the water before this storm hits."

I set to work, attaching the yellowing penis to a hook the size of my hand. We drop it into the dark water, then sit back and wait.

The silence between us unnerves me. She's looking out at the water, but I can see that she's deep in thought. I have to think of a way to buy some time and throw her off until the last day. If I can discover why I killed her brother, maybe I can convince her that it was justified.

Then she places the partial solution into my lap.

"What was Eighties' deal?" she asks. "Is there any chance he could have been the Abattoir Adonis?"

She may have offered an out, but I have to play it cool, so I shrug. "It's possible, I suppose. He was from Texas, but serial killers can travel for work just like anyone else."

Kindra shudders. "Makes me think of the I-90 killer. Did they ever catch that guy?"

"No, and I doubt they ever will. He seems to be on hiatus. They haven't found any new bodies for months."

She sits with this for a moment, then says, "Do you think you'd ever give it up?"

"Not a chance," I say with a shake of my head. "As far as I'm concerned, my need to kill is genetic. My brother and I were killers before we knew about each other, and our father is still an active killer as well."

"Your father too?" Her eyes go wide. "Does he do good work like us?"

This is a topic I didn't want to touch on. It's too shameful. But she asked the question, and I feel safe with her, so I answer. "No. My father and I aren't close for a reason. He kills indiscriminately. He hasn't gone so far as murdering children, so we're still on speaking terms, but he's made some questionable choices that Bennett and I don't agree with."

"I'm sorry, Ezra."

She rests her head against my shoulder and places her hand on my thigh. I'm unaccustomed to these bids of affection and comfort, and only now do I realize what I've missed out on for so long. Then again, I've never craved this sort of attention from a woman.

In reality, I've missed out on nothing. I've just been waiting.

For her.

I place my hand under her jaw and raise her face to mine. She closes her eyes, anticipating a kiss, and I don't want to disappoint her. I place my lips to hers, and her hand travels higher.

"Sorry to interrupt," Cat says beside us.

Kindra pulls away and smooths her hair. "Are you feeling better? You weren't down for very long."

"No, I'm not, and you're about to feel a little worse yourself." She holds her phone toward Kindra. "The email was sent two days ago, but the signal on the island is pretty non-existent. I guess we got some brief blast of signal, because this just came in."

Kindra takes the phone and studies the screen, her face growing paler with each word she reads. She's drained of all color by the time she finishes.

"Guess I'd better start looking for a new job," she says.

"What's the issue?" I ask.

Cat and Kindra take turns telling the story of how they ended up here and why Kindra's job is now in jeopardy.

"My boss is asking for an update, and I have nothing to give him," Kindra says. "I've been too busy riding your dick to focus on the reasons why I'm here."

"I didn't know how secretive she'd have to be when I set this up," Cat says. "It's all my fault."

Unlike Bennett, I won't kick the blonde when she's down, though she had to have reached max-level ignorance to believe Kindra could write a story about anything on this island.

Then again, maybe Eighties is the solution to every problem.

"I might have an answer for you. I'll be right back," I say.

I hurry to the wheelhouse as a plan takes shape in my brain. It could work, but it would rely heavily on Bennett's help, and I'm not certain he'll offer any assistance after my little jab on deck.

Grim is fast asleep behind the wheel, his hands resting in his lap and his chin pressed against his chest. Soft snores burble from his thin lips every few seconds. Bennett glances up from a gun magazine as I enter the cabin.

"Are we ready to head back, or do you need to bring up more of my past first?" he asks.

I motion for him to keep it down, then sit next to him. "Actually, I need to ask a favor."

"Mighty bold of you, all things considered. You also have no bargaining chip. I already get to kill Gary."

"Just hear me out," I say. "I need you to take the meat hooks from my room and hide them in Eighties' villa."

He already knows where I'm going with this, and his head begins to shake before I can finish. "No, absolutely not. You're thinking with the wrong fucking head, Ezra. You plan to lie to this girl, and she doesn't deserve that. I'd help you fuck over the blonde all day, but I like Kindra, so I won't help you deceive her more than you already have."

"I still plan to tell her on the last day. That hasn't changed. But I just want a little more—"

"Time to dick her down? I get it. But the answer is still no."

"No, that's not what I was about to say. I want to know why I killed her brother, and I need more time to figure that out. This will buy that time for me, and it will help Kindra."

I explain her situation with her boss and how Eighties' death can be a solution to that problem. We just need Jim to sign off on revealing Eighties' identity, and Bennett has more opportunity to get that approval.

Bennett sighs, and his head drops to his hands. "Fucking fine," he says through a groan. He pulls his hands away and looks into my eyes. "But I'm doing this on one condition. No matter what happens, you'll tell her the truth before the hunt on the final day."

"Why before the hunt? Can't I do it at the airport right before we part ways?"

A smile slides onto his face. "No, you can't. If you want me to help you dig the hole, I want you to fight your way out of it. You have to do it the right way for her, not the easy way for you. She needs time to cuss you up one side and down the other, and I want to see it."

"So your payment will be my public humiliation?"

"Yes."

"That means I'll probably be too distraught to go on the hunt."

He claps his hand on my back. "I thought of that too. That's when I plan to kill Gary, and with you out of the way, there's no risk of you 'accidentally' taking my kill."

"It happened one time, Bennett. One time."

"And that's one time too many." He gets to his feet and stretches. "Go spin your little web of lies. I'll place the fly in the trap once it's dark."

I hurry back to the girls, but I'm happy to see they didn't need me around to get a fish on the line. Kindra holds the rod's tip in the air, moving it up and down as she and Cat laugh. But as I draw closer, I realize it's not a fish at all. It's one of the Cattle from below deck.

"Kindra rammed a hook through his scalp and cut off his feet to draw sharks," Cat says. Her blue eyes gleam with childish mischief.

I peer over the side of the boat as Kindra brings the man's head above water. He gasps through his nose before sinking into the red water again. I also spy a weight belt around his waist, and his hands are fastened behind his back.

"The line isn't rated for something as hefty as a man. Or a shark," I say. "It'll probably snap soon."

As if I willed it to happen, the line breaks, and the wriggling body begins to sink to the depths.

"Bon voyage!" Cat yells to the receding man.

Kindra slides the fishing pole back into its holder, then turns to me. "Did you figure something out?"

I pull her into me, not caring that Cat can see. "I think I have a solution to your job problem, but Bennett has to talk to Jim first. As for the other, I want you to meet me at my villa around midnight. We have some reconnaissance to do."

Kindra beams up at me with a genuine smile. "I'll be there."

Chapter Twenty

Ezra

With some of the weight lifted from her shoulders, Kindra seemed a lot lighter after the boat ride back. She even joined me for a round of mini golf before heading back to her villa for a nap. I don't blame her. We were up very late last night.

After she headed to her room, I sought out Cat. She would be my alibi so that Kindra wouldn't suspect I'd put the meat hooks in Eighties' villa. After spending several hours with her, I'm not sure why my brother doesn't get along with her. She's pleasant enough to be around.

She's no Kindra, though.

I haven't stopped thinking of my raven-haired goddess since we parted ways this morning. Even now, sitting at the tiki bar with Cat as the sun sets over the water, my thoughts are with her. I'm ashamed to admit that many of these imaginings are X-rated in nature, and I've worked myself into a proper case of blue balls.

Tonight isn't about sex, though, and I'll need to take care of this raging lust so that I can focus. If I don't rub one out before she shows up at my villa in a couple of hours, I'm liable to rip off her clothes before she even gets through the door. That's how badly I yearn for her.

"It's been fun, but I need to get back and prepare for tonight," I tell Cat as I rise from the bar stool.

Her lower lip forms a pout. "I wish I could tag along."

"I know, pal. You'd get bored, though. We'll just be poking around a dead man's things."

She groans. "Stop it. That sounds so exciting."

Has she lived under a rock for her entire life? Nothing about this sounds exciting to me—aside from being with Kindra. That's always exciting.

"Don't forget your drink," she says as the bartender arrives with the piña colada I ordered almost thirty minutes ago.

I grab it from her, nod, and head toward the strip of villas.

A full moon would be fitting for a night like this. It's always a full moon in the books and movies, but this is real life, and a slender crescent of light hangs in a sky full of stars. The storm stayed far offshore, but the storm inside me rages on.

As I clear the steps on the little porch, I'm already undoing my khaki pants with my free hand. The door clicks shut behind me as I place the piña colada on a side table and grip my cock. With all the shutters closed, this seems like a good enough place to jerk off and clear my head.

Leaning my weight onto the side table, I work my dick to thoughts of Kindra. I imagine tying her up. Biting her soft flesh. Licking her pussy until she begs me to stop. I even imagine drowning her again.

The way she looked when she came from that . . . I can't describe it. Beautiful. Perfect. Nothing seems to fit. Even though I can't put a word to what I've seen, the images burned into my brain bring me right to the edge.

Right as I hear footsteps on the stairs outside.

I'm too close to stop now, so I lean over the glass rim of the piña colada as come jets from the head of my cock. Despite being the same color, it doesn't blend or sink to the bottom. It just floats like an ominous glob on the surface.

Oh god. It looks like phlegm.

I nearly break my neck as my head whips around, searching for something to disguise it. My eyes land on the tiny purple umbrella lying beside the glass. I mix it up, the contents blending just as I hear a knock on the door.

I fasten my pants and continue stirring the evidence into the drink as I open the door. It's too early to be Kindra, yet there she stands, looking incredible in a skin-tight all-black outfit. She's even smudged a bit of dark eyeliner around her eyes. She's the picture of an assassin.

God, if I ever have to die by someone's hand, I hope she's holding the blade.

"You're a bit early," I say as she enters my villa.

"I'm happy to see you, too," she says. "I couldn't sit still, so I figured I'd come over."

She goes for my drink, and I pull it out of her reach. She looks dumbfounded and, frankly, a little bit offended as I tip it against my mouth and force some down my throat.

"I really need a drink, Ezra."

"So do I," I say, because I for sure do now. I'm sacrificing my own taste buds to preserve hers.

"Don't be a dick," she says, wrapping her hand around the base of the glass and tugging it toward her.

I relinquish it. I did my best to keep her from drinking the monstrosity now in her hand.

I watch with bated horror as she brings the rim of the glass to her mouth and takes a long gulp. This is a come-laced defeat if I've ever seen it. She moves the liquid around in her mouth, as if she's savoring a fine glass of merlot on a fancy wine tour.

"What is this?" she asks, taking another sip for good measure. "Did you make this yourself?"

"You could say that." I try to take the drink away, but she pulls it against her chest once more.

My chest tightens as if I might have a coronary right here. Sweat drips down my temples and rolls toward my cheeks. All I want is for her to stop drinking it so that she doesn't ask me any more questions about it. It's not my proudest moment, that's for sure.

"Let me have one more swig. I'm under a lot of stress right now." She tips it back and downs a quarter of what was left, then coughs. "Well, that was a little tangy . . ."

"Because it's a piña cum-lada."

She blinks and looks up at me. "Come again?"

"I don't think I can because I already did. In that glass. Just before you arrived."

To my surprise, she shrugs her shoulders and takes a parting sip. "Is that why you look so ill?"

"I do not look ill."

"I didn't realize a human could sweat this much. You'd be less distraught if police were questioning you about your murders."

She's right about that. I wipe the sweat from my brow.

"Besides, I've already had your come in my mouth," she says. "At least this is more palatable."

I'm too stunned to speak, so I just stand there as she

finishes every last drop. Wonders never cease with this woman. And I don't know how I'll ever let her go.

That's a fucking problem.

Kindra eyes me up and down, examining me from head to toe. "Are you doing recon dressed like that?"

I look down at my shirt and khakis. I didn't think it mattered what I wore to a dead man's villa.

"Yes?" I say.

"No. Absolutely not."

She heads to my bedroom, and I follow because there are things she shouldn't see in my room. In my luggage, to be specific. Which is exactly what she begins dragging onto the bed and unzipping.

I try to stop her. If Bennett didn't make good on our deal, she's about to see something very damning. "I can dress myself, pet."

She eyes me. "Not properly."

"Must we shit on what a man wears to a crime scene? This is a deeply personal choice of attire." I try to squeeze her out of my luggage's personal space, but she won't be moved.

She whips my suitcase open and dives headfirst into the thing. She begins tugging out clothes, ruffling up my perfectly folded fabrics and leaving them discarded on the bed.

"I feel like I'm pulling shit from a Men's Warehouse magazine, dude. Do you have anything that isn't so . . . business casual?"

"I have t-shirts."

She reaches the bottom of my suitcase, and I finally take a breath. Bennett came through for me. Thank fuck.

I step closer to her. "I don't want to look ridiculous, pet. Can't we just go like this?"

"Are you saying *I* look ridiculous?"

"No, that isn't what I meant."

Kindra's eyes widen as she comes up with an idea that I'll surely dread. She leaves me alone with my decimated suitcase, and I hear every cabinet in the kitchen being opened and closed. She reappears with scissors and a devilish expression.

I fear for my life.

She comes at my crotch with the scissors, but I put my hand on her head to keep distance between us.

"What are you doing?"

"I'm making some khorts," she says.

"Excuse me?"

"Khaki shorts."

"I have khaki shorts. You cast them aside."

"Shorter than those."

"I am not rifling through a dead man's things while wearing shorts that your friend would wear. It's not work appropriate."

"You have to."

"I don't have to do any such thing."

"Well, you don't have a leather catsuit, and I won't be the only one dressed *ridiculously*." She darts forward again.

I try to stop her, but she's already at my crotch, and all I can do is defend my balls from the dual blades. The legs of my expensive pants fall, and jagged, frayed fabric hangs at heights it shouldn't. I look like a plonker.

"My khaks," I whisper in mourning.

Khaki booty shorts shouldn't be a thing. For anyone. Ever. They aren't so short that my balls might hang out like Grim's, but they're still a little too Richard Simmons for me to pull off.

But if it makes her feel better and brings that smile onto her face, I'll wear the damn things.

With that settled, we exit my villa and start toward Eighties', which is at the end of the row. Kindra's sneakers are silent on the boardwalk, but my thongs make a racket on the worn boards.

Flip, flop, flip, flop.

Kindra looks back at me and stares at my feet.

"What? I would have looked ridiculous in my nice shoes and these *khorts*," I say.

"You look ridiculous anyway," she whispers.

"I wouldn't have if someone had let me wear what I was comfortable in."

"Try a hoodie next time. I promise you'll never go back. Besides, you look pretty comfortable in those shorts now." She waggles her eyebrows at me.

"Tell you what. I'll buy a t-shirt just for you if you promise you'll never cut my clothes again."

"Make sure it's an extra-large so I can wear it too, please."

When she says that, the light flip-flops become lead weights on my feet. Kindra may not realize what she said, but I did. She's planning for something outside of this retreat. On some subconscious level, she's thinking about a future I absolutely cannot be in. And that's the most tragic part of this whole thing.

We continue on in silence until we reach the villa. His door is unlocked, and we slip inside.

Kindra pulls out her phone and types into an app of some kind, documenting things about Eighties for her article, I guess. Jim agreed she could out Eighties as long as no photographs were involved, and she's holding up her end of the deal. What the organizer's short-sightedness fails to realize is that words can be more powerful than a photograph.

And what my short-sightedness has failed to realize is that I'm only digging myself into a deeper hole.

When she finds those meat hooks, she'll believe she's discovered the identity of the Abattoir Adonis. She'll write an entire article—likely a very extensive exposé—and it will all be for nothing when I tell her the truth on the last day.

If I can figure out why I killed her brother, I might be able to give her the information that will help her process his death, but this? I don't know how I can make up for it.

While she's busy typing away on her phone, I step into the kitchen and realize that Bennett is a lazy sack of shit. He left the meat hooks somewhere, all right. They're plopped under the light on the counter. He had to walk maybe ten steps max to plant these here.

Who just leaves their meat hooks lying around like this? Not me, and I actually use meat hooks.

Kindra steps into the kitchen, and her eyes widen as she leans over and spies the gleaming metal. Her head tilts and pivots as she examines them without touching them.

"Eighties was the Abattoir Adonis?" she whispers, and the slight crack in her voice breaks my heart. Those metal hooks have thrust her back into some terrible memory that I orchestrated. And I still don't know *why* I did it.

"It sure seems that way," I say, and a lie has never tasted so bitter on my tongue.

"He doesn't seem strong enough to have strung up my brother, though. And he's not exactly what I would have considered an Adonis."

Her jab at Eighties' meager physique is a compliment to me, but instead of stroking my ego, it twists the knife in my heart.

"Maybe he used hoists or pulleys?" I reason.

"I didn't see anything that would suggest that."

"I don't know, Kindra. He must have done it somehow. Who else would have meat hooks like this?"

Me. I have meat hooks like this. I have *these* meat hooks.

"Can it be this anticlimactic?" She leans against the counter with the most heartbreaking look of defeat on her face. "I imagined it would be more glorious than this. I wanted to find him and make him suffer for what he did. Maybe not here on the island, but back in the real world. I could have gotten the vengeance my brother deserved."

I feel fucking awful about this. Eighties being her brother's killer is great for me but absolutely devastating for Kindra.

"You got to kill him," she says, her eyes rising to mine. "Not me."

"I'm sorry, pet. If I knew, I never would have killed him. I'd have served him to you on a silver platter."

That's a lie because I'd have to serve *myself* on the silver platter. And for some reason, I'm struggling to do that. Self-preservation?

Or something else . . .

I go to her and put my arms around her. Instead of pushing me away, she leans her head against my chest and winds her arms around my waist. While I don't want to take advantage of this moment of weakness, I'm running out of time to figure out why I did what I did.

"Do you think you could talk about what happened to your brother?" I ask. "I know it's a sore subject, but it might help."

She nods, and I seize the opening.

"When was he killed?" I ask.

"It will have been a decade ago next month." She

mumbles the words into my chest, then sucks in a deep breath. "Actually, I don't want to talk about it right now, if that's okay."

I stroke her head. "That's fine, pet. We don't have to."

It's a hint, at least. Ten years ago. This narrows it down a bit. I believe I killed four people that year. Or maybe it was six. Who the hell even remembers that long ago?

She does, that's for sure, and her brother's murder is slaying any chance of a relationship between us.

Chapter Twenty-One

Kindra

Well, I got the story and won't lose my job, so there's that, but everything I've chased for the last decade has just evaporated in front of my eyes. It should be criminal for anything to end like this. I had grandiose visions of stalking this guy for months before kidnapping him and slowly ending his miserable life. What do I do with all of this anger now?

But then I lean my ear against Ezra's chest, and that anger shrinks away from his warmth. It's pretty difficult to be outraged when I'm in his arms.

"Let's get back to your villa," he says.

He takes my hand and leads me down to the beach instead of back across the boardwalk. Tiny white crabs scurry around our feet and rush toward the incoming water.

"Did you grab the meat hooks?"

"Should I have?"

I guess not. "No, it's probably better this way. If I never see a meat hook again, it will be too soon."

We finally reach my villa door, and he leans in to give me a goodnight kiss. I don't want to be alone right now, though. Sex is the furthest thing from my mind, but I crave his company. Before I can ask him to come inside, a figure appears at the edge of the boardwalk.

"Why are you dressed like . . . that?" Bennett asks as he steps into the circle of light thrown by the tiny bulb by the door.

"Kindra didn't want to look ridiculous by herself."

"So you had to wear sloppily cut shorts," Bennett says. "Got it."

I punch Ezra's arm. "I don't look ridiculous."

More footsteps approach as Cat enters the equation from the opposite side of the boardwalk, but she nearly runs into me because she's so focused on Ezra's bulging thigh muscles as they burst from the short shorts.

"For fuck's sake," Ezra says. "Anyone else coming to this party?"

"I think we're all here," Cat says, "but the rest of your pants are missing."

Bennett and Cat both laugh, and for a moment, we all bond over the atrocity that is Ezra's attire.

"I'm glad you all had a good laugh over my unfortunate state of dress. Excuse me while I go put on some real pants."

"I'm heading to the grotto," Bennett says, catching Ezra's arm. "Change into swim trunks and meet me there."

Ezra's gaze catches mine. "Would you like to join us?"

I planned to return to my villa and be a miserable bitch, but the way he looks at me makes me pretty certain my bitchiness can wait.

Cat grabs my arm with childlike excitement. "Come on, Kindra, the night is young."

"No one invited you," Bennett says, but Cat just ignores him and keeps looking at me.

The night has been shit. But regardless, I force a smile toward Ezra. "I guess it wouldn't hurt to drown my sorrows in some booze. There will be booze, right?"

Cat nods her head.

"Just let me change, and I'll meet you all there."

Ezra heads toward his villa, and Bennett lets out a low groan as Cat rushes off to change as well.

The door closes behind me, and I already regret agreeing to join everyone at the grotto. I'd rather sit alone and sulk. But if anyone can bring me out of this foul mood, it's Ezra. And maybe Cat.

I squeeze into a shimmering silver one-piece suit and drape a black mesh cover-up over the top. After sliding my feet into some cheap flip-flops, I head down the boardwalk.

The Blood Grotto is gorgeous. Colorful tiki torches surround the giant hot tub, and light fixtures stick out of the sand and cast a red glow on the blood-stained stone altar.

It looks almost like a table; one solid slab lies over four fat stones. A channel winds beneath it, stained with the memory of blood as it slithers toward the hot tub. I'm assuming it's so that one could bathe themselves in the blood of whomever was sacrificed on that thing.

I stare at it and wonder what my brother's killer looked like when he lay there. How much blood did he lose before he died? Did it hurt? I hope so.

I hope it was agonizing.

"Kindra!" Cat screeches beside my head, and I envision dropping her onto that altar.

"What?"

"I've been trying to get your attention, and you're staring off into space. I asked you if you wanted a drink."

I have never needed a drink so badly, but preferably not one with Ezra's special sauce in it. "Yeah, I'll have a glass of red."

Ezra comes up behind me and grabs my shoulder. I lean into him and take my eyes off the giant rock.

"Wine for my pet," he whispers as he places a glass in my hand.

I turn around and look at Ezra. He's traded my creation for a pair of swim trunks that fall past his knees.

"Who's up for a game of truth or dare?" Bennett asks as he walks over. He's double-fisting beer bottles, one of which he hands to Ezra.

"Are we twelve?" Ezra clips.

"No, even better," Bennett says. "We're adults."

"I'll play," I say, and everyone turns to look at me.

"If Kindra is in, I'll play too," Cat says.

Bennett scoffs. "Of course you will, little tag-a-long."

Ezra gets another glass of wine because I've already guzzled the first in one swallow, and then we all settle into the hot tub.

Cat turns toward Bennett. "Truth or dare, dickhead?"

"Truth."

"Lame," Cat mumbles.

"No, not lame," Bennett says. "It's smart. You'd probably dare me to jump into a bonfire and count to one hundred."

"I would absolutely do that," Cat says with a sly smirk. "Truth. Um. Tell us your real serial killer name and MO."

Bennett takes a hearty drink before standing up, turning around, and lifting the back of his shirt. Between his shoulder blades, nestled among his other tattoos, are two words.

Chaos. Killer.

"They call me the Chaos Killer," he says.

"By they, he means me and him," Ezra says.

"Don't hate me because my chaos is what makes me so unknown. That's my MO. It might be a hammer this time, but next time, it might be an ax. Maybe fire."

Cat curls her lip. "You tattooed your own killer name on your body? That is—"

"Why don't you let me know what you do once you kill at all? As of right now, you're someone who desperately wants to be part of this little group, and you aren't." Bennett's smile widens as Cat's fades. "You probably won't ever be one of us."

Maybe it's the glass of wine I chugged as soon as it was placed into my hand. Maybe it's the absolute absurdity that has become my search for my brother's killer. Either way, the way Cat's lip wobbles as Bennett's words hit home strikes a nerve inside me.

I sit forward and take another pull from my wine glass. "Do you always have to be so goddamn cruel, Bennett?"

He spares a quick glance at Cat. She's already stuffed her pain deep down inside her, and she's done so at such a brisk pace that I can tell she's had a lot of practice.

"Let's move on," Ezra says, trying to keep the game going.

Bennett turns toward Ezra. "Truth or dare."

"Truth."

I don't miss the devilish gleam that runs through Bennett's eyes when he says, "How did you get the name Crumpet Killer?"

"I'm not getting into this again." Ezra shakes his head

and lowers himself into the water until only his head sticks above the bubbles. "Give me the dare."

"I dare you to show Kindra your tattoo."

"Absolutely not," Ezra says, and my curiosity is piqued.

I've seen Ezra's body. Most all of his body, I think. But I haven't noticed an embarrassing tattoo. Then again, I was pretty busy looking at other things.

"Don't be a poor sport," Bennett says.

"Fine, you twat."

Ezra stands up, turns around, and lowers his swim trunks. On his left cheek is a greenish . . . snake? I think it's supposed to be a snake. I squint really hard because it looks like a penis sitting on top of a red rose.

"Who did this to you?" I ask, dropping my hand from my mouth.

He raises his swim trunks and slips back into the water. "When I first moved to the States, my brother and I got drunk and decided to get tattoos. He got his stupid name on his body, and I picked out a cobra on a rose. That tattoo 'artist' clearly hasn't seen a cobra in his life, so now I'll look like I have a dick on my ass for the rest of eternity."

"That's not even the best part," Bennett says through a laugh. "When he dies, the coroner is going to flip him over and come face to face with that beauty."

"Oh, fuck off," Ezra says.

"If it makes you feel any better, I almost got a drunk tattoo myself," Cat says. "I ended up throwing up all over the guy before he could start."

"It doesn't make me feel better, but thanks," Ezra says with the cutest pout I've ever seen. "My turn. Kindra, truth or dare?"

While I have a nice little buzz going, I haven't imbibed

enough to play this game. I shake my head and wave for him to pick someone else, but he levels me with a pointed stare that tells me I'm not getting out of this.

"Truth," I say.

"Tell us about your brother's death."

I study Ezra's face, but I find no malice in his eyes. So what possessed him to ask such a painful question?

"Well . . . I found him in the garage. His killer bled him out and hung him from meat hooks."

"Don't forget the other details," Cat adds. "It might help to talk about it."

It won't. Years of therapy proved that.

I shake my head and swallow the rest of my wine in one gulp. "I think I'm ready for another one," I say as I jiggle the glass toward Ezra.

He doesn't press me to continue. Instead, he grabs my glass and goes to the bar for a refill. Cat also helps things along by reminding me that it's my turn.

"Right," I say with a forced smile. "Bennett, truth or dare?"

"I'll go with a dare this time." He knocks back his beer, then sends the empty bottle rolling across the concrete.

Ezra returns with my wine, and I'm grateful that he's brought the bottle with him this time. I take a long sip directly from the glass neck as I consider what to do to Bennett.

Cat scoots closer and cups my ear with her hand before whispering, "Dare him to take off his swim trunks and jump into the pool."

I nod my head and turn to face him. "Strip and give Cat a good eyeful of your junk."

Cat swats my arm. "That's not what I said!"

But it's too late. Bennett has already pulled off his trunks and brought his flaccid cock within an inch of Cat's nose. He pretends to stretch his back as she squirms and squeals beside me, trying to escape the impressive (and pierced) penis that threatens her sanity.

"Why is it looking at me like that?" she squeals.

"Put it away," I say through a belly laugh. "She's seen enough, and so have I!"

I sit back and relax as the four of us share a laugh as a group, but life has taught me that laughter only lasts for so long. Like a storm cloud, Bennett brings the mood down once again.

"Kindra, I'm shooting it back to you," he says. "Truth or dare?"

"Truth," I say, unwilling to race down the beach while baring it all.

He thinks for a moment, then says, "Did anything stand out about your brother's death? Anything strange?"

Ezra places his hand on my arm. "You don't have to answer that. I never should have started that line of questioning."

"But you did," Bennett says. "Now inquiring minds want to know."

"No, it's fine." I take a deep breath and relay the dirty details, including the missing eyes and the number scrawled into his cold skin.

"Oof, he was mutilated?" Bennett says. "Whoever killed your brother was a real asshole."

No one is laughing now. The topic of my brother's death has effectively killed the vibe. Ezra stares at me. Bennett gulps his beer. Cat sits back, unable to meet my eyes. Yeah, no one is having fun anymore.

"On that note, Kindra, I'm going to go to bed," Bennett says, wiping spilled beer off his chin.

"I guess I am too," Cat says.

They climb out of the hot tub and head opposite ways as they start toward their respective villas.

"I guess I should go to bed too," I say to Ezra. "We accomplished a lot tonight."

He nods, but he's stopped staring at me. Now, much like Cat, he won't even look at me. "I'll walk you to your villa."

We trudge through the sand. After lounging in the steaming water, the air feels like ice. The thin wrap doesn't help, so I start to shiver.

Ezra doesn't even notice. His gaze is glued to the ground, and he nearly takes himself out on a sign in front of him. I didn't think talking about a murder at a retreat full of killers would make everyone so uncomfortable. You'd think they'd all have enough experience with death by now.

We hit the edge of the light from the bulb above the doorway. Bugs circle above our heads.

"Do you want to come in?" I ask.

I hope he does, as I could use the company. I've brought myself down just as much as them. More, probably.

Ezra steps into me and kisses my forehead, and it's not a yes-I'll-come-in kind of kiss.

"I'm not feeling too well," he says. "I think I'm going to head back myself."

Are you kidding me? I've found my brother's killer. I've told my story in front of everyone. There's a weight off my chest that's finally letting my heart beat a little more freely. And now he's going to leave? Now?

I'm speechless.

"Go inside, Kindra. I'll see you in the morning."

"Yeah. Night."

I watch him leave, his hands slipping into his pockets as he disappears into the darkness. And isn't that always the way? The moment I let my walls down, the man decides I'm no longer worth the effort.

"At least I still have you," I say to the wine bottle in my right hand. And that's when the tears come.

Chapter Twenty-Two

Ezra

They weren't sevens.

That's the pervading thought that circles my exhausted mind as I blindly stumble toward my villa. Those little lines I carved into his skin weren't meant to represent the number seven, though I can understand why she would have thought that was the case.

I carved him up when I had him tied to a table, long before the family discovered him, so each symbol would have appeared upside down once I changed his orientation and draped him from the hooks.

But they weren't sevens. They were letters. More specifically, dozens of capitalized letter Ls.

Letters or numbers, it didn't matter either way. She and her mother wouldn't have made the connection because they were blissfully unaware of what their beloved son and brother had been up to in his free time. The missing eyes wouldn't have made much sense, either. But now I know everything I need to know.

I killed Kindra's brother.

A terrified mother brought him to my attention all those years ago. She didn't hire me to kill the man who'd been molesting her child, though. She only wanted me to ferret out enough evidence so that he could be brought to justice. Instead, I meted out justice myself.

My methods haven't changed much over the years. Someone brings a name to my P.I. firm, and I sally forth and return with the evidence they require. But, on rare occasion, that evidence secures my right to kill, and that was the case with Kindra's brother.

His name was Reese Amato, and he paraded around as a community do-gooder. No one questioned a twenty-some-thing youth pastor who just wanted to help the neighborhood kiddies with their batting average, especially when that man had been the star of the local baseball team in high school. Someone should have been asking some questions, though.

A week of investigative work gave me more details than I could stomach. The mother had been right to worry. He'd been doing horrible things to her son, but he'd been molesting other boys on the team as well. Unfortunately, I learned her son had been his personal favorite since he was eight years old.

After warning the child's parents, I stalked Reese for three days, waiting for the right moment to strike. When that moment never presented itself, I got tired of waiting. Just knowing he did such vile things to such innocent children tipped the scales of rage in my heart. It was the only time I've ever lost myself to a kill.

It was stupid to stray so far from my MO, which usually involves careful planning and rigid execution, but I couldn't help myself. I really wanted to hurt that asshole, so I snatched him from his bed one night and hauled him back to my place.

That's where I tied him to a table and carved those letters into his skin. That's where I removed his eyes with a melon baller, all while he was still alive. He would die with that child's brand on his skin, and he would never look at another innocent babe with lust again.

I wanted to do so much more. I wanted to shove his stumpy cock into his mouth, wait for him to shit it out, then feed it to him again. I yearned to pull each of his nails from his fingers and toes, then drip acid into the open wounds.

There just wasn't enough time. There never is.

So, I loaded him up in my car and took him to his mother's address, where I hung him in the garage and proceeded with exsanguination. That's where Kindra comes in, I guess.

Now, knowing all this, I'll be forced to explain everything to the woman I'm falling for. I have no way to prove anything to her, as all the evidence in my possession has been destroyed, so I can only hope she believes me.

If we were back on the mainland, I'd just call up the families and ask them to corroborate my tale, but that isn't possible here. The cell connection is too spotty, and the internet is about as accessible as a pious nun's knickers.

Which is to say, not at all.

I sigh and lean against the door to my villa. My heart has done a very stupid thing and attached itself to someone who can't possibly return the affection. Once she learns that I killed her brother and lied about it, she'll never want to see me again.

That means I have one more day with her. I promised Bennett I would tell her before the hunt on the last day, so I still have tomorrow. But is that fair to Kindra?

"No, it's not," I whisper as I turn around and break into a run.

Trees and tiki torches rush by in a blur. If I don't tell her everything right now, I don't know if I ever will. It won't be easy, but it's better to rip off the Band-Aid now and give some time for the wound to heal. Kindra's a smart girl. She'll do her own digging, and once she discovers the truth, she'll come around.

I stop running when a strange sound reaches my ears. It's almost like a gentle wail riding in on the wind, but the sea swallows the keening cry before it fully reaches my ears. As I draw nearer to Kindra's villa, the sound grows in strength.

Is she . . . weeping?

Light catches on her hair. She's seated on the porch, right where I left her, and yes, that sound is coming from her. I know this because the sound stops when she tips the wine bottle against her lips, then begins again when she's done guzzling.

"Is everything okay?" I ask.

Not the most brilliant move on my part. My voice startles her, which sends the wine bottle flying directly at my head. I duck just in time, and the bottle collides with the sand behind the boardwalk. Incredibly, it remains intact, but I don't fetch it. Kindra doesn't need any more wine.

As I approach, she swipes her hands over her eyes, desperate to conceal any lingering hint of vulnerability. This poor, poor creature. How terrible to go through life as you hide your emotions from the world. And I would know.

"I didn't mean to frighten you. I just . . ." I step onto the small porch, still searching my mind for the words that must be said. "There's something I need to tell you."

She waves her hand and purses her lips. "No, no. You

don't need to say anything. I already know. Now that I'm falling for you, you've lost interest. It's cool. I'm cool. You're cool."

"No, pet. That's not what I wanted to say at all." I rush to her side and brush the sweat-soaked hair from her tear-stained cheeks. "I haven't lost interest. On the contrary. My interest in you has only grown from the moment I laid eyes on you."

I want to lean forward and kiss her, but I also recognize that this isn't the right moment. Not when she's this sloppy. She's liable to spill her guts in the most unappealing sense. Instead, I sit beside her, guide her head to my shoulder, and wrap my arm around her.

"I'm so sorry I've made you feel as if I've lost interest," I say, then kiss the top of her head. The sun set hours ago, but I can still smell the sunshine in her hair.

She shakes her head and sniffles. "No, I'm the one who should apologize. I'm a miserable, closed-off, antisocial mega-bitch. How can I expect anyone to find something to like about me when I'm in a constant state of fuck-off?"

"The right person sees through the rough exterior and spots the promise within." I pull her against me and brush my hand up and down her arm. "You haven't scared me off yet, love."

This sets her off again, and she wails against my bare chest. Had this been any other woman—and I speak from experience, mind you—this show of melancholy would be a major turn off. I'd be squirming in my skin, looking for the exit.

But now?

Now, I want to let her cry. I want to hold her until she's let it all out. I want to be her source of comfort. When the world is at her back and she feels she has nowhere else to go, I want her to run to me.

Even though I have no right.

I've been the source of her pain for so many years. It's not right for me to keep this secret from her any longer, regardless of what the truth will do to me.

"Kindra, I really need to be honest with you about something." I try to peel my arm from behind her, but she clutches my wrist and pulls it back into place over her shoulder.

"No," she mumbles. "Whatever it is, I don't want to know right now. I just want to stay like this for as long as possible. Just hold me, Ezra."

So I close my eyes and I hold her. I rub her arm and let her rest against my chest as the stars cut a path through the sky. If she wants me to wait to tell her, I will, but I don't feel great about it.

"Truth or dare?" she says after a long stretch of silence.

My lips form a lazy smile. "Truth."

Sitting up, she rubs her eyes, then looks into mine. "Have you thought about what happens after the retreat?"

I know what she's asking, but I decide to toy with her. "Well, I don't have to think about it too much. I already know what happens. Jim has a clean-up crew that comes in and takes care of the bodies. A cannibal tribe from—"

"What? No!" She smacks my arm. "You know what I mean."

"Oh, you mean with us? Yes, I've given it a bit of thought, but it's still early days, so I wasn't sure if it would be weird to bring it up. Plus, you seem to enjoy flying solo, and I didn't want to wreck your carefully curated mystique."

"Carefully curated mystique? Do you ever listen to what you're saying?"

She laughs for the first time since the crying fit, and I've never been more relieved to hear a sound.

"I've been alone a long time," she says, then sighs. "I don't mind it, but sometimes I get lonely. Maybe it wouldn't be so bad to have someone to call at the end of a long day."

"Are you asking for my number, Kindra? How forward."

She giggles, and it's music to my ears. "Maybe I am. Do you think we could be anything outside of this place?"

"I think we could."

Once we get past the whole I-killed-your-pedophile-brother bit.

She sits up and begins picking at the side of her thumb. "If that's the case, there's something you need to know about me."

Now I can see her logic. Now I understand why she didn't want me to tell her anything that could derail this train of paradise we've set rolling down the tracks. Because now I don't want her to speak. Whatever dark secret she hides, let it remain hidden.

"I don't want to know," I say.

She ignores me and cocks her head to the side, then bites her lower lip. "I'm the Heartbreak Killer."

If the flirty, drunken way she's looking at me wasn't enough to get blood to the down below, her words certainly do the trick.

I've been fucking my idol!

The killer I've been obsessed with, the murderer I've fantasized about meeting, has had my dick in her mouth.

I nearly come in my pants.

"You . . . are the Heartbreak—"

"Killer, yes. Are you okay? You look a bit pale."

"It's just my British complexion. I'm perfectly fine. Shocked, but fine." I run my hands through my hair and look at her again. "*The* Heartbreak Killer?"

She nods and sits back on her side of the bench. In her inebriated state, she nearly topples to the porch. I catch her arm and pull her forward again.

"Maybe we should get you to bed, HBK." I help her to her feet, and she leans against me.

"Yeah, that doesn't sound like such a terrible idea."

Once inside, I help her undress and ease beneath the sheets. Being a good boy is difficult, especially when her perfect nipples brush past my lips as I'm helping her out of her swimsuit, but I remain steadfast. And painfully hard.

"Can you stay with me until I fall asleep?" she asks through a yawn.

I sit on the edge of the bed and run my fingers through her dark hair. "Of course I can."

"I think I'm ready to hear whatever you have to say now," she mumbles. "Even if it's something bad, I'm too exhausted to care."

"It's not something bad," I say, and I'm not being dishonest. It's not bad.

It's horrible.

And now I've lost the courage to tell her I killed her brother, so I say the only other thing that comes to mind.

"Kindra, I'm beginning to fall in love with you."

She replies with a soft snore.

Chapter Twenty-Three

Kindra

I'm seated at the small breakfast nook when I hear a light tapping on my door the next morning. The sun has barely broken the horizon, but I didn't exactly sleep peacefully last night.

After setting my coffee on the table, I fling a light robe around my body and rush to the door. Cat is already halfway down the boardwalk by the time I step into the sunshine.

"I'm up!" I call toward her, and she spins around.

She shuffles back with a sheepish look on her face, probably fearing I'll reprimand her for waking me. Her eyes only widen when I grab her arm, pull her into the villa, and close the door behind her.

"You will not believe what happened after the two of you left last night," I say.

"If I had to guess, I'd say you had more kinky tie-down sex," she says.

I sit at the breakfast nook and grip my mug of coffee

close to my chest. The heat from the ceramic rests just over my heart, where another sort of warmth blooms as I prepare to tell her what happened.

"He said that he's falling in love with me," I say.

Cat squeals and begins jumping up and down, and goddamn me, I can't help but join her. I set down the mug, leap from that chair, and grip her hands, and like two absolute brain-dead ninnies, we jump in a circle and squeal.

"Oh my gosh, Kindra, please tell me everything," she says once we sit down. "What did you say when he told you?"

I pull the mug to my lips and take a long sip. "Well, I didn't know what to say, so I just . . . snored."

"You what?"

"I was shocked, okay? I'd just told him that I'm HBK, and he set it up like he needed to tell me something horrible, but then he said he was falling in love with me. That isn't exactly something I prepared a response for, so I pretended I was asleep."

She jumps up and comes to my side, then wraps her arms around me. "It doesn't matter. Nothing matters. He said he's falling in love with you, and I'm so happy for you!"

I stiffen in her arms, as I'm not normally the hugging type. Sensing my discomfort, she releases me and takes a seat again. Her face glows, and her cheeks have to hurt from smiling this widely. It's as if someone had professed their love to *her* last night. That's how happy she is for me.

And then it hits me.

This is what having a friend is like. This is what it could have been like all along, had I not been such a prickly bitch. It feels nice to have someone in my life who is truly excited about my little wins, and I don't know why I've run from this for so long.

I reach across the table and grip her hand. "Thanks for being my friend, Cat, even when it wasn't easy."

Tears spring into her eyes, but she swipes them away. "Oh, stop it. I didn't make it easy, either. Though I had good intentions, everything I've done has ended in a mess for you."

She's not wrong. But everything has come out right on the other side, so I can't complain.

"Is that why you're up so early?" she asks. "Too excited to snooze?"

"After he left, I couldn't sleep. Then I fell asleep, but I couldn't stay asleep. Around five, I gave up and made coffee."

"Sounds like you need something to occupy you. Would you want to go on the hike this morning? That's why I came by. At the end of the hike, you can push some Cattle off a cliff. It's not the most luxurious way to murder someone, but I figured it's better than not murdering anyone at all. I'm running out of time."

While a hike at the crack of dawn's ass isn't at the top of the list of things I wanted to do today, I don't have the heart to tell her no. She's been kill-blocked at every turn—through no fault of her own—and I want to be there for her when she accomplishes her first murder.

"Of course I'll come with you," I say. "Just let me change clothes."

As I'm easing into a tank top and some jean shorts in the bedroom, I hear another knock at the door, followed by Cat talking to someone with a deep voice. While I have a newfound appreciation for our friendship, the girl could fuck up a wet dream. If that's Ezra on my doorstep, I can't risk her blabbing that I heard what he said.

I hurry to the bathroom to piss before rushing back to

Lauren Biel

the main area and, just as I feared, Ezra is seated on the couch. Judging by his outfit—a pale-blue button up, khaki cargo shorts, and hiking boots—he planned to hike this morning as well.

"I came to see if you wanted to join me on the hike, but I see someone beat me to it," he says. "Mind if I join you girls?"

"Not at all," I say, and why does my voice sound like it's risen three octaves? Do I always sound like this when I talk to him? I clear my throat. "Will your brother be joining us?"

Ezra shakes his head. "Not this time. While he enjoys most athletic endeavors, he finds hiking a bit boorish."

"My day just got exponentially better," Cat mutters. "Then again, if he hates hiking, maybe I'd rather he tag along. I can feed on his misery."

"We should probably ask," I say. "I'd hate for him to feel excluded."

Yes, I need to make nice with my future brother-in-law, I think to myself, then immediately chastise my wild imagination. He said he was falling in love with me, not that he was *in* love with me.

And we aren't exactly dating. Are we?

How will I know if we are? Is that a question I ask, or is that something he'll clarify?

But will I seem too needy if I ask? What if I *am* needy?

Oh god. It's been so long since I've been in a relationship. I don't even know if—

"Kindra?" Ezra looks at me with his eyebrows pulled together. "Have you heard anything I've said?"

"She's probably a little tired because—"

"Because I slept so hard!" I say before Cat can completely blow my cover. "You know how it is. Sometimes you sleep so well that it takes longer to shake off that groggy

214

feeling." I cover my mouth as a yawn parts my lips, and then I smile at them.

Cat seems to get the memo without having it spelled out for her. She's evolving.

"I was saying that we can certainly drop by his villa and ask him to join, but he'll still say no." Ezra looks at his watch. "But we'd best crack on if we want to make the hike. It starts in less than forty-five minutes."

We hurry and craft a bag filled with trail mix, bottled water, and sunscreen. Ezra plays the part of pack mule and carries it.

Everything seems a little brighter as we step into the morning sunshine. I've unearthed the identity of the man who killed my brother, and though it didn't end quite as I'd hoped, it's still a chapter of my life I'm happy to close. I've gained a friend and an assistant, and I've gathered the necessary info to begin a multi-part exposé on Eighties.

And, yes, the man of my dreams has confessed that I've affected him, and maybe that's fucking with the vibrance of life a little more than usual.

Cat and I walk across the wooden boards, sticking close behind Ezra as we make our way down the row of villas. Maudlin Rose sits on her porch, wearing nothing more than a sun hat and a smile. She waves as we pass.

I don't think I've heard the old woman speak since we arrived. I don't even know if she *can* speak.

When we reach Bennett's villa, "It's Not Unusual" by Tom Jones pours from the open windows as a breeze ruffles the curtains. I cover my mouth to stifle a laugh. I never would have pegged Bennett as a Tom Jones fan. Then I catch the faintest sound, like someone tapping against the wall to the beat of the song.

Ezra looks as confused as I feel, but he shakes his head

and knocks on the door anyway. Bennett doesn't answer, and the odd tapping sound continues.

"Bennett? You in there?" Ezra knocks again, a little louder this time, but no one comes to the door. He looks back at us and shrugs. Bennett probably can't hear us over the thump of bass and smooth male vocals.

"Try one more time," I say, though I'm less interested in convincing Bennett to join us and more interested in discovering what he's doing in there.

Ezra turns back to the door as Cat leaves the porch and goes to the window. Before Ezra can knock, Cat flails her arm and covers her mouth, her eyes wide. She motions us over, and, being the nosy bitch that I am, I rush to her side.

I've seen a lot over the years, but no amount of internet porn could prepare me for what waits beyond this thin coral curtain blowing into Bennett's bedroom.

My brain almost can't register it at first. He's standing in front of the bedroom dresser with his hands firmly planted on the top, bracing himself as he . . . fucks a pineapple. He's wedged the spiny fruit within one of the drawers, positioning it at the perfect height for his dick. With each aggressive thrust, the back of the dresser collides with the wall.

Well, at least I know what the tapping sound is.

As his ass flexes to the beat, I can't contain my laughter. I mean, he is *really* showing this pineapple who's boss, and despite what Tom Jones says, it absolutely *is* unusual.

Then Bennett's head tips back, eyes closed in the throes of passion, and it's all Cat and I can do to stay upright. We grip each other and fall to the sand as tears of laughter fill our eyes.

My entire abdomen aches, and I can't breathe. In fact, I'm fairly certain I'm one wheeze away from pissing myself, but I can't stop. And I don't want to. I can't remember the last time I laughed like this.

Ezra rushes over, trying to shush us through a wide grin, but it's not like his brother can hear us. He's lost to passion, pineapples, and a groovy sixties tune.

When we've composed ourselves, we return to the window. Bennett has removed his hands from the top of the dresser so that he can caress the fruit wedged within the drawer. His thrusts slow, and we all watch in horror as he completes his mission—right inside the pineapple.

But, oh god, it doesn't stop there.

Bennett finishes spilling his load, then drops to his knees. Now I can see that he's cut the bottom of the fruit away and taken out the central core, leaving the perfect slot for his dick. Kneeling in front of the destroyed, pulpy innards, Bennett leans forward and begins licking the outer hole he created.

"I know they say pineapple makes it taste better, but I'm not sure this is what they meant," Cat says . . . right as the song comes to an end.

Bennett's head whips toward us, and, like a bipedal chameleon, he jumps to his feet and shifts from tan to beet-red.

"Why aren't you assholes on the hike?" he screeches as he snatches a blanket from the bed to cover his crotch. But not before we're blessed with a view of his pierced glory.

Another song begins, and Bennett rushes to the stereo to silence Celine Dion's "I'm Your Lady" before disappearing into the bathroom.

Ezra leans into the window. "We wanted to see if you'd join us on the hike."

"Fat chance of that happening now," I say. "After we

caught him with his pants down, I don't think he'll be up for hanging out."

Cat nibbles her lip and giggles. "On the contrary, Kindra. Now he doesn't have a choice. Unless he wants his fruity little secret to get out, he has to come along."

"You clever girl," Ezra says. "My god, this little tidbit of information is going to come in handy."

Realizing Bennett isn't going to open the door, Ezra hoists himself through the window while Cat and I wait outside.

Chapter Twenty-Four

Ezra

It takes some convincing, but Bennett finally emerges from the bathroom once I've closed the windows and assured him the girls are still outside. He rushes to remove the offending pineapple from view, taking it from the room and, I assume, disposing of it. When he returns to the bedroom, he's resumed a more natural skin tone, though he still can't look me in the eye.

"What are you three jackasses doing out this way?" he asks. "I figured you'd all be on the hike or asleep this early."

I sit on the edge of the bed and try not to look at the half-open drawer. "Kindra thought it would be nice to invite you on the hike. She didn't want you to feel left out."

I don't mention Cat's machinations.

"You know I hate hiking," he says.

"I think it would mean a lot to Kindra if you—"

"Why does that matter?" He pins me with a look and lowers his voice. "You're just fucking the girl, right? I mean, you still plan to tell her the truth tomorrow, so it's not like you two can keep seeing each other after this."

I swallow everything I want to say. That she's broken me, well and truly, and I have no desire to tell her the truth. That, for the first time in my life, I've considered what it might be like to attach myself to someone else and forsake all others. He wouldn't understand.

But my silence tells him everything.

"Ezra, you can't keep her. You need to shut down whatever fantasy you've concocted in your mind and be honest with her. And yourself."

"Myself? What's that supposed to mean?"

Bennett begins dressing, trading his boxers for gym shorts and his bare feet for hiking boots. "You know exactly what it means, and I'm going on this hike to make sure you do what's right. Stop deluding her, and stop deluding yourself. This can't be anything more than a memory after today."

"And if I don't tell her?"

My brother's back faces me as he sifts through the shirts hanging in the closet, but his body language speaks tomes. His shoulders droop, and he shakes his head as he pulls a shirt from the shadows.

"Look," he says, "if you can't scrape up the balls to be honest, I won't do it for you, but I'll also lose any semblance of respect I have for you."

I don't see how that's possible. If I'd been honest from the start, we could have somehow worked past the initial hurdle, but now I've only made the problem worse by building a tower of lies. There is no way we can make that leap.

"Does it change your mind if I say that I'm falling in love with her?" I ask.

I expect Bennett to laugh at my admission or chastise me in his brutish way, but he doesn't. He sits beside me on the bed and, for what may be the first time since I found him twelve years ago, really considers what he's about to say.

"No, it doesn't change my mind. It only reinforces what you need to do." He runs his hand through his dark hair and sighs. "I'm no love guru, and I don't even believe in the concept of commitment, but if you truly love the girl, don't you owe it to her to be honest? What's that old saying? Love is patient, love is . . . I don't fucking know, but I'm pretty sure it says something about honesty."

"It's not a saying. It's a quote from the Bible," I say.

He laughs and smacks my shoulder. "I better go wash my mouth out before I burst into flames, then."

And that's the end of the conversation. We stand and walk toward the villa's front door as if we weren't just having a heart-to-heart in the same room where Bennett molested a pineapple.

I glance at my watch on the way out the door. We've wasted too much time, and we're bound to miss the hike if we don't put a little fire under our feet.

The girls begin laughing again as soon as Bennett steps into the sunshine. We'll never make it if we have to stop for a giggle fit every five seconds. I also worry their poking will agitate him to the point of saying something I really don't want him to say.

"Let's give it a break," I say to the girls, but they continue laughing until tears brim from their black-lined lids.

Unable to speak through the laughing fit, Kindra points toward Bennett and wiggles her finger, urging me to turn and look.

So I do.

What I see behind me can only be blamed on the room's dimness and Bennett's inattention to detail while in a deep discussion. I can't imagine my brother made this decision with any forethought.

I stifle a laugh as I look at Bennett, unwilling to add any fuel to the fire. "You might want to change your shirt, but be quick about it. We're running late."

He looks down, and the bright shade of red returns to his face when he realizes he grabbed a Hawaiian shirt with pineapples all over it.

"I genuinely hate all of you," he says as he retreats into his villa.

By the time he emerges again—this time wearing a plain white t-shirt—the girls have gotten their laughter under control, and they've been warned to keep quiet about the pineapple incident. For right now, at least.

We set off at a jog down the boardwalk. When we reach the last villa, we turn right and start down the jungle path. Tomorrow morning, this path will be closed to allow Jim and Jeff to set up for the hunt. The remaining Cattle will be released into the jungle, and we'll all be set loose to destroy them.

Well, most everyone will, but I doubt I'll be among them. I'll probably be holed up in my room, nursing a pint of something frothy and wishing for a time machine.

To be clear, I would still kill her brother, but I would also come clean about it a lot sooner, accompanied by iron-clad proof of her brother's guilt.

As I dodge encroaching branches and hop over wandering tree roots, my brain navigates its own obstacles. There has to be a way to prove my actions were justified. Once we're back in the continental US, I can scrounge up every ounce of proof if Bennett will just grant me some time.

Speaking of Bennett, he's pulled pretty far ahead of us. The jungle is a maze, especially if you aren't familiar with the nearly invisible trails, so I stick close to the girls so they don't get lost.

As we near a break in the trail, I hear a loud thud behind me, followed by a feminine grunt. I turn and see Cat on the ground, her hands clasped around her ankle as tears stream unbidden from the corners of her eyes. She's not crying, mind you, but the pain burgeoning from her ankle is so intense that she can't stop the tears.

Gritting her teeth, she flops to her side and groans. "I think I broke something."

Kindra kneels at her friend's side and looks up at me, pleading with her eyes.

I kneel beside Cat and take her ankle into my hands. It's already swollen, and the skin is beginning to bruise, but I don't feel a break. "I think it's just a nasty sprain, but you'll need to rest it today. No hike for you, I'm afraid."

"How can we get her back to her villa?" Kindra asks.

"I'll carry her," I say.

I assume Bennett realized we weren't behind him, because he comes jogging up to us as I'm lifting Cat into my arms.

"What's the hold up?" he asks. "Did the kitten get too weak to continue?"

Cat shifts in my arms so that she can face him. "Does someone smell pineapple? Weird."

"Enough," I say. "Both of you."

Kindra steps forward and points to Cat's ankle. "I think it's pretty obvious that she isn't being a wuss, Bennett. She's hurt. Ezra is taking her back to—"

Bennett shakes his head. "Not necessary. I'll do it. I wouldn't want my dear brother to miss an opportunity."

"An opportunity for what?" Kindra asks.

I step forward and deposit Cat into Bennett's arms, if for no other reason than to shut him up expeditiously. Like her namesake, she digs her claws into my arms and tries to remain in my hold.

"What if he stuffs me in a drawer and tries to fuck me to 'What's New Pussycat'?" she pleads, though her fear is a blatant put-on.

Bennett rolls his eyes and starts walking. "I wouldn't fuck you with Grim's dick and Ezra pushing. Just shut up and hang on."

Cat mouths something to Kindra that looks like, *Please don't leave me with this fruit fucker.* I would think I misread her lips if we didn't walk up on Bennett doing precisely that.

"I'll be by to check on you after the hike!" Kindra calls out as they disappear around a leafy bend in the path. Then she mumbles, "If we can even make the hike."

I look at my watch. The hike started five minutes ago, and we're only halfway to the start. Jim and Jeff are highly anal—and not in a fun way—so she's probably right.

"We could still go on a hike," I say. "We can go as far as Galloway's Bridge, anyway. There's a nice waterfall near there, and I'd be happy to show you."

"Can't cross the bridge because of your fear of heights?" she asks.

"I've mostly conquered that fear, but when you see the bridge, you'll understand. It would be nice to spend the day just the two of us, don't you think?"

With a nervous laugh, she forces a smile. "If I didn't

know better, I'd think you were treating this as our last day together. Is it?"

She's asking questions I don't have the answers to right now. If it were up to me, we'd never have a last day together, but it's out of my control. Bennett is holding my nose squarely in my piss spot, and I've been forced to obey.

So, I say the only thing I can without adding more lies to the growing pile. "If I have any say in things, it's definitely not our last day together."

She smiles and holds out her hand, and I take it in mine as we venture deeper into the jungle.

Chapter Twenty-Five

Kindra

As the sun rises higher, so does the humidity. When I couple that with the strange chirps and calls whistling over the whisper of our footfalls on the overgrown path, I can almost imagine I'm deep in the Amazon rather than an island in the middle of the ocean.

Speaking of the overgrown path, it appears we've gone off trail. Tree roots twist and stretch underfoot, and I can't see the sky through the foliage.

"Do you even know where we are?" I ask as I swat a large leaf away from my face.

"Of course, pet. I've been coming to this island since the Sinners Retreat began."

Fair point. Not all of us are here on false pretenses, after all.

We travel a bit further. The trees begin to thin, and water rushes somewhere in the distance. Up ahead, the ricketiest bridge I've ever seen dangles between two cliffs.

Gnarled knots hold together the planks of weathered wood that make up the footholds.

Ezra leans back on the balls of his feet and smiles. "Welcome to Galloway Bridge. Want to know how it got its name?"

"The blind man who made it was named Galloway?"

Ezra laughs and shakes his head. "The first year it was Bridge Five-Three-Eight because Cattle number five-three-eight fell to his death during construction. The second year it was Fisherman's Bridge. The Fisherman was a serial killer who also had very poor balance. Now, it's Galloway Bridge. Last year, Jim brought in a silent investor. Needless to say, it was more than just the deal that fell through on that one."

Well, that's fucking dark.

I peer past the bridge, at the dense growth crowding the other side. "What's over there?"

"That's part of the hunting grounds."

"What's the hunt? I've heard it mentioned a few times now."

"The highlight of the resort stay. Jim takes all the remaining Cattle to this isolated part of the island and sets them loose. They disperse here and across the bridge."

"So if I sleep in tomorrow, the only thing between me and a rapist is a little bit of jungle and this poor excuse for a bridge?"

"It's nothing to worry about, pet. Jim has a few goons who like to lurk the perimeter. They take out anyone who tries to slip by."

"Point taken. But what happens if they stay out in the jungle? Like, can they survive out there?"

"If anyone survives—and that doesn't happen often—they get an opportunity to work on the island. They're fitted with trackers so that Jim knows where everyone is at all times. The cannibal chef? He's the rare survivor."

"What if your friend survives?"

"Gary? No, Gary won't survive. Bennett won't let him after what he's done."

"How are you even so sure of what he's done?"

"I have more than enough proof for his death warrant. I'm a PI, remember?" Ezra grips a branch, holding it out of the way as I duck under it and step closer to the bridge.

"Oh, right. That's how you found your brother."

I have plenty of time to get to know the skeletons in Ezra's closet, so I stop with the personal questions. Right now, I'm more interested in seeing what waits on the other side of that bridge.

"Can we go over there? To the hunting ground?" I ask.

Ezra clams up, though it takes everything in him to play it cool. He stuffs a shaking hand into his pocket, but not before I witness his rare weakness.

"There's only one way over to that section of the island," he says, "and it involves taking the bridge."

"Is the big bad Crumpet Killer afraid?" I walk my fingers up his chest and touch his chin.

He smirks and pulls off his glasses so he can clean them on his shirt. "I don't want it to be the Ezra Carter Bridge next year, so why don't I show you another of the island's hidden gems?" He holds the branch out of my way again, and we return to the jungle.

We follow the same non-existent path back the way we came, but then Ezra takes a right at a tree. I'm not sure how he knows where to turn, as all the trees look identical to me. I'm about to ask if he's sure he knows where he's going when the sound of rushing water reaches my ears again. Then we step into a clearing, and I can hardly breathe.

I never should have doubted him.

Stunned into silence, I stand in awe of the island's hidden beauty. Massive hibiscus plants have been left to grow wild near the water, dotting the greenery with bright splashes of red, orange, and pink. Moss grows on the rocks jutting from the water, which is a blue so dark and deep I can't see below its rippling surface.

A waterfall rushes down the side of a tall cliff and lands in a large basin below. It's not Niagara Falls, but it doesn't have to be. It's a tropical oasis for Ezra and me.

Ezra begins stripping off his shirt, and now I'm stunned into silence for another reason. Does he plan to go for a swim?

"I didn't wear a swimsuit," I say.

"Neither did I." He pulls off his shorts.

No. He certainly did not.

He slips his fingertips beneath the hem of my shirt, and, with a featherlight touch, he begins to lift. I slam my hands over his to stop him as my eyes scan for the people who could be hiding behind all these rocks and trees. He's gotten me to loosen up quite a bit, but I'm not sure I'm ready to go skinny dipping.

"I can't strip here," I whisper. "Someone could see me."

Ezra looks around, turning a full circle and giving me a glimpse of his perfect backside and that horrible tattoo. He even has those sexy dimples above his ass cheeks. I still can't believe this British choirboy has such a devilish streak to him.

When he faces me again, he shrugs his shoulders. "I can scare the birds off if you're that shy, but I'm not sure what I'm expected to do about the fish."

"Why don't you be a good boy and go for a swim while I sit on this rock and watch you, hmm?" I move to sit, but he grabs my arm and pulls me against his naked body.

"A good boy, eh? I can't say I've ever been very good."

He hardly completes his sentence before his mouth presses against mine. I relax in his hold and lean against his sun-soaked body as sparks zip through my limbs.

As he pulls away, my knees weaken.

"I'm not going to win this one, am I?" I ask.

He kisses my forehead. "Not a chance. Now strip."

After situating his perfect bare ass on the very rock I wanted to sit on, he turns his full attention to me.

I've never stripped for a man in the middle of a fucking jungle, so I hope he can bear with me as I gather the nerve. I start with my shirt. It seems the easiest place to begin. There isn't much to it, so I just rip it off.

"Slowly, my pet," he says. "We have nowhere to be."

Giving him my back, I unfasten my shorts and ease them down my thick thighs. I can't see him, but I hear the deep groan he utters as I bend at the waist.

"Have I ever told you how much I adore your body?" he asks.

"Possibly," I say as I untie my laces and toe off my boots. "But a girl never gets tired of hearing it."

Wearing only a thin lace bra and some barely there panties, I step into him. His erection speaks as loudly as his words, showing me just how perfect he believes me to be.

He leans forward and nips my stomach. "Take off the rest. I want to see all of you."

"You said to go slowly, so I was thinking maybe I could swim in this, then take off the rest when we're back at the villa." I rush to get the words out as his kisses travel lower. "But maybe I can just take them off."

I reach behind me to unfasten my bra, but he stands and

swats my hands away. I expect him to use one hand to do that snazzy fuckboy trick where they unfasten your bra with the flick of their dirty fingers, but he doesn't. He fumbles with the clasp like a gentleman.

As the lace falls away, my breasts relax. His hands are there to cup them, gently squeezing as his fingertips seek out my pebbled nipples. Heat courses between my legs.

He leans over and begins kissing my breasts, then moves down my body. His mouth guides the way, cutting a path toward my panties. Then they're gone too.

Realizing how naked I am, I hurry for the water and nearly slip on a rock. Ezra is right behind me and catches me before I can crash down and break my neck.

"First day on your new legs?" he asks.

I grip his hand for dear life and step forward again. "No, but if I'm not careful—"

The rocks cease to be, and down I go. Apparently, it was impossible to see the bottom of the basin because it doesn't fucking exist.

I sputter upward and swipe the hair from my face. Ezra holds out his hand for me, but he doesn't stop laughing as he hauls me back onto the rocks in the shallows.

"Let's walk a little further away from the falls," he says as he guides me. "The water is a touch deep over there, but not as deep as the well you just fell into, Timmy."

I swat his arm and laugh along with him. What else can I do? Despite feeling and looking like a sack of kittens just saved from the river, something about Ezra just makes me . . . happy.

At the edge of the pool, we ease into the water together. I press my back against a large rock that almost creates a sort of chair. His hands slide down my body, and I brace myself against the rock as he lifts my hips and dips his head below the surface.

Bubbles rise between my legs, and the tickling sensation feels like one thousand touches against my bare skin. Then his tongue glides between my lips, encasing me in warmth.

I reach back and grip the rough rock while catching a glimpse of my reflection in the water. My rippling rolls stare back at me. My nipples are mildly off center, and my breasts are a bit too saggy for my liking. How can he see me the way he does?

But then his tongue washes away any insecurity as he devours me beneath the water.

Seconds later, he breaks the surface and takes in air. His mouth engulfs my nipple, sucking and nipping, but it's not enough.

"Please," I moan. "I need more."

"My pleasure."

He disappears again, and goddamn, it feels amazing to have him between my legs. Ezra never shuts up, and that skill seems to translate to the way his tongue moves on me. Like he's telling a story on my clit.

While I'm still cross-eyed with pleasure, he pulls me lower so that I'm floating on my back while he devours me. The water muffles all sound, and I can't help but squeeze my thighs around his head and blink as I see stars.

Just as I teeter on the edge of an orgasm, he comes up for air again.

"Haven't you ever heard of engaging in foreplay like a normal person?" I pant.

"Nothing about either of us is normal, pet. There's a time and a place for boring sex, and a time and a place for waterfall foreplay."

I can't argue with that.

Lauren Biel

Ezra moves his hand from my lower back, and I let my body sink. He pulls me into him. With my legs around his waist, his length presses against my pussy. Despite the chill in the water, he's had no trouble maintaining a rock-hard erection.

Unwinding my legs from his waist, I smile up at him. "Your turn."

Using his powerful body like a buddy line, I lower myself until my mouth meets his dick. Whenever I let go of his hips, however, my body begins to rise to the surface.

Ezra recognizes the problem and scoots back so that he can sit on a rock while holding me below the water. We work out a system. I suck him until I'm nearly drowning, and then he pulls me up.

It's going swell until I'm ripped out of the water by my arm.

But then I look down and realize Ezra is still sitting on the rock, the look on his face showcasing the perplexity I feel. As I dangle above the water, nude as the day I was born, I turn to identify my captor . . . and I come face to face with Ice Pick.

"You can't drown the other participants!" he shouts as he starts to drag me to shore. I wriggle in his hold, but I can't get free.

"I was letting him!" I shout, and his meaty hand finally releases my arm.

I tumble into the water, but I don't bother fussing about my predicament. I just sink lower to cover my breasts. Humiliated doesn't begin to cover it, least of all my nudity. If the heat from my full-body blush sends the water into a rolling boil, I won't be surprised.

"Ice Pick," Ezra says with a smile. "I wasn't actually drowning her, though I think she'd like that."

I swim closer to Ezra and punch him in the side. *Shut up*, I mouth.

Ice Pick spins his namesake in his hand before he sets it in the grass. Then he whips his shorts down his sunburned legs. God, I've seen enough dicks on this vacation to last a lifetime.

Though I haven't spent much time with Ice Pick, I know he isn't fabulous at reading the room. He proves me right with his next action. Completely nude, he takes a running leap into the basin.

Water rushes toward me and slams into my face. As I'm sputtering and scraping pond water from my eyes, I can only imagine some sort of *Jaws*-meets-porn mashup. I scoot closer to Ezra so that I'm practically in his lap. If Ice Pick wants to bite anything of mine, he'll get a bite of Ezra right along with it.

Ice Pick pops up with a hearty laugh, water dripping from his mustache. "You're a pretty thing, sunshine," he says with a smile as he drifts toward me.

Ezra calmly slips between us. "That pretty thing is *mine*, Ice," he says with a smile. "I like you, but I don't like you enough to share her attention."

Ice Pick raises his hands in a placating gesture. "I didn't realize you had a claim staked already. No disrespect intended, Ezra. I guess I missed nearly the whole damn retreat, including your budding romance. I've been holed up in my villa since shortly after the Olympics. I think I ate something bad the first night."

Ate something bad? Like a person, perchance?

Ezra nods. "At least you didn't miss the hunt."

"Even if I wasn't feeling better, I wouldn't miss the hunt for anything." Ice Pick moves closer to us. A little too close. I can see his tiny soldier underneath the water, and he's little more than a helmet. God bless it.

"It's sure to be a big to do," Ezra says with a nod.

How is he just casually carrying on a conversation right now? I couldn't be more uncomfortable with our group nudity. Three's for sure a crowd.

"Well, I read this wrong," Ice Pick says with a fading smile. "I think I'd better head back to the beach. Chef's making a sandwich board for lunch."

Did he think this would end up being some group orgy? No thanks. I'm surprised I've let one psychopath sink inside me. I'm not a fucking pin cushion of self-loathing here. I don't accept all comers.

We say our awkward parting words, and Ice Pick swims back to shore. He dresses and departs as Ezra and I look anywhere but at each other.

"Well, that was beyond uncomfortable," I say once we're alone. Our amazing sexcapade is a distant memory now.

"Sorry. We killers are a bit shit at reading social cues."

"What part of this said to join us?" I ask, motioning between us.

"If I were him, I would have tried as well." He swipes his hand down his face. "I'm guessing you want to head back now?"

I begin swimming for shore. "Yeah, that sandwich board is sounding mighty good."

Chapter Twenty-Six

Ezra

The incident with Ice Pick had the potential to completely derail the rest of our day, but Kindra takes it in stride, laughing about it on the way back through the jungle. We reach the pavilion right at noon and take a seat.

Maurice's assistant bustles past us, setting a sandwich board before us and refilling the missing ingredients at other tables. A variety of sliced breads stands at each end of the large wooden board. The meat selection makes my mouth water: turkey, ham, and what I hope is cow-derived roast beef. Each cut of meat has been rolled up and layered around a bowl of mayonnaise.

Kindra picks up a knife and gestures toward the creamy white substance. "This is actually mayo, right?" she asks the assistant as he flutters by again.

The assistant stops his buzzing and stands completely still, a look of horror on his face. He didn't look this concerned when he served us *viande d'homme*. It's not a far cry to assume that they could be using . . . other things back there in that kitchen.

I back her up. "Honestly, it's a valid question. It's really just a yes or no answer."

"Sick!" he belts in his thick French accent.

"So is eating people," Kindra says under her breath as he runs off, completely flustered.

I want Kindra to enjoy her lunch, so I take one for the team. I grab the knife from her hand, dip the tip into the mixture, and taste it.

"It's mayo," I say with a sigh of relief.

"Thank fuck." She plucks the knife from my fingertips and begins building a sandwich.

"Afternoon," Bennett sings as he comes into the pavilion and has a seat in front of me.

If my brother is here, where is his arch nemesis? His sing-song welcome makes me worry he did in fact stuff her in the dresser . . . but not to fuck her.

Please tell me he didn't kill her.

"Bennett, where's Cat?" I ask.

He grabs a few slices of bread, cheese, and meat, and slaps it all together. "The kitten is asleep."

Not permanently, I hope. But then I remember Bennett brewing Gary a sleepy-time cocktail. "Did you drug her?"

"Drug her?" Kindra's eyes go wide.

"Calm your tits," Bennett says. "Her ankle looked pretty painful, so I thought it would help her sleep."

I give my brother a knowing look. Kindness doesn't exist in his repertoire.

He clears his throat and adds, "Plus, someone can only listen to a person sing a vulgar version of the *SpongeBob SquarePants* theme song for so long."

Kindra chuckles and begins humming the tune under her breath.

"Do I have to drug you next?" Bennett asks.

"Over my dead body," I say as my spine instinctively stiffens.

"She can shit on me, but I can't dish it back? Quit your posturing." Bennett grabs a rolled-up piece of turkey and shoves it into his mouth, but not before I catch the sparkle in his eye as a thought strikes him. "Did you know Midnight Masochist is coming for the hunt?"

I choke on my spit.

"Who's that?" Kindra asks as she pats my back.

I continue coughing.

Bennett smiles. "He's a good friend, isn't he, Ezra?"

She gives me an odd look, and I get it. Who reacts like this when they hear of a good friend's imminent arrival?

Instead of pressing the issue, Kindra keeps patting my back. I'm still choking on my panic when she stops and stares at me.

"Okay, I'm going to get you a drink before you drown on air," she says. "Is water good?"

"Splendid," I say with the most pained smile I've ever plastered on my face. Regardless, she doesn't notice as she heads to the outdoor bar. I immediately turn to face Bennett. "Since when is Maverick coming?"

"Jim mentioned that he finished his assignment early, so I shot him an invite. He couldn't be more pleased to come, honestly."

This is a low blow if I've ever seen one. Maverick is a good friend of ours, and we've known him almost as long as we've known each other. Which means he knows I'm not the Crumpet Killer.

Which means this could all blow up in my face.

"What the hell did I do to you, Bennett?"

"You didn't do *anything* to me. Except announce my STD history to the entire island."

"You invited Maverick because I . . . Goddamn it, Bennett."

"No, it has nothing to do with that." Bennett grabs some bread from the board and starts slathering it with mayo. "I just don't think you're going to tell her. You said you'd tell her *before* the hunt, so he shouldn't fuck anything up. She'll already know."

I need to get to him before he gets here and tells her everything I don't have the balls to tell her. The selfish side of me wants to keep her in the dark for the foreseeable future. It's bloody unfair. Now that I've finally fallen for someone, she'll be ripped away from me. But do I have any right to keep hiding this from her?

Because I am the villain here.

Not because I killed her brother—the piece of shit deserved his death—but because I've lied to Kindra. But I don't know how to stop.

"Bennett—"

"No, Ezra. Do *not* try to get me on your side here. You've played with that poor girl's heart and vagina long enough." He begins grabbing each type of meat and at least two different types of cheese, all of which he crams onto the pile of mayo.

"You don't understand. You have no idea what it's like to have someone care about you."

"Plenty of women have cared about me, Ezra. The feelings have *not* been mutual."

"Then you don't know what it's like to be in—"

"Hey, guys, what are you talking about so angrily?"

Kindra asks as she sets a bottle of water in front of me and takes her seat.

Bennett and I answer in unison. Unfortunately, our responses differ as I shout *sports* and he cries *politics*. For people who thrive at concealing their misdeeds, we're really making a mess of this.

"Sports *and* politics," I clarify to Kindra.

"Sounds awfully boring."

"It won't be for long," Bennett says with a smile as he takes a bite of his sandwich.

I swear he wants me to have a coronary. Right here.

My whole world is on fire and nothing is okay. I may not deserve happiness, and I may not deserve her, but can't I pretend for just a while longer? I don't expect God's blessing, but Lucifer isn't offering me a deal, either. And I would give him whatever he wants if I could have her.

My soul and eternal damnation in exchange for a single lifetime of her love.

But I can't have that. I can have a few more hours, and then it's over. I'd best make the most of it.

I turn to Kindra. "Do you want to go bowling?"

She lowers her sandwich. "Jim built a bowling alley on the island?"

"Not exactly. It's only a little two-lane job crafted beachside. You use human heads as bowling balls and just chuck them down the lane at some limbs that have been stood in the sand. Jim's macabre creation. To be fair, it's more like bowling mixed with cornhole, but it's a lot of fun and a good way to blow off some steam."

"You haven't even eaten yet," she says as she motions to my empty plate.

Bennett chugs a beer to wash down the rest of his

cholesterol sandwich, then begins making another one. "I don't think he's very hungry right now."

"I'll go," she says through the last bite of her meal. "Sounds like a good time."

I expected more of a fight from her, considering we usually have to pull her teeth to get her to join in. This is a pleasant surprise.

"I feel like I can actually enjoy myself now that I've learned the truth about my brother's killer," she adds, and my heart collapses in on itself like a dying star.

Bennett clears his throat, adding salt to a festering wound. I kick his ankle beneath the table and pray the next sandwich takes him out.

We say goodbye. Well, Kindra says goodbye to Bennett. I just walk away.

This isn't what I pictured when I sought my brother all these years ago. I figured we'd share a brotherly connection and support each other, and for the most part, we have, but for someone with no moral compass, he appears to feel very strongly about my dishonesty. Or maybe it's deeper.

Maybe Bennett is afraid he's losing me.

Kindra and I head down the beach. My mind races with ways to keep my charade intact, but I'm running out of time. Regardless of Bennett's reasoning, he's determined to see Kindra and me separated by a monumental divide.

We reach a mound of severed heads and recognize some of them from the games we've participated in. Others have decayed past the point of recognition. Flies swarm the macabre pile.

Two lanes have been cordoned off with rope, and at the end, dismembered arms and legs poke from the sand. Metal rods have been driven into the flesh to keep the limbs upright. Rigor doesn't last forever, after all.

I step toward the pile of heads and pluck one from the top. I choose a fresher one for Kindra so that the skin doesn't slough away when she touches it.

I place the head in her hands, then motion down the lanes. "The goal is to pick up a head, toss it, and knock down as many pins as you can."

Kindra studies the head, then decides to go for it. She sticks two fingers into the nose and one into the mouth. She steps toward the first lane, raises the head, then stops.

"Everything okay?" I ask.

She lowers the head and turns to face me with a shrug. "I'm not sure. You've hardly looked at me since we left the pavilion, and you were quiet on our walk down the beach. It feels like something is off. What changed?"

"Not a thing, pet. I promise. I've just been thinking about the hunt. That's all."

"I'm really excited about that. Now that everything is behind me, I feel so much better. Lighter. And it's all because of you." Kindra looks back at me with a smile as she grips the severed head and throws it down the lane, knocking six arms and legs onto their sides.

But with her words, she's knocked everything out of *me*. *All because of you.*

Yes, her ten years of agony. Every tear she shed over her brother. Her struggle to connect with others because she's lost her trust in humanity. All of that is because of me.

Typically, I love to see her smile, but now her smile is my death sentence. Tonight, before anyone else has the chance, I need to tell her the truth. It won't be easy, but it's my last shot at redemption.

Maverick wouldn't tell her out of malice. He's not like Bennett. But Maverick is young, and he isn't as tight-lipped as he should be. In his youthful exuberance, he's liable to slip up and call me AA, even if I explain why he shouldn't.

For now, I need to make the most of the time I have left. If I can make these final hours memorable, maybe it will be enough to help her forget what I've done.

Chapter Twenty-Seven

Kindra

After a few rounds of bowling in this heat, I'm more than ready to cool off, so we head toward the dock to participate in a water activity. After losing out on the first few days of the retreat, I'm eager to give the experience a real effort for what time I have left.

Ezra seems to have shaken off the funk he was in after lunch. I make a mental note to avoid the topics of sports and politics since they seem to sour his mood.

We board the fishing boat and travel below deck to change into wetsuits and scuba gear. Ice Pick, Maudlin Rose, and Grim are already dressed and waiting in the wheelhouse.

Before pulling out the wetsuits, Ezra gives me a crash course on scuba diving. I know more about the hobby than when I first boarded the boat, but I still don't think I know enough to participate. Then Ezra hands a neoprene suit to me, and I'm more afraid of the attire than the actual activity.

"How the hell do I squeeze into this?" I ask as I hold up

the wetsuit. "Cat's smaller than me, and even *she* wouldn't fit in this thing. It looks like it was designed for a stick person."

Ezra holds up his suit. "They're meant to fit snug, pet. It creates an insulating barrier so that you don't freeze. It's also advised that you piss in the suit for warmth."

"Piss insulation. Got it."

He chuckles and helps me into my suit, and it's not that bad. No worse than wearing a waist trainer, which I tried in my late teens before I embraced my fuller figure.

Looking like demonic, emaciated Teletubbies, Ezra and I make our way up the stairs and onto the upper deck. Ezra shields his eyes from the sun and looks toward the wheelhouse. Grim gives us the thumbs-up, and we motion back that we're ready to haul anchor and kill some Cattle.

Ice Pick comes down, and he and Ezra fool with the anchor while Maudlin Rose and I take a seat and watch. I steal glances at the silent woman beside me. Right now, covered head to toe in neoprene, she could pass as anyone's grandmother. You'd never know she's a highly sought-after serial killer who also enjoys sunbathing her butthole.

"It's very warm today," I say.

She smiles and nods.

"I hope the water cools us off."

More smiling and nodding from Rose.

"What did you think of—"

She rises from her seat and walks away, heading toward the wheelhouse. Apparently, Ice Pick isn't the only one who can't read a room, as I've annoyed the poor woman to the point that she had to get away.

Ezra returns to my side, and I'm glad for his company after that awkward interaction.

"Why doesn't she speak?" I ask him.

"Maudlin Rose?"

I nod.

"Have you never noticed the scar on her neck?"

"No. Most times, she's been nude, so I haven't wanted to look too closely."

A deep laugh bubbles out of his chest and melts the crotch of my wetsuit. God, does he do anything that isn't sexy?

"She can't speak, love," he says. "Many of us have some sort of trauma that catapults us into this line of work. She's no different, though she isn't a discerning killer like you or me. She targets men, and having a penis is the only requirement."

"So what set her on her path?"

"She married at the tender age of fifteen, and the man was a monster in more ways than one. He tried to slit her throat in a drunk fit of rage soon after the honeymoon. She survived, but her vocal cords were too damaged to repair."

My hand rises to my throat. "Oh my god, that's horrible."

"It truly is. That's why we don't ask her any questions unless they have a yes or no answer."

"Well, fuck. That explains why she walked off. Now I feel like a shitbag."

He wraps a comforting arm around my shoulders and pulls me into him. "Don't worry. You didn't know, and she won't hold that against you. But that's why she sticks with Grim on these retreats. They have some weird sort of language. They can communicate without speaking."

"How beautiful and sad," I say. "At least they've found each other. Do they have a relationship outside of this?"

Ezra shrugs his shoulders. "I'm not entirely sure. They neither leave nor arrive together, so I'd say not."

I can't imagine finding someone who understands me in a way no one else does, then only seeing them for a few days each year. Then I look at Ezra and realize I might be *forced* to imagine it.

We haven't talked much about what happens when we leave the island. I'm not sure what he wants or expects, and I'm too afraid to ask. If he says he just wants this to be a fun fling, I'll be heartbroken because I want more. I didn't at first, but now . . .

He has me rethinking everything.

I've pictured myself in a wedding dress, for fuck's sake! I've even picked out what Cat—my only bridesmaid—will wear, along with what I'll say to convince her to walk down the aisle beside Bennet. I've imagined a house, a dog, and many happy nights spent before a roaring fire as we wear nothing but the clothes God gave us. No kids, though. We can't raise children while we're busy concealing our favorite hobby.

I'm only missing one important thing, and that's Ezra's input. He's the main character in my fantasies, after all.

The boat comes to a stop before I can muster the courage to broach the topic. Ezra places a chaste kiss on my lips, and then he and Ice Pick begin their anchor duty.

Grim descends from the wheelhouse and joins us on the deck. He's no longer wearing his wetsuit. Instead, he's stripped down to his beloved Speedo.

"Rose and I have decided we'll stay on the boat while you swim," he says. "We may join you in the water, but we may not. Have fun."

He turns and retreats up the steps, but not before I feel like I'm the reason they're staying behind. I need to make this up to Rose somehow.

Ezra, sensing my downward spiral, sidles up to me and

leans close to my ear. "This isn't because of you," he says. "To be frank, they're probably staying behind to fuck."

Images of their naked bodies slamming together rush unbidden through my head, and I feel a bit queasy. I'll chalk it up to seasickness if he asks.

"Let's just get in the water," I say.

Once we're weighed down with gear, we head to a lower deck and make our way to the rear of the boat. A white buoy bobs in the wake nearby. I can only assume this marks the activity area.

Needing no assistance, Ice Pick covers his face with a diving mask, grips a machete to his chest, and drops back-first into the water. Despite his large size, he doesn't float back to the surface. In fact, in the span of only a few seconds, he's disappeared from view.

Ezra fiddles with the tanks strapped to my back, assuring everything is connected and working properly. "Just remember that you shouldn't hold your breath. We won't be very deep, but just keep breathing, especially when we're coming to the surface."

"What, will my lungs explode or something?" I laugh as he comes around to face me.

He doesn't so much as crack a smile.

"Ezra? Will my fucking lungs explode?"

"We aren't going that deep, pet."

He grips my hand and tries to lead me to the boat's edge, but my feet are massive lead weights.

"I don't know if I want to do this anymore." I back up a few steps. "Maybe I should stay on the boat. You know, in case there's an emergency."

Instead of laughing at me and saying I'm being ridiculous, or shrugging his shoulders and leaving me to listen to the elderly love making, he pulls me into him. His powerful arms wrap around me, and he places a kiss on my head.

"We don't have to do anything you aren't comfortable doing. Besides, if we want to drown some Cattle, we could always have Jim set something up at the pool."

He inadvertently digs a knife into my pride. I'm not a wuss who needs a kiddie pool set up for playtime. I just don't want my lungs to, you know, explode.

I take a deep breath and pull away from him. "No. I'm fine. Is there anything else I need to know aside from everything you've already told me?"

"Just stick close to me. I won't let anything hurt you. I promise."

Drawing the mask over my face, I nod. "Let's fucking do this."

I don't sound nearly as cool as I did in my head. The mask pinches my nose and gives my voice a nasal quality.

"Breathe in and out regularly," he reminds me as he lowers his mask. "I'll be right with you. If you panic, just give me the signal."

I step to the edge of the short deck and take a deep breath. Small whitecaps break near the boat. Overhead, the sky is a cloudless blue, broken only by the occasional offshore bird who dares to venture out this way. I suppose this is a beautiful day to die if I must.

I turn to face Ezra.

"You can do this," he says. "I've only known you for a short time, but it's long enough to know you can do anything you put your mind to. You're stubborn as an ass and as bold as an Irishman after a few pints."

I close my eyes and place the regulator into my mouth as Ezra steps toward me. His warm lips press against my forehead. Well, the sliver of forehead peeking between the top of the mask and the wetsuit's hood.

I assume the position, which is this weird crouch with my back to the water. Now I'm supposed to simultaneously lean forward and fall backward at the same time. Gripping the regulator with my left hand and the back of the mask strap with my right, I drop into the water.

Water surrounds me, and I swim a few feet away, pop to the surface, and give Ezra the thumbs-up so that he knows he can safely enter the water without landing on top of me. He gives me a wave and steps into the water instead of doing the lame backward roll he had me do.

Treading water at the surface, I wait for him to emerge in front of me. Seconds drag on and turn to minutes. Surely nothing happened to him . . .

I dip my face below the water and peer into the depths, right as a cloud of blood rushes toward me.

Chapter Twenty-Eight

Kindra

When I was busy worrying about my lungs exploding, I failed to consider the other dangers in the ocean. Like sharks. That's the first thing I think of when I see the blood.

I don't take time to think about how weird it feels to breathe underwater. I kick my legs and swim down. I don't know what I plan to do if I find the shark with my half-eaten lover in his mouth, but I'll figure it out when I find them.

The blood begins to clear, and I have a better view of what waits below. Instead of discovering a shark, I find myself in a minefield of people chained to anchors. They float in the underwater current, their hands secured behind their backs and a chain bolted around their ankles. They all wear scuba gear that looks identical to ours.

One of the Cattle is missing its head, which explains the blood. A large, dark figure freely swims near the body. That must be Ice Pick, but where the fuck is Ezra?

I feel a tug on my ankle and look directly below. One of the Cattle has managed to break free from the bindings around their wrists, and now they have a firm grip on me. And they're pulling me down.

The hands claw at the wetsuit, and I let them bring me close enough that I can slash my flipper against their head. I'm trying to knock their regulator loose, but these damned flippers make it difficult to put any real force into a downward kick. It's like fighting in a fucking nightmare.

Then, just as quickly as the hand grabbed me, it releases its hold. I look down again. Using Ice Pick's machete, Ezra has chopped my assailant's arm clean the fuck off. He looks up at me and waves with the disembodied arm, and I can't tell if I want to kiss him or kill him.

In one smooth motion, Ezra cuts the Cattle's airline and motions for me to follow him. We swim away from the writhing, one-armed asshole and head toward the less volatile group.

There are no markers to indicate which of the Cattle are our preferred targets, so I'm hesitant to make an unprovoked kill. Drowning an innocent won't give me the warm fuzzies.

Another red cloud creeps toward us as Ice Pick slashes the stomach of one of the Cattle. A school of flashy silver fish move in unison toward the organs spilling from the gash in the wetsuit. Like shining metal needles, they dart in and out of the lengthening rope of intestines. Despite the heavy blood loss and the fish literally eating them alive, the injured figure continues to squirm.

Did they deserve that fate? The uncertainty eats away at me, and I turn away from the horrific scene. It boils down to this: I'm not the hardened killer most people believe I am.

I don't enjoy death, but I do enjoy punishing someone who deserves it. The motive matters.

Sensing my hesitancy, Ezra motions for me to come closer. I swim nearer, and he points to the back of each Cattle's diving mask. The straps are color coded, just like the jumpsuits, and now I can see that Ice Pick attacked red.

My body relaxes, and the creeping nausea recedes.

I give Ezra a thumbs-up and swim to another floating figure. Once I check the strap color, I pull the mask from the Cattle's face. I want to see the fear in his eyes when I end him.

Ezra and I didn't bring any weapons along, so an old-fashioned drowning will have to do. Instead of removing the regulator from his mouth, I swim behind him and cut the oxygen at its source. The effect is almost immediate.

His legs begin to shift and strain, and he struggles so frantically against the binding around his wrists that the skin begins to slough away in white strips. The nearby fish make quick work of the snacks on offer, and I feel like a princess in some twisted underwater fairytale.

I swim to his front again. Despite the lack of air, the Cattle holds the regulator firmly between his teeth. His jaw clenches, and his cheeks cave inward with each desperate pull for a breath that won't come. A dark cloud fogs the water around his crotch, and I realize he's shit himself.

With a flick of our fins, Ezra and I move down the line, pulling regulators as we go. When we turn and face our creation, I have to stifle a laugh. The wiggling bodies look like participants in an underwater rave. The bubbles pouring from the gaping mouths catch bits of light, and the fish moving around them flicker with shades of pink, silver, and orange.

A few more Cattle bob in the current further down, but

we leave those for Ice Pick. He seems to be having a grand time with his machete as another head drops to the ocean floor in a cloud of red.

Ezra grabs something from the sand, then motions for me to follow him. As we swim, the water brightens as the seabed rises a few feet and a reef comes into view.

Coral, seaweed, and colorful fish spread in front of us. The water shifts from a murky blue to a bright azure, and it's as if I've been transported into another place entirely. Then Ezra shows me what he grabbed from the killing field. It's the arm he chopped away.

Ezra wiggles the arm toward the fish, and I understand what he means for me to do. I only feel bad that he can't feed them as well. Then again, I guess he does this sort of thing every year.

As I take the arm from him, his cheeks lift into a smile. He's so excited to share this little moment with me. His hand moves up my arm, and he shows me how to wiggle the stump at the limb's fleshy end to entice the fish closer. Bits of blood and tissue disperse into the water, and the fish turn toward us.

We're surrounded, lost in a swirl of flashing colors. I recognize none of the species, but they're each unique and beautiful. In their own little groups, they dart forward and snag bits of flesh before zipping in another direction.

Goosebumps rise on my skin, and I tear up. This is truly a magical moment.

A shadow moves over us, dark and threatening, and I look toward the surface. I expect to see a shark looming overhead, but what I discover is so much worse.

Mere feet above my diving mask, Grim's wrinkly cock cuts a path through the waves. Beside him, her hand gripped firmly in his, swims a naked Maudlin Rose. Her pale nipples cling to the ends of her sagging breasts and do their best to stay attached as they wave in the current. Instead of scuba gear, they've chosen to wear only snorkeling masks and flippers.

They look down at us and wave with their free hands. Ezra and I return the greeting, though I look away as Grim's balls bob into view. I've opened myself up to getting closer to others, but this is a little too close.

The magic moment ruined, I motion to Ezra that I'd like to surface. He gives the signal, and we begin to rise. I make a point to keep my eyes averted from the pair of butts floating by on my left.

Ezra pulls the regulator from his mouth. "Are you ready to head back to the boat?"

I nod and do the same. "Yeah, Grim's dangling doodle kind of killed the mood."

"Understood," he says with a laugh.

We swim back to the boat, and hauling myself out of the water takes the last of my strength. I didn't realize how many muscle groups I use to swim, and I'm sure to be sore tomorrow.

Ezra leads me below deck once more, and we hang up the gear and change into our clothes.

"When we first entered the water, I thought a shark had gotten you," I say as we leave the small room. "There was all this blood, and I couldn't find you."

He grips my hand at the bottom of the stairs and turns me so that I'm facing him. "I didn't mean to worry you, pet. I thought you were right behind me. But just out of curiosity, what would you have done had that been the case?"

"I guess I would have been fighting a shark."

"Buzzing," he says before kissing me. "I'm absolutely

Lauren Biel

buzzing, pet. My tough little American is willing to take on a shark to save her man."

A blush blooms on my cheeks as he makes me feel like a teenager in love. It's not a familiar feeling, but I refuse to be confused by the butterflies and fireworks. I'm just going to embrace this moment and hope he feels the same.

We ascend the stairs and sit on the upper deck. In the distance—thankfully too far off for me to make out any details—Grim and Rose continue floating through the water. Red clouds occasionally stream upward, which means Ice Pick is still busy below them.

For this moment, it's just the two of us.

Difficult questions crowd my mouth, but my lips are a steel trap. I'm too nervous to ask him what we are or what we could be. As much as I want the truth, sometimes the truth hurts.

"You're cute when you're lost in thought. Did you know that?" he says. He leans closer and brushes my hair over my shoulder. "You do this cute little thing with your mouth where you push it to one side and chew your inner cheek."

I hadn't even realized I was doing it, but I stop now that it's been pointed out.

"What's on your mind?" he asks.

"Everything," I say. "I don't want to bother you with my silly girl thoughts, though."

"None of your thoughts are silly, and if it's bothering you, I want you to share it with me. Talk to me, Kindra."

"Okay, for starters, why? Why do you want me to share my troubles with you?" I turn to face him.

The light clicks on in his head, and he understands what this is really about. "I want you to share your thoughts with me because I care about what you think. I care about *you*."

"Do you mean for this trip? Or does that care extend beyond tomorrow?"

He cups my chin and raises my lips to his. "I care about you for this trip, yes, but I want to care about you for much longer. Maybe even for as long as you'll let me."

I close my eyes and lose myself in his kiss. His hands move through my hair, pulling my head closer, but I feel him everywhere. When we kiss, it's as if our souls touch.

"I'm falling for you," he whispers against my lips. He pulls back and runs his thumb over my cheek. "No matter what happens, I want you to know that this moment is real. Don't ever question it."

"No matter what happens?" I cough up a nervous laugh and lean back. "Is there something you aren't telling me?"

He stares into my eyes, but he doesn't answer me.

Chapter Twenty-Nine

Ezra

I've made a real dog's dinner of this. My need to be honest with her quarrels with my need to protect what we have. Now would be a good opportunity to lay out the facts. We're on a boat, so it's not like she can run away. She'd have to face this head on, as would I.

But I can't do it. The truth will shatter her, and who will pick up the pieces? I would gladly paste her together again, no matter how long it might take. Even if her sharp edges leave deep wounds, I'll bear the pain if it means she can be whole again. If only she'd let me.

Knowing she would never, I'm forced to keep this going.

"I meant nothing by it, pet," I say. "I just want you to understand my sincerity. That's all."

Her shoulders relax, and she lets out a soft sigh as she places her hands on my chest. "So this isn't just a fling for you?"

I shake my head, unable to form the words to explain what this is.

"We aren't so different, you and I," I say. "We've both been running from attachments for so long that we're terribly awkward at this."

"I can think of one area where we aren't *terribly* awkward." She climbs over me and straddles my lap. "How long do we have before the others return to the ship?"

I run my hands up and down her sides. "Not long enough for all the things I want to do to you."

"What about when we get to shore? Maybe we can set up our own activity back at the villas?" She grinds herself against my lap, and the friction sends a pleasurable jolt up my spine.

"As tempting as that is, we can't miss tonight's dinner. Per the great director, attendance is mandatory."

She groans and tips her head back, giving me a view of her perfect neck. I remember how she looked tied up, and maybe Jim's wrath would be worth it if it means I can see that again.

"We could always show up fashionably late," I say.

With a shake of her head, she slides off my lap and sits next to me. "No, I completely forgot about tonight's fancy dinner. I'll need time to get ready, and depending on Cat's mental state after your brother drugged her, she might need help as well."

"Dinner won't last all night," I say as I put my arm around her shoulder and pull her closer. "But *I* might."

"Ezra Carter!" She smacks my chest. "My room or yours?"

"Mine." I lean toward her ear and lower my voice. "And I want you to bring your toy."

"The Priest-Exorciser Five Thousand?"

"That's the one." I nip her ear, and she rewards me with a soft moan.

Her palm brushes over my hard length, then squeezes. I have an almost Pavlovian response to her presence, and it takes every ounce of my willpower to keep myself from climbing on top of her and ravaging her right here. Actually, that doesn't sound like such a bad idea.

I'm a millisecond from lowering my zipper when footsteps clomp up the stairs and Ice Pick appears on the deck. Ever the oblivious one, he tromps over to us and sits beside Kindra, nearly close enough to touch. I can almost hear the steam rising off my cock as it deflates.

"You guys didn't stick around very long. You missed all the fun." He reaches over and eases Kindra's hair away from her face. As he tucks the strands behind her ear, she recoils from his touch.

"Give her a little space," I say.

Ice Pick chuckles, then stands and stretches. "Sorry. I forgot you already sank your *hooks* into her."

I grit my teeth when I'm overcome by the urge to stand up and ram my fist into his smug face. He has the audacity to threaten me after touching what belongs to me? How quickly he forgets who I am.

Standing to my full height, I ball my fists at my sides and step into him. The shining crown of his bald head barely clears my clavicle. As I pull my glasses from my face and hand them to Kindra, Ice Pick seems to remember his place in the pecking order. He holds out his palms and gives me his most placating smile.

"I was just joking around," he says. His wheedling voice grates on my nerves, and I crack my neck to release the tension building there. "C'mon, Ezra. No harm meant, pal. I was just having a little fun, but I'll lay off. Scout's honor."

I clap a hand on his shoulder and lean into his face, speaking so that only he can hear me. "If you so much as look at her for too long after this, I'll sink my hooks into *you*. Are we clear?"

His thick earlobes wobble on the sides of his head as he nods. "Crystal."

I smile. "Good. Now let's raise that anchor, shall we?"

"Sorry, Kindra," he says as he shuffles past her, and I'm pleased when he keeps his gaze trained on the teak beneath his feet.

"What was all that about?" She holds my glasses toward me, and I pluck them from her fingertips before situating them on the bridge of my nose.

"Just protecting what's mine," I say. "Unless you have a problem with a possessive partner, in which case, we may not be such a good fit after all. I hate sharing."

She motions to her voluptuous figure and laughs. "So you want the party-size bag of chips, but you want them all to yourself?"

"I'm a very hungry man."

"Say less." She parts her thighs, giving me a glimpse of heaven. "The buffet is always open."

My god, I want her so badly that it physically hurts.

I rush to the front of the boat. The sooner we haul anchor, the sooner we can finish dinner and move on to dessert.

Chapter Thirty

Kindra

As I head back to my villa, I'm walking on air. It's incredibly stupid to throw caution to the wind, but I've tossed all concern into a hurricane and wished it well. The walls are down, and it's official.

I'm falling in love with Ezra Carter.

And what isn't to love? He's handsome, intelligent, and witty. He looks at me the way every woman deserves to be looked at, and I feel like I'm enough when I'm with him. Most of all, he makes me happy.

Now I'm about to get dolled up for a fancy dinner date with Mr. Perfect. My current self kicks my past self for bringing such a limited selection of formal wear, but how was I to know I'd meet the love of my life on this trip? When we first set out, I was so determined to keep my head down and my heart protected. I treated everyone so cruelly, especially Cat.

Cat!

I need to check in with her and make sure Bennett didn't

kill her with an accidental overdose, so I skirt past my villa and make a beeline for Cat's place. It's already late afternoon, so I can only hope she's had enough time to sleep off the drugs. She loves dressing up, meaning she'll want to attend the dinner.

Pale orange curtains flap in the window, but I see no lights on inside Cat's villa. At least Bennett had the wherewithal to ensure she had a breeze. I rap on the door, then peer through the window when she doesn't answer. I don't see her in the living room. Not wanting to wake her if she's still sleeping, I ease open the door.

A blanket lies across the couch, as if someone had been beneath it only moments ago. The bedroom door stands open, giving me a clear view of the empty bed.

Where the hell is Cat?

Then I hear a sound, like metal scraping against glassware. I freeze and close my eyes, listening as the clinking commences again. It sounds like it's coming from the bathroom.

I step toward the door, but there's no little rectangle of light beneath it. The lights are off in there. Figuring I imagined things, I take a step back, but the sound freezes me in place again.

Scrape . . . scrape.

Placing my fingertips against the door, I ease it open. "Cat?" I whisper.

"In here," she says from the shadows. "It's the only place where the light doesn't reach."

"Is there a reason why we're skulking outside of the Pridelands, Mufasa?"

That earns a small chuckle, followed by the most pitiful groan I've ever heard. "Please don't make me laugh. My head is killing me. I think Bennett drugged me."

"Oh, I know he did. He told us so." I feel around in the dark until I find the stack of washrags stacked beside the sink. I run one under the cold tap and move toward her voice. "Are you in the bathtub?"

"Yeah. The cold porcelain feels good." She grunts, followed by some squeaking sounds, and then she's beside me. "Let's go into the living room."

She follows me out of the bathroom, and as the sunlight finds her face, I'm shocked by how pretty she is when she's at her worst. At my worst, I look like a bridge troll who played chicken on the I-90. Meanwhile, she looks like she's ready to pose for a two-page spread in Cosmo about the benefits of a natural glow.

I drape the cool cloth over her neck. In her hand, she holds a glass bowl and a metal spoon. That explains the sound I kept hearing.

"Were you feeling a little peckish in the dark?" I ask.

She scoops something from the bowl and shovels it into her mouth. "Yeah, I guess I was hungry after missing lunch. Thanks for making this for me."

My eyebrows pull together. "I've been with Ezra all day. I didn't make that."

"Hmm?" She chews what's in her mouth and swallows. "Really? Then who did?"

I peer into the bowl and discover what remains of a fresh fruit salad, complete with miniature orange slices, shreds of strawberry, and a heaping helping of pineapple.

Cat and I make the connection at the same time, and I catch the bowl as she drops it and races for the sink.

"No, no, no!" she screams. "Not the pineapple, Kindra. Not *the* fucking pineapple!"

"Surely it's not the same one. I mean, you saw the way

he was fucking that thing. I don't think there would have been this many solid pieces left."

She spits into the sink, then dips her mouth beneath the running faucet. My emotions vacillate between horror and humor as I watch her frantic motions, and I come to one conclusion. This is horrifyingly humorous.

"He doesn't know how to do something nice," she says as she gulps air before going back under the faucet for another rinse. "He fed me his fucking lover, Kindra!"

I hold the bowl to my nose and dare to take a sniff. It just smells sweet, like fruit. "I think you're safe. I don't detect any undertones of salt or ball sweat."

"The pineapple probably hides it." She snatches the washcloth from her neck and dabs it on her forehead. "I don't want any part of that man inside me in any way. Even the thought of ingesting a single skin cell from his body makes me sick."

I dump the remaining fruit—of which there is sadly little—into the wicker trash can, then set the bowl on the counter. Cat wipes her mouth on the back of her arm and retreats to the couch to pout. She pulls the blanket over her shoulders so that only her head sticks out.

Sitting beside her, I place my hand on what I hope is her knee. "I'm sorry I can't relate. I'm on the other end of the emotional spectrum. Instead of hating Ezra, I'm falling in love with him."

I brace myself for a squeal of joy and a hug that doesn't come. Maybe she's still in shock after eating Bennett's fruit salad. I turn to look at her, but I can't read her face. She's lost in thought, with her bottom lip tucked between her teeth and a faraway look in her eyes.

"Did you hear me?" I ask.

Cat sighs and lets the blanket drop. "I heard you, but

did you ever think that maybe things are moving a little fast with Ezra? I mean, what do you even know about him? You two have been spending a lot of time together, and I don't want you to get hurt."

Though her voice is gentle and her questions are valid, what she says sinks into a sore spot. Isn't she supposed to be happy for me? Why this sudden change of demeanor?

Is she jealous?

It's the only thing that makes sense. She was obsessed with me before the trip, and now that we're friends, she doesn't want to share my time. Why else would she bring up how much time I've been spending with Ezra?

"I don't understand," I say. "I thought you wanted me to hook up with him. What changed?"

She gets that faraway look again, like she's doing battle inside her head, and her fingers start tapping beneath the blanket.

"Just spit it out, Cat."

"When Bennett thought I was sleeping, he said some things that worried me. Things about Ezra." She picks at the corner of the blanket. "I just think you should be careful, that's all."

"Bennett? The same Bennett who would snatch an ice cream from a child and stomp it into the concrete if he thought it would wipe the smile off the child's face? *That* Bennett?" I scoff and shake my head. "I don't trust anything that comes out of his mouth. He probably knew you were half-awake and just wanted to plant a seed of contention."

"I don't think so, Kindra. He—"

"No, I don't want to hear it." I get to my feet and pace around the coffee table. I'm too angry to stay seated. "Bennett is a snake, and I won't let his lies get to me. I trust Ezra. He's a good guy, and he's good *for* me."

"Bennett said something about a secret. I can't remember exactly what, but it's something about his brother's identity. Please, just be careful."

I stop pacing. "His identity? He's a private dick and a serial killer. He has no romantic attachments, no children, and no pets. He owns his home and drives a Mini Cooper because it reminds him of the UK." I count the points on my fingers, then look at her. "What am I missing?"

Her tiny shoulders lift in a shrug. "I don't know, but you're missing *some*thing. A little distance may not be a bad thing. You and I could get ready for dinner together, and we can hang out for the evening without the guys."

"You and Bennett are more alike than you realize." I fold my arms over my chest. "He's jealous of Ezra, and you're jealous of me. Now you're both working to rip us apart."

Cat looks like I just slapped her in the face. I expect her to start crying, but she steels herself and says, "I'm sorry you feel that way."

She retreats to her bedroom, and as the door clicks shut behind her, it feels like we've closed the door on our friendship.

Chapter Thirty-One

Ezra

I check my watch for the third time and pace the mansion's front hall. Kindra said she would meet me here. I'm not sure if it's the anticipation of seeing her or the dread of knowing tonight may be our last night together, but my heart won't stop hammering against my chest each time I hear footsteps in the corridor.

Once she finds out I'm the one who ruined her adult life, I'm done.

I've put this off for far too long, and now I've run out of room to hide. Especially with Maverick's impending arrival. If he gets to Kindra before I can get to him, he'll unwittingly blow this entire thing out of the water.

Bennett was right about one thing. It's best if she hears the truth from me first.

Heels click against gleaming hardwood floors, and I turn to face the sound. The moment she rounds the corner, any chance of my heartbeat slowing is gone.

Black hair frames her face in gentle ringlets and soft

waves, and though the Caribbean humidity tried to sabotage her locks, it hasn't detracted from her beauty. A purple dress flows over her curves like glistening water. Tiny jewels catch the light and cast glimmers of shifting color on her skin.

She's stunning.

When I finally stop acting like a twelve-year-old boy who just saw a beautiful woman for the first time, I raise my eyes to her face. Her smile usually gives me life, but something seems off. The joy formed by her lips and perfect teeth is a lie.

I offer my arm, and she slides her hand into the crook of my elbow. She's shaking.

"Is everything okay, pet?" I guide her to a quiet corner and swat a massive houseplant out of my face. "You seem upset."

Her lips pull into a tight line, and tears spring to her eyes. She shakes her head. "Cat and I got into a fight. She seems to think you're hiding something from me." She swipes away the tears beneath her eyes before they damage her makeup. "Apparently, Bennett said some shit when he thought she was sleeping."

My spine feels like it's going to collapse in on itself. What would he have told her? And why? I know my brother has a big mouth, but I never thought he would wield it in such a way.

"Friends fight, pet. It will all blow over. I promise."

I can promise her that her friendship will mend itself, but the relationship I share with Kindra bears no such guarantee.

This entire situation feels like I'm standing at the gallows. I know my fate, yet I'm forced to march toward it. I'm forced to pretend the last few hours with Kindra won't be the last. I would almost prefer an actual death sentence at this point.

Kindra shifts her weight and rests her forehead against my chest. "She said that Bennett thinks you're no good for me."

I'm not. And she's too good for me. But I say nothing. I won't add to the lies I've told thus far.

"Then again, she was on a lot of drugs. Maybe she just misheard him," she says. She releases a deep sigh and leans back to look at me. "I should probably apologize to her for biting her head off, huh?"

"I think that would be a good idea. I don't know her as well as you do, but I doubt she had any harmful intent. The poor girl doesn't seem capable of malice toward anyone other than Bennett."

Kindra groans. "You're right. I'll apologize after dinner."

A figure pops around the corner, and a hand waves at me. It's Jim. He's always been the type to greet his guests, which is unfortunate at this moment. I really wanted to get more details on what exactly Bennett said to Cat, but I guess it will have to wait.

Jim has chosen a tux with tails this evening, and he looks absolutely ridiculous. The black-and-white Oxfords adorning his long feet look more akin to clown shoes. If he had a walking cane and monocle, he'd pass as the Planters Mr. Peanut mascot.

"How are we this evening, Ezra?" Jim asks as he claps a hand on my shoulder. His fingers move against the fabric, pinching and rubbing. "What is this? Brioni? Sartorio Napoli?"

"I'm afraid I don't make enough to afford one of those," I say with a laugh. "I just choose what hangs well on my frame, regardless of label."

Jim eyes me up and down, then licks his lips. "Yes, well, it certainly fits well, doesn't it?"

Kindra covers her mouth to stifle a grin. We've long suspected Jim prefers to play for the other team, but he's from a different time. He doesn't realize it's safe to come out of the closet, so we let him stay there, pretending we don't know.

The lusty look fades from his eyes. "Well, you'd best be seated. Dinner is about to begin!" He claps his hands together with a gleeful smile, then turns for the dining room.

Kindra and I follow him through the thick mahogany double doors. I have to do a double take once we're inside. The room has been transformed from a traditional—though luxurious—dining room into a themed dining experience.

Strands of glistening crystals swoop from the ceiling in delicate arcs that connect to each of the three chandeliers over the table. They create a dazzling curtain of light. More crystals lie along the table. Chrome charger plates with intricate filigree in the outer rims adorn each place setting, and the table runner appears to be made of woven silver. Jim's pockets are deep, so it wouldn't surprise me.

The guests surrounding the table are just as fabulous. Ice Pick has squeezed himself into a black suit with a red rhinestone tie. Grim and Maudlin Rose sport matching suits, both fabrics the color of the sea on a clear day. Flashy suits and sequined gowns appear everywhere I look.

Then my eyes fall on Kindra again. It's as if everyone is playing at being glamorous, but she truly is. A woman has never captured my attention so fully.

I grip a chair, and its legs squeak against the floor as I ease it out for her. Once she's seated, I take my place beside her. The two seats across from us—where Cat and Bennett should be—remain vacant.

I lean near Kindra's ear and whisper, "I wonder where Cat and my brother have got off to . . ."

Could they be hanging out? Plotting against me, maybe? Who the hell knows.

"Cat seemed like she planned to come," she says. "I hope our fight didn't change her mind. I probably should have gone to her villa and apologized before dinner. I'm new to this friend stuff."

The defeated look in her eyes breaks my heart.

I place a hand on her thigh and give it a comforting squeeze. "She'll forgive you and all will be right with the world, don't you worry."

She smiles up at me. "I hope you're right."

Metal clinks against metal as servers enter the dining room, pushing gleaming silver carts. Appetizers are placed before each guest. It appears to be some type of sushi roll. Judging by the color of the meat, it's some sort of fish.

"It's safe," I whisper to Kindra.

She heaves a relieved sigh and tucks in.

Glasses clink as wine is served, and hushed conversations vibrate the air. The chairs across from us remain empty, however. I look around, hoping Cat and Bennett may have arrived without my notice, but they aren't here.

The servers enter the room again, this time pushing much larger carts. The scent of seared meat reaches my nose, and I close my eyes and pray that it's beef. I'm famished.

A man in a black dress shirt places a plate in front of Kindra. A bloody cut of steak lies beside a scoop of mashed potatoes and steamed broccoli. Kindra eyes the meat and clears her throat as she places her hand on the server's arm.

"I've had a bit of indigestion today. Would it be possible to request a salad? I'd like something a bit lighter than meat for dinner."

The server looks back at the kitchen before nodding and scurrying off, but not before sliding my plate in front of me. I stare down at the hunk of meat and cock my head as I examine it.

I've cut up enough humans and strung them on meat hooks that I should know what a cooked human might look like. I should be able to tell what kind of meat is sitting in front of me. I've been eating meat for thirty-something years, for fuck's sake. But no. I'm stumped.

Too scared to try the steak, I aim my fork at the potatoes, being careful to steer clear of the bloody puddle edging along the fluffy perimeter. Kindra eyes my plate with a longing look, and I offer her a bite of mashed potatoes, which she accepts.

"God, that is so good," she says as she tips her head back. "Maybe I should have kept the plate and eaten around the potential chunk of man."

"You're not a fan of salad?"

She motions to her body. "I didn't get this voluptuous physique from eating like a rabbit."

The server appears again and places a massive plate of greenery in front of Kindra. Her face turns a similar shade of chartreuse.

"Would you prefer this?" I ask, gesturing toward the mayhem on my plate.

She plucks up the fork and shoves a bit of lettuce into her mouth while forcing a smile around the tines. "No thanks," she mutters past the mouthful.

"Ezra," Jim says as he taps his glass, "you're the only one

who hasn't taken a bite of this meticulously prepared steak. You really must try it."

I shift in my seat. I don't like having the spotlight on me like this. "What cut of meat is this again, Jim?"

"Maurice has prepared a scintillating cut of Wagyu, straight from Japan." Jim grins and shoves a hunk of meat into his mouth. As he chews, a bit of red juice dribbles onto his chin.

"Wagyu?" Kindra whispers as she picks at her salad. "I regret my decision."

Jim swallows, clears his throat, and swipes a cloth napkin over his chin. "I think his name was Phil. Bill, maybe?"

"Never mind," Kindra whispers. "Spoke too soon."

My stomach tightens. I haven't eaten the human delicacies since the first year at the retreat. I learned to mistrust anything that emerges from Maurice's kitchen.

Jim points at me with his fork. "We won't continue with dinner until you've eaten."

"Go on, Ezra, eat away," Kindra says with a smile. She picks up her glass of water and brings it to her lips to keep from laughing.

My vegetarian lie might have worked on night one, but Jim knows me too well. If I say I've decided to forgo meat, he'll call me out.

With twenty-something pairs of eyes on me and no other way to avoid offending Jim, I raise my fork, cut into the meat, and bring a small bite to my mouth.

An embarrassing pep talk blares in my mind. I imagine a big, juicy cow walking in a field with a chunk of its rump missing as I open my mouth. My throat threatens to close, but I fight it and win.

Sorry Phil . . . or Bill, I say in my mind as I chew and swallow.

Whatever is going on with my face makes Kindra let out a soft chuckle beside me. She's trying so hard to stay in control.

I choke down two more bites before people turn their attention back to their own meals, freeing me to drop the fork and snatch up the napkin to dab a bit of sweat from my forehead. A swig of merlot helps me wash the taste from my mouth, and I devour the potatoes and broccoli to cushion my roiling guts. It doesn't help.

As everyone finishes the main course, the servers are back again, this time with delicate cups of rich coffee and beautifully caramelized crème brûlée.

Kindra leans close to my ear. "This isn't made with breastmilk or anything weird like that, is it?"

"If it is, I can't be bothered to care. You won't either once you've tried it." I sink my dessert spoon into the cup and ready my tastebuds for the second-best thing I'll ever taste in my life—the first being Kindra.

She digs in as well, and we polish off both cups in record time. Our bellies full, we stand from the table and bid our farewells to the host and the other guests.

The chairs across from us still remain empty.

With an uneasy feeling in my gut, I guide Kindra toward the front of the mansion. Jim's butler nods as we pass, then closes the door behind us as we step into the cool evening air.

"You enjoyed that, didn't you?" I say as I place my hand on the small of her back and lead her toward the walkway lit by tiki torches.

"Your torment? Absolutely. It's payback for the first night."

I grip her hand and spin her so that she's pressed against my body. Her chest heaves against me as I lean closer for a kiss.

"No, Ezra, gross!" she says with a laugh.

She squirms in my grasp, but I only kiss her harder, spreading her lips with my tongue. If I have to have the taste of a human being on my tongue, so does she.

Her fight diminishes, and we soon forget about my betrayal of humanity in the dining hall.

"Get a room!" Bennett says as he comes up behind me.

We turn to face him, and I expect to see Cat beside him, her claws fully extended, but he's alone.

Kindra's smile falls as she stares past Bennett, looking for her friend. "Where's Cat?"

"Gone."

"Gone like . . . you killed her?" I ask.

Kindra sucks in a sharp breath as her hands press against her stomach. Before she can launch herself at him, he scoffs and shakes his head.

"What? No, asshole. She's gone, as in, she left the island. I just got back from taking her to the airstrip."

Kindra swallows loud enough for me to hear, and my heart hurts for her. "She's gone?"

"Yeah. Said she didn't want to be on the island anymore. I was happy to get rid of her, honestly. Did I miss dinner?"

"You did," I say.

"Well, hopefully they have that banging cream pie for dessert again tonight," Bennett says.

Kindra doesn't move. She doesn't speak. She just stares at the jungle as the darkness deepens.

"Kindra," I begin, but her hand rises to silence me.

"I'm not feeling well. I'm going to go back to my villa."

Before I can argue, she starts down the path. She doesn't even give me a chance to beg her to stay.

My head rotates on a swivel, bouncing between Kindra's retreating figure and my brother. I need to comfort her, but I also need to talk to Bennett.

"I'll meet you back at your villa!" I yell toward Kindra.

Her hand rises in a halfhearted acknowledgment as she keeps walking.

By the time I turn around, Bennett has already made it up the mansion's steps. I rush to his side before he can open the door.

"Why the fuck are you running up on me?" he asks as he turns to face me. "Don't you have something you're supposed to be telling someone?"

I reach his side and lower my voice. "What did you tell Cat?"

A crease forms between Bennett's eyebrows as he tries to puzzle out what I'm referring to. "When I dropped her off? I told her I hope the plane crashes."

"That's horrible, but no, not when you dropped her off. What did you say to her after you'd drugged her?"

His shoulder lifts in a nonchalant shrug, and he reaches for the door again. "I don't know, man. She was out of it, and I was just muttering to myself about how fucking dumb this entire debacle has turned out to be. Now, if you'll excuse me."

"No, I won't excuse you." I step closer, putting myself directly into his personal space—which my brother can't fucking stand. "You hurt Kindra, Bennett."

Bennett slowly turns to face me, a look of exaggerated indignation on his face. "*Me? I* hurt her?"

His hand shoots forward and wraps around my arm. In the time it takes to blink, he's dragged me inside and begun hauling me straight toward the large mirror taking up a wide stretch of the wall between the double staircases. His grip shifts from my arm to my chin as he faces me toward my reflection.

"If you want to know who's hurting that girl, you only need to look straight ahead. If you want to hate someone, hate yourself." Looking in the mirror, he straightens his tie. "Now, if you'll leave me the fuck alone, I'd like to have some dinner."

I hate that he's right, but he is. I'm hurting her.

I turn back for the door. The only place I can think of going is Kindra's villa. She's just had one blow for the evening, since her friend chose to escape in the dark of night, and I want to be there for her one last time. I want to comfort her and hold her until morning comes.

And then I have to break her heart all over again.

Chapter Thirty-Two

Ezra

By the time I reach Kindra's villa, she's already changed into sweatpants and a large t-shirt. Through the window, I watch as she swipes her eyes and paces circles around the couch with her phone held toward the ceiling. She is the picture of a panicked woman.

Without knocking, I ease open the door. She stops pacing and sucks in a breath when she sees me, then bolts for my arms. I hold them wide, encircling her within them when she reaches me.

"This is such a fucking mess," she cries against my chest. "This is why I don't make friends. I suck at it."

I brush my hand over her hair, comforting her in a way I've never comforted a woman before—in a way I have no right to comfort this one now.

"If it weren't for you, I'd want to leave right away," she adds.

The sentence twists the knife in my gut, but it also

sparks an idea. I could take her to the airstrip when the pilot returns and see her off the island. I could tell her I'll contact her as soon as I'm back from the retreat. Then I could hop across the pond and make a life for myself in the UK.

I never have to tell her the truth and break her heart.

Or mine.

Instead of being a regret, I could be a fond memory. She might grow to hate me, but that's okay. It sure as hell beats her feeling something much stronger than hate for me.

But then she leans back and looks into my eyes, and I know what it means to love a woman completely. It means being honest, even to my detriment.

"I don't like to see you hurt," I whisper as I brush a tear from her cheek. "What can I do to help you?"

She lets out a humorless laugh and rests her head against my chest again. "Unless you have a time machine that can take me back a few hours, I don't think anything *can* be done."

A time machine would solve so many problems.

I lead her to the couch and guide her onto my lap as I sit. She nestles against me and lets out a contented sigh. Her hair smells like a Tahitian sunrise with a hint of sunscreen. I breathe it in and commit the scent to memory. These are our final hours, and I'll need these memories to get me through.

"It's hard to even stay in this villa," she says. "I keep seeing things that remind me of her. Why does this feel like a fucking breakup?"

"In a way, losing a friend is like experiencing a breakup. But I don't think she's gone for good. Maybe she just needed a little space."

"I still don't know how I'll sleep tonight, even if you're with me. I can see her villa from my bed."

"Why not stay at my villa tonight?" I suggest.

My reasoning is twofold. Yes, I want to help her, but I've also seen the vast repertoire of weaponry she brought along. I don't fancy getting gored by a longsword when I tell her the truth, even though I deserve it.

"A sleepover would be nice," she says. "It'll take my mind off of everything, and I won't have to see a constant reminder of my fuck up."

She wiggles off my lap and retreats to her room. She returns a few minutes later with a small bag about the size of a tote. I rise from the couch, and we start toward my villa.

I've had visions of our last night together, and we were naked in all of them. To say I'm not disappointed in the turn of events would be a lie, but her tears cause me more discomfort than the ache in my balls. Sex is likely the furthest thing from her mind right now, and I won't press the issue.

After a silent walk, we reach my villa and step inside. The air conditioner's low hum greets us as we head toward the bedroom. Kindra flops onto her back on the bed. I divert my attention away from her nipples pressing against her shirt and begging for my touch.

"Is it too cold in here for you?" I ask. "I can turn down the air."

She shakes her head. "No, it's perfect. If it's not as cold as a well digger's ass, I can't sleep."

"Turn over," I say. "Let me rub the tension out of your shoulders."

She rolls onto her stomach with a chuckle. "Don't think I don't know what you're doing, though."

I straddle her full ass and grip her shoulders. "I'm not trying anything, if that's what you're insinuating."

"How disappointing," she mutters into the mattress.

"I just figured you'd be too upset to indulge in carnal desires." I squeeze the muscles, and she lets out a soft moan.

"I'm never too upset for that. Besides, an orgasm will help me sleep. If you keep rubbing my body like that, I'm liable to come before you can even get your dick wet."

God, I love her vulgarity.

Having received the green light, my cock hardens against her ass. She lets out another soft moan and grinds against my length.

"Let's play with the ropes some more," she says. "I want to be used right now."

I nearly choke on my own spit. How is this woman real?

"If that's what you want," I say, "then that's what you shall have. But first, let me relax you so that you'll be limber. I want to put you in compromising positions."

I raise her shirt and move down so that I can place my lips against the small of her back. My tongue laves her skin, pressing and moving against her twitching muscles. Her moans fuel me, and I travel higher and higher until I reach her neck, all while my hands continue massaging her.

The muscles shift from concrete to liquid beneath my fingertips.

Once her tension has loosened, I ease her onto her back and remove her shirt. The small lamp by the bed provides the only light, and it bathes her round lines in the perfect mix of brilliance and shadow. She hasn't worn a bra, and her relaxed breasts make my mouth water.

I dip my head, take her nipple into my mouth, and suck the hardened bead until she squirms. Fearing I've been too rough, I go to pull away, but Kindra yanks my head down again.

Noted.

I repeat the action, this time nipping the sensitive skin as well. That earns a louder moan.

"Fuck, that feels so good," she breathes. "I want you inside me."

"Soon," I rasp against her breast.

I pinch her other nipple between my fingers as I continue to nip and suck the first. Her hips rise, pushing her pussy against me. Warmth radiates from her.

After releasing her from my mouth, I go for my bag and pull out rope and two sets of black fur-lined cuffs. What I have planned will keep her tied up for a bit, and I want her to be as comfortable as possible.

"Look in my bag too," she says, and the playful lilt to her voice sends a pleasurable zap up my spine. I already know what I'll find before I pull back the zipper.

I also know exactly how I plan to implement it.

"In due time, pet. Right now, I'm going to use you."

I return to the bed and fasten the cuffs around her wrists. If we had more time, I'd wrap her from head to toe. I can just imagine how beautiful she'd look as her flesh pushes through a net of gaps. But there is no time. My pet has a need, and I must fulfill it.

I strip away her sweatpants and panties, then affix the rope to the cuffs and tie her hands to the bamboo bed frame. I do the same to her ankles, positioning her so that she's spread open for me with her knees near her head. Signs of arousal glisten between her legs like runway landing lights.

I strip off my shirt and drop onto my elbows so that my face is mere centimeters from heaven. The salt on her skin reaches my nose, and my mouth waters. My tongue drives forward and slides through her slit.

"Fuck, fuck, fuck," she whimpers.

Her pussy clenches around nothing as I find her clit and

tease it with the tip of my tongue. I'm not trying to make her come. Not yet. Not until this position begins to wear her out.

I continue licking and sucking until she's a quivering mess, but I always stop just before I send her over the edge. Her frustration begins to build. She probably thinks I've lost my ability to dine out, but this is all part of the plan.

"Okay, it's getting harder to breathe like this," she says.

I smile against her mound, but I don't stop licking, sucking, and biting.

"Ezra, I'm serious. I think it's time to let me out of this now. Positional asphyxiation is a thing."

The slight panic in her voice tells me that it's time.

Without a word, I stand and go to her bag. I pull out her toy and turn to face her. "I'll let you out of that, but you have to come first."

"I don't think I can," she says, her eyes widening. "I'll suffocate before I get off!"

I flick the switch, and the device buzzes to life. The tiny machine shakes so violently that it nearly leaps from my hand. The priest's look of fear doesn't seem so far off base now. I'm liable to fracture her pelvic bone with this thing.

"Is this what you regularly use?" I ask.

"Yes, now let me out of these ropes!"

Panic has her in a chokehold now. Her legs jerk against the restraints, and she snatches her wrists back and forth. She doesn't yet realize it, but I've just constructed the best orgasm of her life. It's amazing what you can learn about a woman if you just listen when she speaks.

I step forward and trace her pussy lips with the toy, holding it just close enough that she can feel the movement of air. She relaxes again as she realizes that an orgasm may not be such a bad way to go.

Full transparency: I would never allow her to perish at my hand. I've tied the ropes with a quick release. If I feel she's in any danger, I'll cut her loose.

But she doesn't need to know that.

Using my left arm, I press against her thigh and make it a bit harder for her to breathe as the toy drifts closer to her clit. She tries to get a gulp of air, but it won't come. Her chest doesn't have enough room to expand.

"Fuck, I . . . really can't . . . breathe," she pants.

"Then you'd best come."

I lower the toy, and the reaction is immediate. She lets out a cry as her body tenses and writhes. The ropes pull taut as she loses control and strains against the cuffs. I release the pressure on her leg, allowing her more air.

Her hands flex, opening and closing, and her toes curl until I'm certain they'll snap right off. Her chest jerks up and down, but I keep the toy pressed against her clit, milking every ounce of pleasure from her body. She gasps in quick bursts, which is all she can manage. Standing at the brink of asphyxia only enhances her orgasm.

As she begins to come down, I silence the toy, lean over her, and unfasten the ropes. Her arms and legs flop to the bed. Her eyes stare at the ceiling as she smiles and gulps oxygen into her lungs.

"Are we feeling a little better now?" I ask.

She licks her lips and tries to answer, but no words come, so she nods.

"Good," I say, but I'm not finished with her yet.

Kindra

I'm still seeing God when I hear the sound of Ezra's belt buckle coming undone. Normally, I'm good to keep going after I come, but before tonight, I've never had someone make me come so hard that I was afraid my internal organs might shut down.

His zipper falls.

Shit.

I open my mouth to let him know that I need a minute, but he's already on me. When I look up into his face, it doesn't matter anyway. I forget what I wanted to say.

"Has anyone ever told you how beautiful you are after you've come?" he asks, and my god, he could file nails with the rasp in his voice. "Because you are. You are absolutely stunning, pet."

His accent cloaks his words in silk, and I'm finding myself more amenable by the second. Maybe I can survive one more orgasm . . .

Needing no more encouragement, I reach between his

legs and easily find the steel pylon that is his dick. A groan rumbles in his chest as my fingers encircle his girth. With a gentle tug, I guide him toward my entrance.

As he settles his head inside me, he sucks air through his teeth. "You're so wet and warm for me."

His praise sends a jolt of pleasure between my legs, and my pussy tightens around him. His hips jerk forward, pushing him deep inside me and creating a painful ache.

"I don't think I'll ever get used to your size," I say through a moan.

"And I'll never get used to how incredible you feel." He draws his hips back and glides inside me again, allowing me to experience every glorious inch.

He pulls out of me completely, and I feel so empty. I look up at him, begging for more, but he just smiles down at me before flipping me onto my stomach.

"Arch your back for me," he says, and I respond by poking my ass into the air. "Perfect, pet. Stay just like that."

Heat settles behind me, and his hand winds through my hair. With a tug, he raises my chest from the bed. I'm a bit tender headed, so pain zings through my scalp and causes my muscles to tense.

"Relax into it," he says as he enters me. "Just close your eyes and feel everything, but don't think."

I do as he says. I separate myself from the pain and pleasure and just float in my mind until everything crashes together. With each forward thrust of his hips, he snatches back on my hair, keeping me right where he wants me. His balls slap against me, and it's so weird to get more turned on by that, but here the fuck we are. I'm a sloppy mess between my legs.

And then I spot the toy.

Most men I've been with were too insecure to allow me

to use it during sex. I would reach for it, and they would shoot it down, claiming their skills were far superior and I wouldn't need it.

They lied.

Ezra doesn't seem like the type to be so insecure, though, so I reach for the vibrator. His thrusts slow when he sees it in my grasp, and I worry my assumption was incorrect and he'll stop and tell me to put it away.

"I was hoping you'd make use of that," he grunts as he picks up the pace again. "Make yourself come on my cock."

Say less. I flick the button and press the toy against my clit.

Bright colors explode behind my eyelids as I try to hold back the tide. I don't want to come yet. I want to experience the ride to the top and the sudden drop, but my body has other ideas.

Ezra pounds into me, moving the toy with each driven push and making it dance over my throbbing clit. My fingers dig into the sheets, and I bury my face in the pillow as I let out a scream.

As my eyes spin like pinwheels, my thighs begin to quiver and turn to jelly. Waves of pleasure shoot through every muscle until I'm certain I've reached the crest of the hill, but it just keeps coming.

I just keep coming.

Ezra's hips stutter behind me, and he releases my hair to grasp my hips with both hands. "Fuck, you're going to make me come."

Turning my head to the side, I pull in a lungful of air as the orgasm finally releases its hold. "Fucking fill me," I whimper. "Please, I want you to come inside me."

"I didn't want to go this quickly," he says through clenched teeth.

"We have all night. And tomorrow night, if you're free."

He pauses, and his hands loosen their grip on my skin.

Did I say something wrong? Did I overstep? When he talked about seeing me outside of the retreat, was he just placating me so that he could keep sleeping with me?

His grip tightens again, and he pushes into me, sending my chest against the mattress. "For you, I'm free for the rest of my life."

As his hips hammer forward, I nearly lose consciousness. I've never been fucked with such ferocity and need. Now I understand why he likes thicker women. He needs all the cushioning he can get as he jackhammers my sore pussy.

Just as I'm about to cry uncle, he thrusts a final time as warmth floods me. When he's finished painting my insides, we both collapse in a breathless heap of legs, balls, arms, and boobs.

"You . . . are incredible," he pants against the nape of my neck.

Turning onto my side, I grip his hand and pull it up to my mouth so that he can feel my smile. It's not the first time a man has given me such a compliment, but it's the first time I've heard the sincerity behind it. He isn't using me for sex or betraying me in any way.

He genuinely likes me.

For me.

He leans forward and places a kiss on my cheek, then fetches a rag so that I can clean up. With that handled, he settles in behind me. We lie together, naked, as we listen to the distant sound of the waves brushing against the sand.

A few minutes later, his breathing levels off to a light snore. I don't mind. If we can't fuck all night, that's okay. He's promised me tomorrow. He's promised me forever.

I close my eyes and smile. I've never allowed myself to want something like this, let alone indulge in the amount of vulnerability I've given this man. It doesn't even feel risky at this point. With my heart in his hands, I've never felt safer.

Once I smooth things over with Cat, all will be right again. I still don't know how I'll apologize, though I know I need to. But what do I apologize for? Her information was incorrect. Bennett was just being his usual insufferable self. He spread a—

Thud . . . thud, thud . . .

I freeze and hold my breath as feet stomp across the porch outside the villa.

Without waking Ezra, I slide from beneath his arm and grab a robe from my overnight bag, though I nearly tip over in the process. My legs have forgotten how to function. Once I've covered my body in the thin silk wrap, I tiptoe to the front of the villa and peek through the gauzy curtain.

A tall man stands just outside the door. I don't recognize him. He looks much younger than Ezra. He's possibly younger than Cat. His sandy blond hair is short on the sides and longer on the top, which gives him the look of a government employee.

My stomach tenses. If he's a fed or a cop, we're in serious shit.

He raises his hand to knock, but I open the door before he can. I don't want to wake Ezra unless it's absolutely necessary.

"Can I help you?" I ask.

The light catches his face, revealing a set of perfectly straight teeth that definitely came from years of pricey orthodontic work. His eyes are light, though I can't tell if they're blue or green, and he could cut steel with that jawline.

"I'm looking for Ezra. Jim said this was his villa, but I must have picked the wrong one." He brushes his hand through his hair, then offers it to me. "I'm Maverick, the Midnight Masochist."

My brain registers the name, and the alarm bells stop ringing. "Oh, gosh! Yes, Bennett mentioned you'd be here for the hunt, but I don't think Ezra was expecting you until tomorrow morning. I can wake him if you don't mind waiting for a second. He's not . . . decent."

Maverick lets out a deep laugh, then waves me off. "No, no need. I'll see him tomorrow morning. Jim let me stay in one of the vacant villas, but I found some of Ezra's things in there and wanted to return them to him. I can just leave them with you, though."

He reaches behind his back and pulls something shiny from his waistband. As he brings it around to the light, I realize it's the set of meat hooks we found in Eighties' villa.

"Oh, those aren't Ezra's," I say. "They belonged to a guy named Eighties, who, as it turns out, was actually the Abattoir Adonis. Jim must have put you in his villa."

Maverick turns the hooks in his hands, a look of confusion on his face. Then he looks at me. "Ezra isn't gonna like it when he finds out someone has been pretending to be the Abattoir Adonis."

"Pretending? I don't follow."

"Eighties couldn't have been AA. *Ezra* is the Abattoir Adonis."

Chapter Thirty-Four

Ezra

I wake the next morning, blessedly sore in all the right places. My limbs sing with utter relaxation as I stretch them and open my eyes. Light peeks over the horizon as the sun begins to rise on another glorious day.

Turning onto my side, I look for Kindra, but her spot on the bed lies empty. The ruffled sheets and the errant come stain tell me last night wasn't a dream, but where has my little minx got off to?

I sit up and swipe my hand down my face, then reach for my glasses on the bedside table. Once I have them on, I look toward the bathroom. The door is ajar and the light is off, so she isn't in there.

Then the scent of fresh coffee slips under the door and finds my nose, followed by the sound of something sizzling on the tiny stove. Is she making breakfast?

With a smile, I rise from the bed and hurry to the bathroom to make sure I'm presentable. I can't exactly greet the love of my life with a puff of dragon's breath.

To be fair, the morning after is a new experience for me. Most of my conquests don't stay the night, or if they do, they're gone before I wake. They understood the assignment.

Now, the assignment has changed. I want this to be one morning of many that we spend together.

My breath fresh and my dark hair shaped into something manageable, I dress in a thin button up and a pair of khaki shorts. As I fasten the last button, my good mood falls.

No. It doesn't just fall. It plummets, collides with the ground, then disintegrates on impact.

Because it's time to come clean.

I've toyed with keeping this a secret forever. I've come up with plans and schemes, and I'm certain they'd work, but our foundation would be built on a lie. Losing her forever is better than lying to her forever. She deserves nothing less than my honesty.

Plus, there's still a chance I could salvage this. If I'm the one who comes clean to her, she has to see the merit in that. Maybe not right away, but eventually.

I'll wait forever.

With a steeling breath, I open the bedroom door and step into the main living area. It takes a moment for my brain to register what I see because it varies so greatly from my expectation.

Instead of Kindra swaying her hips in front of the stove, it's Maverick. Instead of Kindra holding a warm mug of coffee toward me, it's Bennett.

"Drink this now," Bennett says. "You're going to need it."

I push the mug away. "What are you on about? Where's Kindra?"

Maverick's hand stalls mid-flip, and the eggs land on the stovetop. Then I spot the gleaming meat hooks on the counter.

"What the fuck did you do?" I bellow as I launch myself at Bennett.

Because this is all his fault. He's wanted to split us apart since the moment he realized this was more than a fling.

Gripping his shirt collar in my fists, I sling him against a wall and begin choking him. Incredibly, he puts up an abysmal fight, merely clutching my wrists as his face shifts from red to purple.

Arms wrap around my torso, and a lean body presses against my back. Maverick might be nearly twenty years my junior, but he lacks my unmitigated rage at the moment. With a quick turn, he's off me.

"This isn't your battle to fight!" I shout at him before I turn back to Bennett and press my forearm to his chest, pinning him against the wall again. "What the fuck did you do?"

"I didn't do shit," Bennett wheezes. "You should have told her. None of this would have happened if you'd listened to me."

"Why are my meat hooks on the fucking counter, then?" I press my arm into his sternum a bit more, and he winces.

"Ezra, it was my fault," Maverick says behind me.

I release Bennett and turn to face the traitor. "Why? What the fuck were you thinking?"

"I didn't know you were keeping your identity a secret!" He rushes back to the pan on the stove, which has produced an impressive cloud of thick smoke.

Cue the fire-prevention system.

The lights cut off, and the villa becomes a concert of shrill beeps and flashing exit lights. Seconds later, the sprinklers come on, drenching us in a cold spray of iron-scented water.

Maverick rushes the pan toward the sink, and though he douses the charred eggs under a running tap, the sprinklers and alarms rage on. The damage is done.

In more ways than this.

We file from the villa and drip onto the boardwalk in silence. It seems no one knows what to say, least of all me. Because all of this is my doing. I can try to pin blame on everyone else, but I'm the lynchpin holding this flaming fiasco together.

I want to cry, but no tears will come. I want to rage and break something, and the boardwalk railing looks mighty tempting.

Instead, I ask a single question.

"Maverick, what happened?"

He explains everything. Jim handed the villa keys to him. Upon discovering the meat hooks, he thought I left them as a sign to come see me as soon as he got here. Being none the wiser, he told Kindra the truth about my identity.

"Where did she go?" I ask. Some small piece of me still hopes I can fix this mess.

"I don't know, man. She grabbed her bag and said she needed to get back to her place, so I can only assume she meant her villa." Maverick covers his face and groans. "Bennett explained how bad I fucked up. I'm sorry."

I sigh and look out at the horizon. "No, you didn't fuck up. And neither did you, Bennett. You were right. The blame rests squarely on my shoulders."

"So what do you plan to do now?" Bennett asks. "The

hunt is in an hour, and as much as I'd love to sit around and eat a pint of Ben and Jerry's while we commiserate, I'm not missing my chance to end Gary."

"I'm not going on the hunt," I say. "I need to pick up the pieces and try to put this back together. There's always next year's hunt, but there will never be another Kindra."

Bennett nods his head and slaps his hand on my shoulder. "I figured you might say that. Go get your girl."

Shocked, I can only blink and stare at him. Hasn't he been against this the entire time?

"I know what you're thinking," he says. "It wasn't that I didn't like the girl, though. I just didn't like the lying. Why do you think I haven't gotten into a relationship? You have to tell chicks everything, and I am not an open book."

"Neither was I," I say.

"Yeah, she ripped your cover wide open." Bennett laughs and shakes his head. "I'll miss having you as my wingman, but I won't stand in the way of your happiness. So go get her. You have my blessing."

It's all the encouragement I need. I turn and break into a run.

"Sorry again!" Maverick shouts at my retreating back as I race toward Kindra's villa.

I pass the entrance to the jungle path just as a line of Cattle disappears into the greenery. The Cattle wear masks to cover their eyes so they don't know where they are, and their wrists are shackled around their waists. An old-school chain connects their ankles to the Cattle in front of and behind them.

Jim brings up the procession's rear. "It's too early to head in just now," he says as I race past him.

I raise a hand to acknowledge him, then keep running.

The hunt is the furthest thing from my mind. Hell, if Kindra commanded me to never kill again, I would give it up without a second thought. I will pay whatever price I must to earn her forgiveness.

Her villa appears around the next bend. I'm out of breath as I nearly fall up the stairs and rap my knuckles against the wooden door.

"Kindra, please let me speak to you! There's more to the story than what you believe!" I open my fist and slam my palm against the door. "Just let me tell my side. If you never want to speak to me again, I'll respect that."

I say this last to myself more than her. Because it's futile. If anything, she probably needs more time to come to terms with things before she'll be open to hearing anything I have to say.

Then, just as I'm turning to leave, I spot something fluttering against the porch banister. It's a piece of paper, held against the wood by the tip of a knife.

Kindra's knife. I recognize the handle.

I pluck the blade from the paper and set it on the railing, then grip the note before the summer breeze can blow it away. As I read, each word taps a stake through my soul.

> AA,
>
> Thanks for ruining my fucking life, you absolute sack of dog shit. If Cat can go home early, so can I. Do not contact me. Ever. If you see me on the street, keep walking.
>
> Also, fuck you.
> HBK

So that's it, then.

She's left the island, and I'll never see her again.

With my head hung low, I start back toward my villa. This is the end of something magical, and fuck, it hurts. I love her. With every fiber of my being, I love Kindra. So I have to let her go. I must respect her wishes and leave her alone.

I'll just wait for her for the rest of my life. No woman has ever come close to making me feel this way, and no one ever will.

Bennett and Maverick are still standing outside when I return. They see everything on my face. The despair. The heartache. The loss of a will to live.

"Didn't go well, I take it?" Bennett asks, and I appreciate that he doesn't have any snark in his tone.

I produce the scathing letter from my pocket and hand it to the guys. They huddle over it like two schoolgirls with a note from a crush. Maverick even uses his finger to trace each line. I don't mind. As long as I don't have to relive the words myself, I'll be okay.

Bennett clears his throat and hands the letter back to me. "Absolute sack of dog shit? Damn, that's harsh."

Okay, as long as I don't have to relive my failures, I'll be okay.

"I mean, you did lie to her for damn near a week about her brother's killer, though," Bennett adds. "You also had an elaborate setup for keeping her fooled. So I get it."

"You're not helping," Maverick whispers.

"Okay, okay," Bennett says as he turns his attention to me. "I don't know why you're here, though. The pilot refuses to fly before he's had his lunch. If she's down at the airstrip, then . . ."

His face pales, and the letter drops from his hand. I scramble to grab it before the wind can snap it up.

"Fuck," he breathes.

"What?" Maverick and I say in unison.

"Oh, I fucked up." Bennett grips the boardwalk railing and leans into it. "I fucked up bad, Ezra. You have to get to the hunting grounds."

I shake my head and stuff the letter into my pocket. "No fucking way. I'm not going on—"

"No, you don't get it. The entire reason I was at your villa this morning was because Kindra knocked on my door and asked which way to the airstrip. I jokingly pointed toward the hunting grounds and said I took Cat that way. I figured she was just asking a question, and me, being my asshole self, decided to make a joke."

"And she took you seriously," I say. "If she's in that jungle . . ."

Bennett covers his face with his hands. "Fuck. I didn't even think anything of it. Then I came to your place, and Maverick filled me in on what happened, and I filled him in on what actually happened. I forgot all about seeing her this morning."

"Meanwhile, Kindra is out there in a jungle filled with nonces! Bennett, what have you *done*?"

Maverick holds up his hands and steps between us. "Before another brotherly brawl breaks out, let's use our logical minds. Kindra is a serial killer. She can take care of herself out there."

Yes, maybe against one or two, but I saw the conga line headed into the jungle. Most of their suits were red or pink. The child abusers might not go for her because she's aged out of their sick perversions, but the reds . . .

"Don't do anything crazy," Maverick says. "Just find Jim and have him hold off until she's found."

"It's too late. I saw them heading into the jungle moments ago when I went to Kindra's villa."

Bennett shrugs. "Then I guess we go on the hunt and if we see her, we'll send her to the correct airstrip instead of the imaginary one."

I'm glad he can be so nonchalant about all of this. I may be responsible for the majority of my woes, but this one? This one falls squarely on my brother's shoulders.

"I have to go after her," I say.

Before they can argue, I'm already headed toward the jungle.

Grim and Ice Pick stand at the trailhead when I reach it. I stop running and plant my hands on my knees while I try to catch my breath. There's no use asking if they've seen Kindra. She went into the jungle at least an hour ago, maybe longer.

"There are plenty of Cattle to go around," Ice Pick says through a chuckle. "No need to run. Maudlin Rose hasn't even gotten here yet, and we can't start without her."

I wave my palm at him and shake my head. "No . . . I'm not here . . . for the hunt." I point into the dense vegetation. "Kindra . . . out there."

Much to my surprise, they get the immediacy of my plight with so little information. Their eyes go wide, and they look at each other before turning back to me.

"Let us help you find her," Ice Pick says. "She's a good girl, and I wouldn't want to see anything happen to her."

I give him a thumbs-up. I'll take all the help I can get.

We aren't supposed to step into the jungle until Jim fires a pistol from Mount Jim—yes, he named a small mountain after himself, but he owns it, so I guess it's his right—but I don't have time to stand around and wait. I'll have to risk his wrath.

"I'm heading in," I say. "You all can wait until Jim fires his pistol, but I can't."

"We understand," Grim says with a nod. He holds out his hand, and I shake it. I let the gravity of that handshake settle in.

Then I head into the jungle.

Chapter Thirty-Five

Kindra

Well, I'm fucking lost. There's no way around it. I've been walking through this godforsaken jungle for over an hour, and I've seen nothing that looks like an airstrip. I can't even find the fucking path at this point.

Instead of paying attention to my surroundings when we first arrived on the island, I was too busy drooling over that liar's muscles and good looks. Now look where that's gotten me. Lost in a jungle, with a broken heart and mosquito bites in places I can't scratch in public.

Fuck this island.

Fuck these miserable bugs.

Fuck the horrific humidity.

And most of all, fuck Ezra Carter.

I sling my travel bag over my shoulder and head in a different direction. My rolling luggage snags on a tree root and topples over, nearly taking me with it.

"Shit, shit, shit," I say beneath my breath.

After righting the suitcase and wiping a waterfall of sweat from my brow, I look around and forget where I came from and where I planned to go. What an accurate depiction of my actual fucking life.

When I set out on this journey, I should have stuck to the plan. My brother's killer should have remained my sole focus. Instead, I wound up in bed with the man I have hated for ten years. If he's smart, he'll stay far away from me. If I ever see his perfect face, I'll make it imperfect.

With a loud groan, I drop my bags and lower myself onto a fallen log. I need a break from walking and getting lost. Just once, can't something go right?

Somewhere nearby—I can't tell which direction because sounds travel weird in this wet atmosphere—a twig snaps under heavy weight.

I hold my breath and keep still. Something is headed right for me, and until I know if it's a search party or a wild animal, I don't want them to know I'm here. If it turns out to be Ezra, I'd rather die in the jungle.

A flash of yellow breaks through the trees, and a wild-eyed man tumbles into my tiny clearing. Twigs and leaves cling to his balding head, and red scratches mark his face.

The hunt.

I completely forgot that was happening today, and only now do I realize the danger I'm in. There is no airstrip this way. Bennett fucking tricked me.

The man's eyes land on me, and I'm not surprised. When I set out this morning, I didn't don camo and reconnaissance gear. I'm in a neon-blue tank top that practically screams for attention. Blending in isn't an option.

Fighting is, though.

I reach for my overnight bag and scramble for my

favorite knife. Then I remember I used it to pin the note to the boardwalk. Fucking Ezra. He's still screwing me over.

"Hey, you don't have to kill me," the man says with his palms held toward me. "Just let me keep going. I'll hunker down somewhere until this is over."

He's not wrong. He's in a yellow jumpsuit, which means I don't have to kill him. I can let him keep going toward his own fate while I try to figure out mine.

But then my eyes fall to the gash in his side. Blood surrounds the tear in the fabric, but when he moves, his skin looks undamaged beneath the stain.

"You're injured," I say as I pull my overnight bag onto my lap. "I have a first-aid kit in here. At least let me help you."

He takes a step back. "Why would you want to help me? Aren't you here to hunt me?"

"I only hunt pink and red," I say. "You're yellow, so you're safe. Some of us follow a code."

"Right, yeah. I'm yellow."

He steps closer now. He's near enough that I can see the way the blood vessels have burst in his thick nose. I glance down at his shoes, which, aside from some dirt and a few small leaves, look brand new. He keeps his injured side turned away from me.

I keep digging through my bag.

"So how did a pretty girl like you end up in a shit hole like this?" He sits beside me on the log, and the hairs rise on my arm. He's too close.

"Oh, you know. Life." I offer a laugh that I hope sounds more convincing to him than it does to me. "Let me see your injury."

He doesn't move, and that only solidifies my decision.

With a deep breath, I wrap my fingers around the

handle of a dagger, then pull it from the bag and jam it into his neck. Before he has a chance to register what's happening, I twist the blade so that it's horizontal, then yank to the right, opening his entire throat.

A red waterfall pours down his chest. His hands scrabble upward, trying to stop the death tide, but he only succeeds in pushing his head backward. He's barely attached at this point.

As his body slumps to the jungle carpet, I step over him. Red foam gurgles around his open trachea as his body continues to function. This won't last for much longer, though. Not with the way he's bleeding out.

"I had my suspicions when I didn't see a wound on your side, but what really sealed the deal was your shoes."

His mouth opens and closes, trying to form words, but I've severed the connection. I don't want to hear anything he has to say.

"With an injury to the side, you should have been bleeding like a stuck pig," I continue as I wipe my blade with a velvety leaf. "Your shoes were spotless. That's when I knew you'd killed one of your fellow scumbags and stolen their jumpsuit. Thanks for playing, though."

I drop the leaf onto his face and return to my log. While he's busy boarding a slow train to hell, I sift through my bags. Participating in the hunt wasn't on my bingo card, but here the fuck we are.

My overnight bag houses several weapons, as well as my weapon belt. I fasten it around my waist, then begin sliding daggers, throwing stars, and throwing knives into their pouches and slots. Once that's situated, I reach for the big guns in my luggage.

They aren't actual guns, but they're what I consider my heavy artillery. I strap my spare bowie knife around my thigh, pop a large switchblade into my pocket, and consider strapping on my sais. I decide against them in the end. I've done very little training with them, and I'm in a life-or-death scenario now. There's no room for error.

"Let's fucking do this."

I look down at my luggage. It'll be incredibly difficult to fight my way out of this jungle while lugging an overnight bag and my suitcase, so I leave them by the log and study my surroundings. If I can remember where I left my things, I can always come back for them.

Or I can just leave them behind, along with my memories of this nightmare vacation.

I toss some leaves and jungle debris onto the bags, shielding them from view. Once I make it out of here, I'll decide if any of my things are worth returning for. The vibrator is tainted now, so it won't be a major loss. Using it will only make me think of him, as will wearing most of the clothes I brought on this trip.

"At least you were faithful," I whisper toward the hidden bag.

An unfamiliar tree with thick green vines spiraling around its warped trunk stands to my right, so I head in that direction. Damp air collects on my arms, legs, and face, where it mixes with my sweat. Mascara runs into my eyes, and I curse myself for wanting to look cute on the plane ride.

In my defense, I blame my warped imagination and the visions of Ezra racing after my plane as it taxied down the runway. I wanted to look from my window and give him a good view of what his actions have cost him.

He's probably still sound asleep.

He probably doesn't even care.

Tears mix with the mess on my face. I grit my teeth to bite them back. He doesn't deserve any more of my pain.

After stumbling around for a few minutes, I come across the body of the Cattle my victim killed. Flies buzz around the drying blood and land near the wound in his side. He's been stripped of his yellow jumpsuit, but I search around and find his shoes nearby. Just as I suspected, the right one is drenched in red.

"Turn around slowly, and give me your weapons," a feminine voice says behind me.

I follow the first command, but she's lost her mind if she thinks I'll give up my gear. She stands about ten feet away from me, with most of her body tucked behind a tree, which is smart. The head is a much harder target than the torso.

"This doesn't have to end in more bloodshed," I say. "You're wearing a yellow suit. I don't have any problems with you."

She points a shaking finger toward the man on the ground. "But you had a problem with my *dad*? Why did you kill him? We were going to get out of this together."

I take a step toward her, and she screams.

"Don't come any closer!" she screeches, but she needs to shut the fuck up. She isn't just dealing with serial killers in this jungle. There are worse fates than death.

I stop walking and hold my finger against my mouth to quiet her. "Listen to me and be quiet. I didn't kill your father. Someone else killed him for his jumpsuit."

"His jumpsuit? I don't understand."

"Some of us killers are picky. We only kill people who we feel deserve to die. Yellow jumpsuits are less of a target than pink and red."

"You're *sick*! All of you are sick, sick, sick!"

312

I roll my eyes. "Look, you have two options. Shut up and move along or keep screaming and I'll shut you up."

"Sick! You're sick! Someone, anyone, help! Get me out of here!"

She appears from behind the tree. In her hand, she holds a stick—a very long stick with an incredibly pointy end. She's crafted a spear, which proves she's resourceful. Unfortunately, she's also out of her goddamn gourd.

I grip the handle of my dagger as she begins her charge. She's wild, unruly, and uncalculated, which works in my favor. As she pushes the stick forward, I simply step to the side and stick out my blade. It catches her in the abdomen.

Now the incessant screaming starts. Having realized her mistake, she looks down at her stomach. Fat pink intestines poke from a gash, which runs about nine inches across her gut. My placement wasn't the best, though. If I'd gone a little higher and a little deeper, I would have snagged an artery.

She drops to her knees beside her father. Blood drips from the wound and patters against the leaf litter.

I won't pretend I don't feel bad for the girl. Whatever she's done, it didn't warrant this kind of death.

I step closer and drop the dagger in front of her. "You'll take a long time to die from that. If you want a quicker exit, there's the door. You were never my target. Whatever you did, it isn't my place to hand down your judgment. You forced my hand."

She reaches for the dagger and clutches it against her chest as she silently cries.

I'm not worried about her coming after me. The blood loss coupled with the pain of disembowelment will make her easy enough to overpower. I couldn't just leave her to suffer, though. That would have been cruel, and I try to treat people with at least a modicum of kindness when possible.

I'm not Ezra.

Leaving the girl with her dead father, I slip back into the jungle and eventually find a path. It might be no more than a game trail, but it's something. Animals need fresh water, and if I keep following this path, I'm sure to come across it. If I can find the water, I can find the waterfall, and if I can find the waterfall, I can get the fuck out of this jungle.

Not that I want to see that waterfall again. It's a reminder of happier times.

After walking for what feels like forever, the trees begin to thicken around me, and I lose the trail. Backtracking is pointless. Everything looks the fucking same! Brown tree trunks and winding greenery stretch for as far as I can see, and if I sit still and listen, I can only hear the wind. No rushing water. No voices. No footsteps.

Feeling more hopeless than ever, I lean against a tree and catch my breath. That's when I spot Ezra.

Chapter Thirty-Six

Ezra

I've been walking this side of the jungle for over an hour, but I've seen no sign of Kindra. Knowing my luck, she's gone over the bridge. Which means *I* have to go over the bridge.

With a deep breath, I turn in that direction. The path is hard to find, but I get there in the end, and now I'm heading toward my greatest fear.

In reality, losing Kindra is my greatest fear, but that bridge is a close second. It's a long way to the bottom of that ravine. I've seen someone make the journey, and it never ends well.

A bit deeper into the foliage, I come across Ice Pick. A fresh kill lies below him.

"Any sign of her?" I ask.

"Not yet." He grunts and pulls his ice pick from the dead woman's ear. "I've been keeping a lookout, though. I saw Grim a few minutes ago, and he said he came across a man who'd had his throat slit pretty good. Whoever killed him damn near took his head off."

"He thinks it was Kindra's handiwork?"

The woman's legs begin to move, and Ice Pick jams his tool through her right eye. The pointed end slides past the eyeball instead of going through it, which forces the errant globe out of her skull.

"That's what Grim thinks," he says as he uses his foot to ram the pick deeper. "Rosie took a bow and some arrows, so it couldn't have been her. Grim has a machete and a few hand grenades. I can do some dirty work with my pick, but he said this cut was clean."

Bennett planned to bring his new toy—a flail—so that counts him out, too. Maverick . . . Well, let's just say that Maverick is far more thorough than a slit throat. There are other killers out here as well, and Jim has been known to favor a blade, but something about this kill screams Kindra.

"Thanks, Ice Pick. I'll keep looking."

We head in opposite directions. I keep moving toward the bridge, while he ventures deeper into the trees.

As I walk along, I keep my eyes peeled for any bodies. I find only one, which is a man. The left side of his skull has been reduced to confetti, and a small rodent of some kind runs off with a bit of his brain as I draw closer. This definitely wasn't accomplished with a blade or any sort of precision.

The chaos screams Bennett.

I nudge the body with the toe of my shoe, looking for any definitive sign that Kindra was here, but I find nothing. I can't stall any longer. It's time to cross the bridge.

A cold sweat slicks my body as I think of that dilapidated mess of boards and ropes. The rocks and shallow water at the bottom make my stomach drop, and I'm not even there yet. Just seeing them in my mind is enough to send me into a panic.

"You have to protect Kindra," I say to myself. "If that means crossing that death trap, so be it. As long as she's safe, nothing else matters."

And if she's on the other side of that bridge, she definitely needs my help. She doesn't only have killers to contend with over there. Jim sets out traps, and if she walks into one, she's as good as gone.

Somewhere behind me, a man screams. Footfalls pound across twigs and leaves. I turn and watch as an older man in a pink jumpsuit stumbles and falls to the ground. A single arrow shaft juts from his right arm.

Like a silent phantom, Maudlin Rose appears from the trees, raises her bow, and fires an arrow into the man's ass. The broadhead connects with bone, and the man lets out another shrill scream as he drops.

"Nice one, Rosie!" I call toward her.

She gives me a thumbs-up and a smile, raises the bow again, and finishes the job by sending another arrow into the back of the man's neck.

"Have you seen Kindra anywhere?" I shout.

Her smile falls, and she shakes her head.

"That's okay. Keep looking!"

She gives me another thumbs-up, then makes a silent exit.

With all of us looking, surely one of us should have spotted her by now, and the fact that no one has only reinforces my need to cross the bridge. We typically hang out on this side for as long as possible, as most of the Cattle stick to this part of the jungle. We usually don't venture over there until we've snuffed out most of the life over here.

And there it is. The Ezra Carter Bridge. That's what

they'll call it next year, because there is no way I'll make it across this thing.

A stiff wind sweeps through the ravine, and the ropes sway against the force. Even the birds avoid the monstrosity by flying around it instead of over it. The ropes are so frayed that a healthy shit from one of the gulls will probably send the thing straight down to the bottom.

Yet I plan to walk on it.

I step to the support posts and grip the ropes on either side of my body. I've never stood this close to the edge before, and I regret doing so now. Some of the boards have begun to rot through. Others are already gone, replaced by a thick knot. This will be like walking across a ladder over the Grand Canyon, but the rungs move and the rails are made of twine.

My love for Kindra pushes me forward. She may be up against something far worse than this rickety piece of shit. If I slip, I might have a chance to call for help, but there is no help for her. She's on her own.

My foot slides onto the first board, and I test my weight. The plank wobbles underfoot, but it doesn't crack or groan. This is a good start.

I take two more steps, and my confidence rises. Until I look down.

A stream cuts through the ground far below me. Rocks of all shapes and sizes line both sides of the water. The stream is too shallow to provide any sort of help, and the lack of vegetation doesn't bode well for me either. One slip and I'm done.

"Watch your step," a raspy voice says behind me. "Wouldn't want to . . . fall."

The bridge sways violently, and I lose my balance. It feels like I'm twisting for an eternity, but then my chest connects with the rope railing. I sling my arms over it and try to find my footing. With one foot on a board, I turn my head and see my attacker.

A woman in a yellow jumpsuit stands at the head of the bridge. She grips a support post with one hand as she leans over with her other hand on her knee. There's a dagger in that hand, and the wild look in her eyes tells me she isn't afraid to use it.

She has a dagger . . .

"What did you do to her?" I ask as I try to steady myself. "If you hurt Kindra—"

"The bitch that did this to me?" She stands upright, and I see things I shouldn't be able to see. Someone has eviscerated her. "If I have to die, I'm taking all of you motherfuckers down with me!"

With a grimace, she grips the rope attached to the post and begins to shake it. My feet scramble to stay put as the bridge rocks under me, but it's no use. My left heel slides and cuts through air. My right foot loses its battle, and now I'm dangling by my hands and sheer determination.

I turn my head to beg the woman to stop, but the rope is no longer shaking. She's doubled over as she tries to shove her guts back where they belong, but they keep sliding out of her.

"As much as I'd love to stay and play, I think I'm running out of time," she rasps. "Bon voyage, motherfucker."

She raises the dagger above the rope securing the bridge to the left post. The same rope I now grip. If she cuts it, I'll be forced to climb it to the other side. I'm fairly strong, but I'm not *that* fucking strong.

There's only one solution. I have to get my feet back on solid ground before she can saw through the threads.

319

With every ounce of power in my arms, I pull myself up until I can raise my legs and get my feet onto a board. As soon as my toes touch the solid surface, she shakes the ropes again and sends me back to my previous position. I don't know how long I can keep this up.

"Did you kill her?" I ask. "At least tell me that. If you did, I can save you the trouble and let go."

"Oh, I killed her all right. Slit her pretty little throat and left her to choke on her own blood."

I smile at her. She's lying. Kindra would never let her get that close. I don't know how she came into possession of that dagger, but I feel confident she didn't take it from Kindra's corpse.

A newfound strength buzzes through me, and I hoist myself back to the board again. I only need to travel across three boards to get back to firm ground, but that's easier said than done when this bitch is halfway through the first rope.

I'll never make it.

"Can you at least give her a message for me," I say as I step to the next board, which isn't exactly simple since nearly two feet of empty space waits between them.

The woman stops sawing and rolls her eyes.

"Tell her that I love her," I say, "and I'm sorry."

She lowers the blade. My heartfelt words got through to her, and she realizes I'm just a guy who loves a girl. She can let me go. Sunshine. Rainbows. Happily ever after.

And than she starts sawing again.

I move to the rope on the other side and hop to the next board. I don't know how this side of the bridge will behave when she cuts that rope, and I don't plan to find out. Only one more step . . . but I'm out of time.

The bridge gives way on the left side. The boards slant toward the water and rocks, and I lose my footing. I grip the rope still attached to the right post, but I'm walking on air now, and not in a good way. With nothing to push myself off of, I'll be forced to edge down the rope these last few feet.

The same rope the woman now turns her attention to.

Hand over hand, I move closer to the cliff's edge, but her blade is poised. If I come any closer, she'll slice through my fingers. I'm also losing steam, and I still need to hoist my body onto land.

Then, like a guardian angel, Kindra appears from the tree line.

Chapter Thirty-Seven

Kindra

"Drop the fucking knife!" I yell, and I hate myself for it. Ezra should fall to his death. He deserves it. But I can't let that happen. Despite everything, the urge to save him overrides my need for vengeance.

Especially after hearing him say he loves me and that he's sorry. I don't forgive him, but I still can't watch him die.

The woman stops sawing and turns to me with a sneer. "You should have killed me when you had the chance, you fat cow."

Okay, shots fired.

I pull a throwing knife from my belt and launch it at her chest. She dodges it, which sends her closer to the cliff's edge, just as I hoped.

"You throw like a girl," the bitch seethes through gritted teeth.

"Thanks," I say, then launch another knife her way.

This one doesn't miss. It lodges itself in her left shoulder, and the handle's weight knocks her off balance. She realizes her misstep too late. Her eyes widen as rock crumbles beneath her shoes, and she slides over the edge.

As she falls, her intestines snag on a rock. I watch and wait for some comical ending where she's stuck hanging by her entrails, but the thin tissue snaps when she's fully unspooled, and that's the last I see of her. Seconds later, a loud splash breaks the silence.

Ezra pulls himself to the end of the rope, then uses his feet to walk up the side of the cliff until he's standing on a ledge. Using his powerful arms, he then pulls himself onto solid ground and flops onto his back.

"Oh, thank god you were here," he breathes. "If it hadn't been for you, I would have fallen."

Don't fucking remind me.

I turn to walk away, but I hear him getting to his feet behind me. Like a stray dog, he thinks he can follow me home and crawl into my bed. Well, he's about to learn something today.

In one fluid movement, I turn and slide my hand into a pouch on my belt, then launch a throwing star at his feet. "Do *not* mistake this for something it isn't. I didn't save you because I want to rekindle whatever relation*shit* you thought you had with me. I never want to see you again."

"Kindra, there's more to this than you realize. Your brother wasn't a good man."

I pull another star from the pouch and fling it toward his nuts. The spinning blades slice the fabric on their way past.

"Don't! Fucking don't, Ezra! I'm done with the lies. For once, can't you just tell the truth? Why did you kill him?"

He runs his hands through his dark hair and pushes his glasses up his nose, then folds his arms over his broad chest.

"There is no easy way to break this news to you. I'm sorry. I wanted to have some proof before I told you, which was one of the reasons I wanted to wait until we were back in New York."

"Proof?" I pull another star from the pouch, but I don't throw it. Not yet. "What proof would you have? Are you saying my brother was a rapist?"

Ezra shakes his head.

"Then what? What did he do that was so terrible that he had to die?"

The look in his eyes answers my question.

"No." I shake my head and launch another throwing star at Ezra. It goes wide. I can't aim with all these tears in my eyes, but I try again. And again. "No! He wasn't a child molester! You're lying again! Stop lying to me!"

Like a flailing man on a tightrope, he dodges everything I throw. A star finally slices across his right cheek, but it's not enough. I need him to hurt just as much as he's hurting me.

"My brother was a good man. He taught little league in his free time, for fuck's sake! He mentored underprivileged children and even sponsored a kid who couldn't afford to play in the recreational leagues. And you murdered him, Ezra!"

I clear the tears from my eyes and pull the bowie knife from my thigh. It's weighted differently than my throwing knives, but it's also more final. And I won't miss.

Ezra doesn't move. He doesn't try to get away or over-power me. He just stands there, awaiting his fate as I prepare to toss the blade. I want him to stop me. If he'll just tell me the truth, it doesn't have to be this way.

"Whoa, whoa, let's just calm down."

I recognize Bennett's voice, so I don't need to turn

around to know that he's behind me. I keep my eyes trained on Ezra.

"What's the truth, Bennett?" I ask. "You knew about this secret all along, so you must know Ezra's motivation for killing my fucking brother."

"It's just like he told it," Bennett says. "Your brother was the worst kind of awful. Do you know how many kids he hurt?"

I take a deep breath because I don't have enough bowie knives to go around. "None. He didn't hurt kids. He loved them."

"This must be really hard to accept, but you're right about one thing. He loved kids." Bennett pauses, and the slight quiver to his voice makes me do the same. "Loved them right into therapy. He loved one so much that the poor kid tried to kill himself at the age of thirteen."

"We have the proof," Ezra says. "If you can just wait until we get back to New York—"

"No!" I raise the blade and secure my grip again. "There is no more waiting. This is on my terms, and the only thing I want is the truth."

Gritting my teeth, I prepare to throw the knife, but Bennett gets to me before I can. Powerful biceps pin my arms to my sides, and I'm useless to fight against him. He might be a tad smaller than Ezra, but he's just as strong.

Before I can scream or land a kick against his legs, a sharp pain pierces my thigh and I drop the knife. Did he fucking stab me?

My six-month obsession with self-defense classes kicks in, and I relax my body. Bennett struggles to grip my dead weight. I slide out of his hold, get to my feet, and dart for the trees. I glance back, but they aren't following me.

Bennett, Ezra, and Maverick stand by and watch as I

disappear into the jungle. They probably realize I'm fast too can't . . .

Huh?

Why are my numb . . . ?

Water. Running water.

That's the first thing I hear as I rise from a thick fog. My mouth feels like a cat shit in it, and pain pounds against my temples.

They fucking drugged me.

I try to sit up, but thin ropes keep me strapped to the bed. I move my hands and discover my wrists have been bound as well. The rope is familiar, and as my hazy mind begins to clear, I realize why.

"Fucking Ezra," I groan.

"He's not here right now," someone says beside me.

I turn my head and try to peer through the shadows. The lights are off and the curtains are drawn, so it's difficult to see much of anything. By the way the bed creaks, I'm fairly certain I'm in a villa.

But whose?

It's not mine. I sprayed my pillows with peppermint oil because it helps me sleep. These pillows smell like expensive cologne, and it's not Ezra's. I also don't recognize the voice, so it's not Bennett beside me, either.

"I've turned off the lights because it'll be easier on your eyes," the man says. "Would you like for me to turn them on now?"

"I would *like* for you to un-fucking-tie me. I'll even give you a five-minute head start before I come after you."

The man chuckles, and a light clicks on. It's Maverick.

"As much as I would love to untie you, I need to talk to you. Bennett figured you wouldn't listen if we didn't strap you down."

"Bennett was right. Where is that sorry son of a bitch and his stupid brother?" I glance around the room, but we're the only ones here.

"They're in Bennett's villa. What I'm about to tell you was news for them as well, and they're trying to process it."

I roll my eyes and consider launching a glob of spit at him because he's clearly in on this. "Whatever you three came up with as a story, I don't want to hear it. I am done listening to lies."

Maverick's shoulders rise in a shrug. "If you don't believe me, that's okay. You wouldn't be the first."

He stands from the chair and steps closer to the bed.

"Do you need to get right up on me when you tell your tale? Personal space," I say, but he only steps closer.

He leans toward my face and pushes the hair away from his forehead. A long white line runs just below his hairline. "Do you see that scar on my forehead?"

I nod.

"Your brother gave me that scar when I tried to fight him off me the first time. I was eight."

Tears fill my eyes. They're taking this lie too fucking far. "This isn't okay," I say. "Children really go through this. It's not a joke, Maverick."

He gives me a wan smile and lets his hair fall. "Fair enough, but my name isn't actually Maverick. I changed my name as soon as I turned eighteen because I never wanted your brother to find me. Until today, I didn't even know he was dead."

"Bullshit."

"My birth name was Landon Rivers. Those sevens on your brother weren't sevens. They were Ls."

"Bullshit!"

This isn't true. None of this is true. My brother was a youth pastor. He . . . he couldn't have done this.

"It's not ironclad proof, but I have pictures if you'd like to see." Maverick sits on the edge of the bed and holds a phone screen toward my face. "This is me as a kid. My first year on the baseball team, thanks to your brother's generous support. No scar in this picture."

He points to a little boy standing beside my brother. The child is all smiles, with a glove in one hand and a bat in the other. I glance between the older and younger versions of Maverick and find them too similar to discount. They have the same dimples and smile, and they both have a dark freckle right below the outer corner of the left eye.

"Now look at this picture, taken just a month later. Notice anything different?"

Maverick flicks the screen, and another picture pops up. The same little boy stands beside my brother, but he's somehow so different. A smile graces the child's face, but it doesn't reach his eyes, which I now see are green. Beneath his hairline, a long gash peeps through strands of blond hair. My brother's arm firmly wraps around the child's shoulders, and I've never seen a more uncomfortable little boy.

My stomach drops and I feel as if I'll be sick. How is this possible? How were my mother and I so oblivious?

"I kept these pictures as a reminder," Maverick continues. "They tell a story in two images, but I'm the outcome. I overcame this, and you can too."

Pictures . . . I remember cleaning out Reese's room after he was murdered. There had been a box beneath his bed, and inside—

"Do you have a birthmark?" I ask.

Maverick's eyes close, and he nods his head.

"On your—"

"On my ass, yes."

I thought it had been a photograph of a girl in a compromising position. When I saw it, I was still fairly young and naïve. I'd quickly closed the box without taking a closer look, then put the entire thing in the trash.

Now I don't feel like I'll be sick anymore. I *know* I will be.

"Trash can," I blurt. "Trash can!"

Maverick rushes to the bathroom and hurries back with the small wicker waste basket. He holds it by my head as I violently retch.

All the pain this man has had to carry because of my brother. I can't even fathom what he's been through. And I've made it worse. I've made it so much worse. I defended the monster to his victim.

"I'm so sorry," I sob through dry heaves. "Oh god, Maverick. I'm so sorry."

One by one, he unties the ropes holding me to the bed, releasing my hands first so that I can hold the basket. When I'm free, I sit up and heave once more. I have nothing left in my system, but my body keeps trying.

"It wasn't your fault." Maverick sits on the edge of the bed. "But it wasn't Ezra's fault, either. He didn't know I was the boy he saved all those years ago."

"How could he not know?"

"He's helped a lot of kids over the years. He can't be expected to remember every face. Plus, I changed my name. When I approached him a few years ago, he met Maverick Eaton, not Landon Rivers. Had he known who I was, he would have told you the truth himself. I firmly believe that. He was just so scared of losing you without proof."

"I didn't exactly help things along," Bennett says as he enters the room. "Sorry to barge in, but Ezra was 'sick with worry.' His words, not mine."

With a sigh, I pat the bed on my right side. "You might as well join the party."

Bennett sits beside me and clears his throat. "I apologize for being so tough on you. It's not easy to feel like I'm losing my brother when I've only known I had a brother for a little over a decade."

"I doubt you have to worry about any of that now," I say. "Ezra probably won't ever talk to me again."

"Is it safe to speak for myself?" Ezra peeks around the doorframe. "Sorry, I was just worried about you. Maverick didn't know how much sleepy juice he'd put in that dart."

"Dart?" I ask.

"Team effort for the hunt," Maverick says. "We thought it would be fun if I darted them with a tranquilizer and Bennett tracked them down and bludgeoned them with the flail. We were right. It was fun."

"Until I ruined it." I cover my face with my hands.

Ezra ushers Bennett out of the way and sits beside me before gently guiding my hands to my lap. "You didn't ruin anything, pet. I'm the one who ruined this. I lied to you. I even planted the meat hooks in Eighties' villa to fool you. If there's any way to make it up to you, I'll do whatever it takes."

"Gross," Bennett says. "If you guys have reached this stage of the makeup, I think it's time Maverick and I take off."

"Agreed," Maverick says as he stands from the bed.

I grip his hand before he can walk away. "Maverick, I

meant what I said. I'm sorry I didn't believe you. Victims shouldn't have to defend themselves."

Maverick squeezes my hand and smiles down at me. "No need for apologies. I'm not a victim. I'm a survivor. Killing is my therapy, and it's done wonders. Each time I take out someone like your brother, I feel a little better. You will too. Just give it time."

He doesn't mean to hurt me when he mentions my brother, but fuck. That stings. I try to meld the brother I knew with the monster he was, and I just can't make it work. It still feels like they're talking about someone else.

But the pictures don't lie. My brother was sick, and Ezra was right to kill him.

Ezra and I don't speak, even once the villa's front door closes and I hear the men retreating down the boardwalk. We sit in silence when we both have so much we need to say. I just don't know how to begin.

My chin begins to shake, and I close my eyes as a confusing mix of emotions buries me. I can't breathe. Shame, regret, grief, and intense heartbreak press against my chest until my lungs buckle.

Ezra pulls me into him, and I don't fight against his touch. "Can you ever forgive me for lying to you?" he asks.

"I could have made it a lot easier to tell the truth."

He places a kiss on the top of my head and strokes my hair. "You make everything easy, especially loving you. The deception is my fault and my fault alone. I suppose if I have anything to forgive you for, it's the new scar I'll bear on my cheek."

"Oh, shit! I completely forgot." I sit up and turn his face so that I can see the thin red line my throwing star gouged into his perfect flesh. It's fairly superficial, which relieves some of my regret.

"Chicks dig scars, right?" he says with a chuckle. "Though I'm only concerned with your opinion. What do you think? Do I pass muster?"

He's asking so much more than what he presents on the surface. He's asking if I can move past this. He's asking if we can still live in the fantasy we created in our minds before reality dealt us a huge blow.

And I have the answer.

"Yes, you pass muster. Now please kiss me."

As his lips press against mine, it feels like our first kiss all over again. Now that we know each other's secrets, now that we have everything out in the open, this *is* our first kiss.

But it won't be our last.

Chapter Thirty-Eight

Ezra

As we sling our bags over our shoulders and prepare to leave the island that late afternoon, the mood is bittersweet. Dating on vacation is one thing, but everything can change when you're back in the real world.

For some reason, I don't think that will be a major hurdle for us. Instead of tackling the big issues out there, we swapped things around and decided to make a dog's dinner of our last day on the island.

But we're stronger for it.

With our bags in hand, Kindra, Bennett, Maverick, and I make our way toward the airstrip—heading in the correct direction this time, of course. Many of us will take the private jet back to Miami, then head off in different directions from there.

Grim plans to go back to Germany. Where in Germany? No one knows. He's private like that. But if you ever see a wiry old man in a Speedo on Hiddensee Beach, keep walking.

Maudlin Rose plans to stay a few more days on the island with Jim and Jeff. We speculate she'll fly to Germany after that, but it's anyone's guess. She keeps her secrets well.

Ice Pick is headed back to Texas, but he plans to come to New York when it snows. He says he's never seen snow, and we've been meaning to invite him to stay with us for years. Now seemed like a good time. As long as he keeps his eyes away from Kindra, that is.

I follow Kindra up the steps to board the jet. The view is fantastic, and I'm not referring to the island. She's chosen a pair of shorts that allow her perfect cheeks to peek out every so often.

We sit much the same as we did on the flight in, though we've exchanged Cat for Maverick. Speaking of Cat, I'm interested to see how she handles our return. Kindra worries she'll never forgive her, but I'm inclined to believe the girl has a heart of gold and will welcome her back with open arms.

I guess we'll find out soon enough.

As soon as we're settled, Kindra grips my hand. "Oh no."

"What's wrong, pet?" I whisper in her ear. She's gone white as a sheet.

She shifts and closes her eyes. "I forgot to take my meds before we left. I always try to remember to take something before flying, and I always forget. Something about being on a plane makes me"—she glances around and lowers her voice to a whisper—"shit."

With a smile, I reach into my pocket and pull out a sachet of Imodium AD. I snagged it from Bennett's travel bag before we set out. "I'll always protect you when I can, even from blowout diarrhea."

She smacks my arm and pulls the packet from my fingers. "Ass. But thanks."

The plane rushes down the runway moments later, and we're in the air. The island shrinks below us, and then it disappears from view as the clouds swallow the silver jet.

Once we're flying level, the flight attendant comes by to close all the windows. Jim doesn't want anyone to know where the island is, and he thinks we're a bunch of topographical geniuses who can discern where we are based on land masses and cloud patterns. He has so much faith in us.

I lean closer to Kindra. "Have you secured the great earthquake machine in your bag? Wouldn't want it to go off again and crash the jet."

"You're really not going to let that go." Her cheeks shift to a bright shade of red, and I'm forced to kiss them.

"God, you two make me sick," Bennett says.

Kindra begins to sing the theme to *SpongeBob Square-Pants*, putting extra emphasis when she says the word *pineapple*. Bennett's lips slam shut, and he turns his head. Kindra's song tapers off to a smile.

"I've always wanted a woman who could give my brother a run for his money," I whisper into her ear. "How are you even real?"

She rests her head on my shoulder. "He gives me a lot to work with."

"That he does."

Within minutes, she's snoring, and I'm not far behind her.

The plane lands in Miami, and the group begins to break apart as if we've never met. As we walk out of the terminal, we must look like a bunch of strangers. Which is good. We wouldn't want anyone to get any ideas.

"Do you want me to give you a call when I arrive in New York?" I ask Kindra as we stand outside the airport. "My flight should land around lunchtime. You could even pick me up, if you'd like."

She bites her lip and smiles at me. "We'll see."

Bennett pulls a rental car up to the curb. Leave it to him to waste money when we could have gotten a cab to the hotel. Maverick gives Kindra a little wave from the passenger's seat.

She waves back and checks her watch. "Well, I guess this is it."

"For now," I say.

"Right. For now." She laughs and wipes a tear from her eye. "Gosh, why am I being so emotional? It's not like I won't see you again. My plane leaves in an hour, and then you'll be back in town tomorrow."

"You have a way of making a minute away from you feel like an eternity."

She smacks my chest and rolls her eyes. "Okay, no need to get all sappy on me."

"You bring it out of me. I can't help it."

As I lean down to kiss her, Bennett lays on the horn. I wave him off and enjoy these moments before we have to say goodbye.

We part ways, and I watch her until she disappears within the airport. She looks back once, and then she's gone.

I slide into the back seat of the rental, and Bennett drives toward the hotel. The ride is much different now that we don't have to listen to Gary.

Gary . . .

"Bennett," I say, "what ever happened to Gary? Did you get to kill him?"

His hands tighten on the wheel, and he shakes his head. "Fuck no. Right before the hunt, Jim finally decided to tell me Gary didn't make it past the first fucking night. The little weasel tried to escape through the air vents."

I wince.

The air vents were installed by Jim as a way to deter the Cattle from escaping. Because the opening is so large and easy to reach, someone almost always tries it the first night, but when the grate closes behind them, all hell breaks loose. If Gary managed to make it past the saw blades, the shrinking room must have squished him. There's no surviving that.

Bennett pulls up to our hotel. It's the same place we stayed that first night in Miami. Memories that seem like they happened years ago rush back to me.

As Bennett and Maverick head to the front desk, I stand by the elevators and check my phone for a text from Kindra. She hasn't reached out, but that's okay. She's probably still trying to get her luggage sorted.

I kick myself for not going with her. I should have changed flights. What if she needs more medicine? What if someone tries to hurt her?

My skin breaks into a cold sweat just thinking about it. How could I have been so stupid? Now that I have her in my life, I have to protect her.

I turn around with every intention of demanding Bennett drive me back to the airport . . .

And there she is.

She smiles and gives me a little wave. "Fancy meeting you here," she says.

I step forward and take her into my arms. "What are you doing here? I thought you'd be boarding your plane by now."

"You aren't the only one who can keep secrets." She tips her head back to look up at me. "As soon as we had cell signal on the jet, I changed my flight. Bennett gave me the details while we were still on the island."

"You little minx." I lean down and kiss her. "I love you."

"I love you too," she says.

Bennett rounds the corner and immediately pretends to gag. "Don't you guys ever get sick of pawing at each other? Give it a rest."

Kindra and I look at each other and laugh. We don't need to say what we're thinking, as we're both thinking the same thing.

Never.

Epilogue

Three Months Later

Kindra

Rain patters outside the window on this dreary October night. I'm busy in the kitchen, trying to carve a pumpkin. Cat thought it would be fun to have a contest and vote for the best one. I think this is just a mess.

But sometimes, a mess is okay. Cat taught me that.

I called her from the hotel that first night back in Miami and apologized profusely. She accepted, and we've gotten even closer since then. We're like oil and water on the surface, but diving a little deeper showed me we don't have to share a million similarities to become best friends. Now, we're almost as inseparable as me and Ezra.

Speaking of Ezra, he's out on the porch with his creation. He didn't want to work on them side by side because he wanted it to be a surprise. I told him I didn't need more surprises, that he was the best I've ever received, but he just laughed and told me to go inside.

I make the final cut, remove the last piece of pumpkin

flesh, and take a step back. It's not great, but I can only hope it looks better once it's lit up.

The front door opens and closes, and Ezra's footsteps draw closer. I spin my monstrous creation so he can't make fun of it yet. There will be plenty of time for that once Bennett arrives.

"Have you finished already?" I ask as he enters the kitchen. "I figured you'd be out there for at least another hour."

He raises an envelope with a puzzled look on his face. "This was in the mailbox. It says it's from Jim."

"Jim? From the retreat?"

He nods and motions for me to follow him into the living room.

We take a seat on the couch, and Ezra pulls the wax seal from the envelope—so extra—and opens it. Inside is a hand-written letter.

"An email wouldn't suffice?" I ask.

Ezra begins unfolding the parchment. "In case the retreat wasn't any indication, Jim is a bit . . . eccentric."

"Understatement of the year."

As he begins reading the letter to himself, his expression shifts from perplexed to overjoyed.

"What?" I say. "What is it? Did he finally get rid of Chef Maurice?"

Instead of answering me, he places the letter in my hand and gestures for me to read it for myself.

Ezra,

Hey, kid. I've been running the summer retreat for a while now, but I've always wanted to expand to something bigger. After all, folks like us shouldn't be relegated to one vacation a year. What would you think about a winter retreat?

I wouldn't be able to run it, mind you. I'm far too busy with work and the island. But I would be happy to fund it. Jeff decided to go on a spree in Europe, so he isn't available, and between you and me, I wouldn't trust him with something this complex.

Would you be interested in taking this on?

I've already scouted a location in Alaska. If you give me the green light, we can start planning. My full account would be at your disposal. Ideally, I'd like you to host the first retreat this winter. Say, after Christmas?

Let me know how this suits you. If it doesn't, scratch out your name and give it to your brother.

Jim

I hand the letter to Ezra. "What do you think? Is this something you'd want to do?"

He pauses and stares down at the letter. Without answering me, he stands and grips my hand. "Come with me. I need to show you the pumpkin I've carved."

I don't really have a choice in the matter because he yanks me up from the couch and drags me toward the front door like a child who's just said *fuck* in church. As I step onto the porch, he turns and grips my shoulders.

Why are his hands so shaky?

"Kindra, when I first met you, I had no idea how you would capture my heart. Your looks ensnared me, but your wit and intelligence bound me to you for eternity. My heart is yours."

He steps to the side, and I see his pumpkin. It sits on a small table. The top has been cut away, and a hand sticks from the opening. Whoever created this fake appendage has a real eye for detail because it looks incredibly realistic. They even took the time to chip some of the nails and add a really convincing yellowish glaze to the skin. And is that bruising?

Ezra pulls the hand—complete with attached arm—from the pumpkin and turns it over. Attached to the palm is a small velvet box.

"Is that the fucking hand from the *beach*?" I screech as realization dawns on me.

Ezra winces. "I wanted to use that one, but the gulls had already destroyed it by the time I went back for it. I had Jim go into the ravine and cut the arm from that woman who attacked me. He shipped it to me, and I've been storing it in the freezer at mine."

I should be disgusted. I should be so repulsed that I throw this rotting arm at him and tell him to fuck right off.

But I'm neither disgusted nor repulsed. I am a woman in love, and Ezra has given me the perfect proposal. All he has to do is ask the question.

He plucks the ring box from the decaying palm and opens it. "I needed to show you this first because if I take on this winter retreat, you'll have to be part of it too. The time for making decisions on my own has passed. Now I want to make every decision together. Starting with this one. Kindra, will you marry me?"

I stare down at the ring. Though Ezra has plenty of money, he's chosen a simple diamond on a simple white-gold band. It's simply me.

Unable to form the word, I nod my head.

He pulls the ring from the box and slides it over my finger, then kisses my hands. "You have made me the happiest man. Now, what do we do about this winter retreat, Mrs. Carter?"

His arms wrap around me as he pulls me in for a kiss. We lose ourselves in each other, and his length hardens and presses against my stomach.

"How much time do we have before everyone gets here?" I ask.

A car door shuts in the driveway, and Ezra groans. "Not enough, I'm afraid."

Bennett charges up the steps and stops in his tracks when he sees us wrapped in each other's arms. "Aw, for fuck's sake. Do you two ever stop? You'll put New York into a condom shortage at this rate."

"Where's your pumpkin?" I ask.

He scoffs. "I'm not carving a shitty pumpkin. That's kid stuff."

Ezra looks behind Bennett and studies his car before turning to him. "Where's Cat? Wasn't she supposed to arrive with you?"

"She wanted to ride with *Maverick*." He uses a whiny baby voice when he says their friend's name. "The girl is barking up the wrong tree with that one. She's not his type."

"Is someone a little jealous?" I ask.

That earns a laugh from Ezra and a scowl from Bennett.

"Whose shit-ass pumpkin is that?" Bennett points to Ezra's pumpkin. "And why is an arm on the ground?"

I look at Ezra, and he gives me a slight nod, so I push my hand toward Bennett.

"Ezra just proposed," I say.

"And she said yes," Ezra adds. "Well, she nodded yes."

Bennett takes a deep breath, and I'm not sure if he's going to turn and leave or explode right here. Then he steps toward me and puts his hands on my shoulders.

"Welcome to the family." He smiles and pulls me in for an awkward hug, though I can feel the sincerity in it.

"Don't touch him!" Cat screams from the car window as she and Maverick pull into the driveway. "You'll get rabies!"

Bennett mumbles something under his breath and swipes his hand down his face. "I was hoping to give you guys some news before the blond squad arrived, but I guess I'll just have to tell everyone."

"We have some news too," Ezra says, then glances at me. "Or we might. I'm not sure yet."

"Don't tell me she's fucking pregnant," Bennett says.

Cat rushes up the stairs. "Kindra's pregnant? What?"

"Congrats, man!" Maverick pushes past Bennett to get to Ezra. He pulls him in for a hug. "If Bennett doesn't want anything to do with it, can I be the godfather?"

Cat grips my hands and starts jumping up and down. "And I can be the godmother! This will be so much fun!"

"Stop!" I shout, and everyone freezes. "Jesus fucking Christ, I'm not pregnant. Ezra and I are engaged, and Jim offered to let Ezra run a winter retreat in Alaska. That's it. That's all the news."

"You're engaged?" Cat shrieks, and there go my eardrums.

I hold up my ring, and she fingers it like it's the Hope Diamond. I'll never stop being amazed by the way my successes become her successes. Friendship is pretty badass, not gonna lie.

"Wait, go back a step," Bennett says. "A retreat in Alaska? I hate snow."

Ezra holds out his hands. "Nothing is set in stone as of

346

yet, but Jim approached me with it, and I'm waiting for Kindra's input before I decide."

"I say we do it."

All heads turn toward me.

"Think about it," I say. "We all met because of the summer retreat, and we made some really good memories. Imagine if we could do that more than once a year. We could get the entire gang back together."

"So you're on board?" Ezra asks, his eyes wide with excitement.

I nod, and his smile nearly splits his face.

"I won't be going," Bennett says. "You all can freeze to death in Alaska this winter. I'll be on a cruise somewhere warm."

"This winter retreat just sounds better by the second," Cat says with a dreamy look in her eyes.

Eyes that are firmly set on Maverick.

"I used to snowboard when I was younger," Maverick says. "Any chance we'll have a little slope action?"

Ezra laughs. "With Jim's budget, I'm sure we can make that happen."

"What about a ride on a horse-drawn sleigh?" Cat jumps up and down. "That would be so romantic!"

"We'll consult you all when we're ready to start planning," I say, "but that may be a ways off yet. Right now, let's get inside. It's getting chilly."

We all head into the house. While everyone settles themselves in the living room, I prepare a tray of apple cider spiked with rum. Ezra and I have learned that alcohol makes the Cat-Bennett dynamic a little more tolerable, though only slightly.

I return to the living room. As we sip cider and talk, the

pumpkin contest is quickly forgotten when Bennett drops a bombshell.

"I think I found a sibling," Bennett says, and we all fall silent. Cat doesn't even have a snide remark. "Daddy Dearest tried to keep a clean trail, but he left a little evidence behind. So far, I only know of one more Carter sibling out there somewhere. No clue if it's a sister or a brother, but they're in the States."

Ezra lowers his mug to the table. "We always knew there were more of us. Father loves women."

"Right," Bennett says, "but we didn't know we had one so close to home. The child was born to a woman named Margaret somewhere in Texas, but I don't have more than that. It could have been last year or forty years ago."

I turn to Bennett. "How do you even know what you know?"

"My mother," he says, though it seems to pain him to speak those two words.

Ezra squeezes my hand in silent communication. *Say no more*, this touch says.

"Why don't we get to the pumpkins?" I stand and smooth the front of my pants. "Ezra, set yours up in the kitchen beside mine. Cat, you and Maverick do the same."

Bennett excuses himself to the bathroom while the four of us busy ourselves in the kitchen. Cat carved a hissing cat into her pumpkin. It's pretty good, but I don't think it stands a chance against Maverick's. The man is an artist. He etched a detailed Ghostface into the orange flesh, and when we cut out the lights, it gets even better. He's hidden a bloody knife within the lighter areas, but it's invisible until the candlelight shines through.

Ezra plops his pumpkin next to Maverick's and we

share a good belly laugh. It's kind of sad-looking when you don't know the story behind it.

Bennett enters the kitchen as I prepare to spin my pumpkin around. It's only fitting that he's here. He's part of this.

I didn't carve something scary. It also isn't very artistic. But it's from my heart, and for the Heartbreak Killer, that's saying something. For nearly an hour, I scratched and scrawled our story into this pumpkin, with a stick figure to represent each of us.

There's Cat, with her big tits and perfect hair, as she struts on the beach. Bennett stands beside her with a flail in his hand and a scowl on his face. I thought about adding a pineapple, but I didn't in the end.

Stick figure Ezra clings to a rope with a smile on his face and a meat hook in his hand. Those metal hooks don't bother me anymore. Ezra made the right decision, and I know that now.

"You put me on there too," Maverick says. "I feel so honored."

Yes, he's there too. Our story wouldn't have had a happy ending without him. His little stick figure holds a phone. The truth set us free.

"But what is your stick figure holding?" Ezra asks me. "What's that in your hand?"

"It's my heart," I say.

Bennett groans. "Fuck, here we go," he mutters.

I won't let him deter me from saying what I need to say. Feelings are hard for some people. I should know. They were once impossible for me.

"This trip gave me so much. A best friend. The love of my life. Some really good banter. And answers." I look at each of the faces in my kitchen. Letting them enter my sacred space wouldn't have been remotely possible before the trip, and now I don't know how I would live without each of them. Even Bennett. "Thank you all for showing me that it's okay to open up a bit."

"Aw, come here, you!" Cat pulls me in for a hug, and I let her. I let them all as I'm surrounded by smiling faces and warm embraces—sans Bennett. Affection isn't his thing.

I get it.

"If this concludes our business, I think it's time for me to get the fuck out of here," Bennett says. "I've got a sibling to find."

Maverick looks at his watch. "And I have a plane to catch. You'll send the details for the winter retreat, right?"

Ezra puts his arm around the younger man's shoulders. "You'll be the first to know, since Bennett won't be joining us."

"I'll be there too," Cat says. "Maybe I can finally get my first kill."

As Ezra and I walk everyone to the door, it almost feels like the last page of a really good book. In reality, our story is still being written.

And I can't wait to see what happens next.

Did you have an amazing time at the retreat? It doesn't have to stop here! **Slay Ride**, book two in the Slaycation series, is available here: Books2read.com/SlayRide

If you want to stay with dark-lite stories, check out these books:

Stranger Session: Books2read.com/StrangerSession
Her Fantasy: Books2read.com/HerFantasy
Last Mistake: Books2read.com/LastMistake
Protect Me: Books2read.com/ProtectMeNovella

If you're ready to dive into darker reads, make sure you check out my hitchhiker romance standalones in my Ride or Die series! These can be read in any order!
Hitched: Books2read.com/Hitched
Along for the Ride: Books2read.com/MFMHitchhiker
Driving my Obsession: Books2read.com/DrivingmyObsession
Across State Lines: Books2read.com/AcrossStateLines
Don't Stop: Books2read.com/Dont-Stop

Connect with Lauren

Don't miss a thing from Lauren Biel! Check out all of her books, social media connections, and other important information at Campsite.bio/LaurenBielAuthor and Lauren Biel.com

Acknowledgments

To my VIP gals (Kimberly, Jessie, Nikita, Lexi, Grace), I love you more than I can explain!

Thank you to my husband for helping me find creative ways to murder fictional criminals.

Brooke, my editor, you're the best, and I couldn't have done this without you.

Thank you to my valued Patrons. Your contribution helped make this book happen.

Courtney, Shari, Electrobean, Cris, Tia E, Tori G, Lymarie95, Sarah S, Helenah J, Amanda T, Tiffany M, Kala R, _____ britneyxO, Tamara M, Suzy A, Tara H, Andie J, Lisa W, Court's Bookshelf, Stacy, Emily S, Sheena E, Queen Ilmaree, SerenaLorraine, Courtney Y, Gini R, Shannan T, Heather C, Kayla F, Jesi D, Charmaine B, Michelle, Karla, Christy P, Cheyanna L, Mickayla F, Kelsey S, Dani C, Sandie W, SweetnSourKandy, Kayla T, Arnica S, Karly W, Cassi K, Gumdrop, Maxine T, Kay, Nicholetta88, Victoria S, Lori R, Jessie, Michelle M, Tabitha F, Lindsey S, Erika M, Laura T, Nicole M, Nineette W, Kimberly B, BoneDaddyAshe, Kimberly S, Sammi Rae, Stjohnreads, Allison B, Andrea J, Chelle, Gabby S, Jennifer H, Jessica G, Samantha R, Sara S, Iesha E, Margaret N,

April C, Amber H, Caitlyn W, Nikki S, Kat De Ann, Inkeddarkreads, Jasmine K, Heather S, Lizzie Borden, CryBaby, Just Jen Here, Mikasa_Kuchiki, Jada W, Briyanna M, Midwest.Kindleworm, Berthie L, Amanda C, Bailey A, YourMomReads, Laura, Eugenia M, bethbetweenthepages, Sharee S, Samantha W, Kelli T, Shelby F, Lauren P, Mackenzie H, Tiannah B, Wombles, Kristiana B, Vero A, Deani, Amanda C, Brooke O, Ashley P, Mandy G, Courtney P, Lisa A, Leslie W, Jordyn J, DJ Krimmer, Kayla M, Marisa, Amber, Tiffany T, Smitty, Anna S, Barrie, Alexandria R, Brianne, Leeat S, DirtyPanda, Callie K, Christine Powell, Erica W, Ashley T, Dia P, Kimberlee A, darkdelightfulreads, Marguerite, Tamika, Tatted Bat, Victoria M, Iris, Pyro, Milan B, Casey K, Lauren S, Carolina S, Faith S, Nada P, Anna, Bonnie F

Also by Lauren Biel

To view Lauren Biel's complete list of books, visit: https://laurenbiel.com/laurenbielbooks/

About the Author

Lauren Biel is the author of many dark romance books, with several more titles in the works. When she's not working, she's writing. When she's not writing, she's spending time with her husband, her friends, or her pets. You might also find her on a horseback trail ride or sitting beside a waterfall in Upstate New York. When reading her work, expect the unexpected. To be the first to know about her upcoming titles, please visit www.LaurenBiel.com.

Made in the USA
Monee, IL
06 February 2025

11611573R00213